MYSTERIES OF
GAME THEORY
AND OTHER ODDITIES

MYSTERIES
of **GAME**
THEORY
and Other Oddities

Joseph Raffetto

NOOVELLA.COM

TABLE OF CONTENTS

Joseph Raffetto
www.noovella.com

ISBN: 978-0-9906149-2-0

Second edition

Cover and interior design by Duane Stapp

Follow Joseph Raffetto on Tumblr and Twitter @ Noovella.

For my Parents

BOWIE AND THE BERLIN WALL

I

WHEN DAVID BOWIE DIED IN 2016, the German Foreign Office tweeted, "Good-bye, David Bowie. You are now among #Heroes. Thank you for helping to bring down the #wall."[1]

What did David Bowie do to help take down the Berlin Wall, a momentous event that signaled the end of the Cold War? Many will point to Bowie's concert at the Wall in 1987, where thousands of East Berlin citizens risked being beaten and arrested to hear him. It was a powerful moment, but Bowie's journey to and association with the Wall started much earlier than even his falling to earth in Berlin in the 1970s, when he put the city on the musical map. He had been breaking down walls his entire life.

Some background on Bowie's early life is helpful in understanding how he went from David Jones to David Bowie to the Berlin Wall.

Bowie was born David Robert Jones in 1947 in Brixton, a district in South London, and he lived there until he was six years old. Brixton had been hit hard by the German Blitz in the early 1940s. Missiles had landed in front of and behind Bowie's childhood home. Children were playing in the rubble of bombed buildings when Bowie was born.

World War II had traumatized the Bowie family. Bowie's mother, Margaret Mary Burns Jones, known as Peggy, and the Burns family had suffered through the nightly shelling from the Luftwaffe, fearing Hitler would overtake England.

Two of Peggy's sisters, Nora and Vivienne, were said to be schizophrenic by multiple sources, but Bowie's cousin Kristina said that this wasn't true and that schizophrenia was a catchall term in those days. Kristina attempted to set the record straight in Dylan Jones's *David Bowie: The Oral History*. Nora, she said, had several serious health problems and illnesses; her aging mother, who was having a tough time handling the situation, gave the go-ahead—without consulting the family—to have Nora lobotomized. As for Vivienne, her doctor said she had become clinically depressed. Kristina was not aware of doctors ever diagnosing Vivienne as schizophrenic.

Kristina's mother, Una—Peggy's sister—was diagnosed as schizophrenic. Kristina explained that it was because the doctors were not aware Una had been hit by a car and suffered a brain injury at the age of nine. They gave Una shock therapy that made her brain injury even worse. She died at thirty-seven.

Kristina clarified that there was no history of mental illness or suicide on Bowie's mother's side of the family. The root cause of their issues had been the trauma of two world wars.[2]

Before World War II began, Peggy fell in love with a French porter, Jack Rosenberg, with whom she had a romance and a son, Terry, who went by Terry Burns. Before Terry's birth in November 1937, Jack abandoned Peggy and his future son. Terry was sent to live with Peggy's mother, Margaret Alice Heaton Burns, when he was a child. Margaret was a difficult person whose anger spared no one, and she treated him cruelly and would slap the boy.

Terry left home in 1955 when Bowie was eight and returned when he was twenty. At some point, Terry introduced Bowie to modern jazz and Jack Kerouac, which Bowie said changed his life.

In 1967 Bowie took Terry to see the band Cream in London. On the way home, Terry fell to his knees and had a vision. Versions vary, but he reported the earth opening and fire spewing out. Terry was diagnosed as schizophrenic and spent the rest of his life in and out of mental hospitals. He threw himself under a moving train in 1985.

"One puts oneself through such psychological damage trying to avoid the threat of insanity, you start to approach the very thing that you're scared of," Bowie reflected. "Because of the tragedy inflicted, especially on my mother's side of the family, there were too many suicides for my liking—that was something I was terribly fearful of. I felt I was the lucky one because I was an artist, and it would never happen to me because I could put all my psychological excesses into my music, and then I could always be throwing it off."[3]

Bowie's grandfather on his father's side, Robert Haywood Jones, was a private in the King's Own Yorkshire Light Infantry in the First World War. He was killed in Northern France at age thirty-four, and they never found his body. Bowie's grandmother, Zillah, was devastated and died four months later, leaving their son, Bowie's father, Haywood Stenton Jones, an orphan at four years old.

Haywood served honorably in Africa and Italy in the Second World War. He worked for more than twenty years as a marketing and promotion professional for a children's charity and was a well-mannered man. He encouraged Bowie's pursuits, buying his son a record player, which was unusual for a child to own in those days. When Bowie was nine, Haywood brought home 45 rpm records, including releases by Fats Domino and Bowie's favorite, Little Richard.

Still, Bowie stated that "it wasn't a particularly happy childhood. My parents were cold emotionally."[4] He also said, "I had a very happy childhood, seriously nothing wrong with it."[5] What is clearly true is that there was an abundance of tragedy and complex minefields in Bowie's family's past that he must have had to navigate growing up.

David Jones changed his name to Tom Jones in 1965 because of the popularity of Davy Jones of the Monkees. The name Tom Jones only lasted a short time because Welsh musician Tom Jones burst onto the scene with a hit record the same year. David Jones found a new identity—David Bowie.[6]

Bowie's name change was similar to that of fellow Englishman George Orwell. Orwell was born Eric Blair in India, where his father was an official in the British colonial government's opium department. Bowie's and Orwell's name changes were significant in what they represented. David Jones would not contribute to bringing down the Berlin Wall, and Eric Blair would not be one of the most important political writers of the twentieth century. Jones and Blair reinvented themselves, creating alter egos who became groundbreaking artists and cultural icons. Bowie developed into the master of reinvention, but not in Berlin. In Berlin he found himself.

In 1972 Bowie admitted to a reporter that he was bisexual. In 1983 he confessed to *Rolling Stone* magazine, "The biggest mistake I ever made was telling that *Melody Maker* writer that I was bisexual. Christ, I was so young then. I was experimenting...."[7]

In the end, it doesn't matter whether Bowie was gay, bisexual, heterosexual, or exploring gender. He had an enormous impact on the LGBTQ+ community that was just demanding its rights when Bowie's androgynous Ziggy Stardust appeared out of the ether. When Bowie put his arm around guitarist Mick Ronson in the 1972 *Tops of the Pops* performance of "Starman," it upset some, but others considered it a statement that it was okay to be gay or different. The gesture made Bowie an overnight sensation.[8]

When Bowie died, tributes flooded in from LGBTQ+ fans, who "shared how the rocker influenced their lives and helped bring queer culture into the mainstream in the 1960s and 1970s. In essays and interviews and on Twitter and Facebook, they told how his rise gave them strength."[9]

In fact, Bowie's wide range of styles and sounds, both spoken and unspoken, moved many demographics, including people who were gay, Black, or Berliners.

Bowie's "plastic soul" album, *Young Americans*, was made in Philadelphia in 1975 with a then-unknown Luther Vandross and guitarist Carlos Alomar (who became Bowie's musical director for the next ten years). It was popular on Black radio, resulting in Bowie becoming only the second white artist to perform on *Soul Train* that same year.

The *Soul Train* audience accepted and appreciated Bowie; they understood he was an outsider and unique. *Soul Train*'s host, the great Don Cornelius, was effusive and generous, even though he had to light a fire under Bowie, who had had a few drinks before the performance.[10]

II

IN 2013 BOWIE GAVE THE "DAVID BOWIE IS" exhibit curators almost complete access to his archives. Victoria and Albert Museum director Geoffrey Marsh said he'd heard Bowie read a book a day.[11] Bowie's son, Duncan, said that his father was a "beast of a reader."[12] Bowie brought four hundred books with him to New Mexico during the filming of *The Man Who Fell to Earth*.

The exhibit released a list of his favorite hundred titles, and with the list, Bowie did something he rarely did: he revealed himself.

More than a few of his favorite reads were related to Berlin, the Cold War, politics, and disenfranchised people. Two books were written by the ultimate Cold War writer George Orwell, who battled fascism, communism, and imperialism. *Nineteen Eighty-Four*, the timeless dystopian novel, is based on Orwell's experiences in the Spanish Civil War and what he witnessed in the 1930s and 1940s. The themes of the totalitarian nightmare of control and conformity, and one man's struggle to be free, had a deep impact on Bowie, and in 1973–1974 he attempted to gain the rights to turn *Nineteen Eighty-Four* into a musical. When the Orwell estate refused to grant him the rights, he came out with the Orwell-themed *Diamond Dogs* album, which included the songs "1984," "Big Brother," and "We Are the Dead."

Inside the Whale and Other Essays contains the first sign that Orwell would become Orwell with the essay "Shooting an Elephant." It is a metaphor for imperialism written while Orwell was a police officer in Burma. In another essay in the collection, "Politics and the English Language" (1962), Orwell writes that political language "is designed to make lies sound truthful and murder respectable, and to give an appearance of solidity to pure wind."

Four of Bowie's favorite books were set in Berlin, three of them dealing with pre-Nazi Germany: *Berlin Alexanderplatz* by Alfred Döblin, *Mr. Norris Changes Trains* by Christopher Isherwood, and *Before the Deluge* by Otto Friedrich. These disparate, brilliant reads evoke a sense of Berlin before the onslaught of the Nazi madness.

Bowie became friends with Isherwood in Los Angeles, and it was Isherwood who influenced his decision to move to Berlin. Bowie lived near where Isherwood had lived in Berlin in 1929–1933 during the last days of the Weimar Republic.

Another Bowie favorite, *The Quest for Christa T.* by East German writer Christa Wolf, is a fluid, experimental narrative about the mysterious life of an East German woman and what happens to the human spirit in a totalitarian state. Christa T. strives to be honest at a time when survival in East Germany requires deception. The book was a sensation on its release in 1968, but it was soon condemned in East Germany. Later Christa Wolf was a speaker at the Alexanderplatz demonstration in East Berlin five days before the Wall fell.

Four books on Bowie's list were about struggles for freedom and from oppression in the Soviet Union and Russia. *Octobriana and the Russian Underground* by Petr Sadecký, tells of a comic book heroine who becomes superhuman in a radioactive volcano and leads the Soviet underground's resistance against Russian and American hegemony. Released in 1971 and only available in illegal magazines at the time, it was important to a generation of young Russian dissenters. *A People's Tragedy: The Russian Revolution: 1891–1924* by British historian Orlando Figes, is a thousand-page tome on the Russian Revolution. *Journey into the Whirlwind* by Russian author Eugenia Ginzburg, documents her eighteen-year imprisonment in the Soviet Gulag after she was caught up in Stalin's purges in the 1930s. *Darkness at Noon* by Arthur Koestler, is the chilling portrait of an aging Bolshevik tried for treason by the same revolutionary forces he once supported.

Bowie also listed nonfiction books related to American politics, including *The Trial of Henry Kissinger* by Christopher Hitchens, who makes the case for Kissinger's crimes of sanctioned murder, genocide, and more when he was the secretary of state in the Nixon administration. *A People's History of the United States* by Howard Zinn, chronicles the history of the United States through the perspective of marginalized people, including workers, women, Black Americans, and Native peoples.

Bowie was an outspoken antiracist in his words and deeds. He famously called out MTV for not playing videos by Black artists[13]—and his support of and interest in the Black experience was reflected in his favorite books. The titles include *Passing* by Nella Larsen, *Black Boy* by Richard Wright, *The Street* by Ann Petry, *Infants of the Spring* by Wallace Thurman, and *The Fire Next Time* by James Baldwin.

Bowie claimed to be nonpolitical, and he rarely, if ever, endorsed political candidates or made a political statement, but he did live at the epicenter of the Cold War and recorded music less than a mile from the Berlin Wall.

The infamous 1976 *Playboy* magazine interview with Cameron Crowe, in which Bowie said he believed strongly in fascism and thought Hitler was the first rock star,[14] has no correlation to anything he said or did elsewhere in his life. It was a narcissistic remark with nothing behind it except his rock star egomania, his sense that he knew better than everyone else, and his need for total control to get things done. "My interest in [the Nazis]," Bowie said, "was the fact they supposedly came to England before the war to find the Holy Grail at Glastonbury... the idea that it was about putting Jews in concentration camps and the complete oppression of different races completely evaded my extraordinary fucked-up nature at that particular time."[15] Bowie wasn't referring to a fascism that would commit genocide against a minority, purge and imprison dissenters, or start a world war.

Still, there was no excuse for his comments.

However, the photo from the same period, allegedly of Bowie giving a Nazi salute to a crowd greeting him, was not true. The photographer had caught him in the middle of a wave.

Bowie was not in his right mind; he was addicted to cocaine and was going through a drug-related psychosis that warped his critical thinking.[16] During this period he didn't sleep for days and ate little, his weight dropping to one hundred pounds. Later Bowie referred to this time as "singularly the darkest days of my life."[17]

III

IN 1945 PRESIDENT FRANKLIN ROOSEVELT, General Secretary Joseph Stalin, and Prime Minister Winston Churchill met at the Yalta and Potsdam Conferences to decide what to do with Europe and a soon-to-be defeated Germany. They agreed to break Germany into four zones: East Germany would be controlled by the Soviet Union and West Germany by the United States, Great Britain, and France.

The phrase *Iron Curtain* entered the Cold War vocabulary in 1946 when Churchill warned of the Soviet Union's expansionist policies and the risk of dividing Europe into two spheres of influence. It was not merely the conflicting ideologies of communism and capitalism that caused the split; it was another totalitarian leader, Joseph Vissarionovich Stalin.

George Orwell was one of the first to see the enemy behind the enemy when he fought against Franco, Hitler, and the fascist coup during the Spanish Civil War. Stalin, who was funding the democratically elected leftist government's war effort, turned on his allies, and Orwell barely made it out of Spain alive. His remarkable memoir, *Homage to Catalonia*, recognized the evil of Stalin early on.

Some historians estimate Stalin's regime killed up to twenty million people in the Soviet Union through starvation, executions, massacres, forced labor, and more.[18]

In 1949 West Germany created the Federal Republic of Germany (FRG). In response, East Germany created the German Democratic Republic (GDR), but it was controlled by the Soviet Embassy and the threat of the Soviet military based in East Germany.

Berlin was an island in the middle of East Germany, but because of its importance culturally and symbolically, the Allies decided that one country should not control Berlin. They carved it up into sectors: the Soviets controlled East Berlin, and the United States, Great Britain, and France controlled West Berlin.

What further separated the two Germanys was the phenomenon known as Wirtschaftswünder—the "economic miracle," when the West German economy boomed in the late 1940s while East Germany suffered economic malaise. Though East Germany was more stable than other Eastern Bloc nations, its economic performance did not compare to that of West European countries. As the standard of living in West Germany rose, many East Germans became even more desperate to find a way to the West.

The Soviets were not happy that a capitalist city flaunting Western freedoms and decadence was in the center of their zone. The existence of West Berlin "stuck like a bone in the Soviet throat," Soviet leader Nikita Khrushchev said.[19]

To solve the problem, they set up a blockade in June 1948 to starve the West out of Berlin. But the Allies responded with the Berlin Airlift, which supplied more than two million tons of food, fuel, and other supplies to West Berlin.[20] The Soviets realized the blockade was tactically and politically a failure; they ended it in May 1949. That same year, the Western powers created NATO, which included Belgium, Great Britain, Canada, Denmark, France, Iceland, Italy, Luxembourg, the Netherlands, Norway, Portugal, and the United States. Greece and Turkey were added in 1952, West Germany in 1955, and Spain in 1982. In response the Soviets instituted the Warsaw Pact, a military alliance that included, among others, Albania, Bulgaria, Czechoslovakia, East Germany, Hungary, Poland, and Romania.[21]

East Germans, many of whom were skilled workers, fled to the West to escape the poor economy and totalitarian regime. In June 1961 alone, nineteen thousand people left East Germany through Berlin. Another thirty thousand departed in July. An additional sixteen thousand crossed over in just the first eleven days of August.[22]

Enough was enough for the Soviets. An order to close the border was signed on August 12, 1961, on the assumption that President Kennedy would not start a war over it. They were right. Kennedy's response was that the Wall was "not a very nice solution, but…a hell of a lot better than a war."[23]

Kennedy did send American troops—1,500 men in full battle gear, and 491 vehicles—through East Germany to West Berlin to show that the West would not be blocked from entering. Still, with the Wall in place, the Soviet regime was in full control of East Germany.

A week before Kennedy's beautifully crafted "Ich bin ein Berliner" speech in 1961, he called Berlin "the great testing place of Western courage and will" and warned that any attack on West Berlin was an attack on the United States.[24]

Kennedy, who was wildly popular in Berlin, attracted a massive crowd of 120,000 to hear him speak in front of the Rathaus Schöneberg (city hall). Schöneberg is the working-class neighborhood Bowie and Iggy lived in.

"There are many people in the world who really don't understand, or say they don't, what is the great issue between the free world and the communist world," Kennedy said in his speech. "Let them come to Berlin. There are some who say that communism is the wave of the future. Let them come to Berlin. And there are some who say in Europe and elsewhere we can work with the Communists. Let them come to Berlin. And there are even a few who say that it is true that communism is an evil system, but it permits us to make economic progress. Lasst sie nach Berlin kommen. Let them come to Berlin." Kennedy ended the speech by saying, "All free men, wherever they may live, are citizens of Berlin, and, therefore, as a free man, I take pride in the words 'Ich bin ein Berliner.'"[25]

Kennedy's defiant words gave West Germany, fearful of the recent Soviet actions, a tremendous boost of confidence and hope and solidified the United States' commitment to Berlin. A few years later, in 1963, Kennedy completed the nuclear test ban treaty, further reducing tensions between the United States and the Soviet Union.

The Wall spanned twenty-eight miles through and seventy-five miles around Berlin. It included hundreds of watchtowers and guard dog runs and was patrolled twenty-four hours a day. Guards had orders to shoot to kill. The Wall was called an "antifascist bulwark" in the East, which was Orwellian and politically deceptive language; the Wall was clearly erected to keep East Berlin citizens from fleeing to the West.[26] East Germany also created a barrier to seal off the 850-mile border between East and West Germany.[27]

Still, from 1961–1989, five thousand East Germans escaped to the West, tunneling under the Wall, swimming across rivers, hiding in cars, and using other methods, like the two families who escaped in a hot-air balloon.

East Germany killed nearly two hundred people attempting to cross the border,[28] and thousands were caught trying to flee. It was not easy to evade the East German secret police, the Stasi; they employed one hundred thousand agents, more than three times the size of the Gestapo under Hitler, and up to two million collaborators. It kept files on one in three East Germans.[29]

IV

BEFORE BOWIE CAME TO BERLIN, he played Thomas Jerome Newton in his first feature film, *The Man Who Fell to Earth*, a role more fitting than any other character he played. He captured Newton's superior knowledge and intellect and the essence of Newton, who was from the planet Anthea and had come down to earth to build a spaceship to transport water back to his drought-plagued planet that had destroyed itself through wars. Newton despaired that the same madness was likely to happen on earth.

Whether it was Roeg's vision, the editing, or the added sex scenes, the film didn't allow the tragedy of Thomas Jerome Newton to unfold as clearly and poignantly as in the book. However, Bowie's and Candy Clark's performances were terrific, and the film is memorable.

Bowie used photos taken during *The Man Who Fell to Earth* as the album art on both his *Station to Station* and *Low* albums. A video from his final album, *Blackstar*, referenced Thomas Jerome Newton, and his final project, the musical *Lazarus*, featured Thomas Jerome Newton as the protagonist. The character of Newton obviously meant something to Bowie.

Newton also recorded an album, *The Visitor*, in the Anthean language for his family, who would soon be dead because of his failure to produce a spacecraft that could save them and his fellow Anthenians. Bowie was supposed to produce *The Man Who Fell to Earth*'s soundtrack, but it never materialized; instead he brought what he had written to Berlin and played it for his band. They were impressed. At least one song, "Subterraneans," ended up on the *Low* album

When Bowie moved to Berlin in 1976, the war was still evident there more than thirty years after Germany's defeat. Empty lots, bullet holes, and partially destroyed buildings scarred the landscape.

Bowie was a member of a new generation that had not been alive during the war. Berlin was a liberal city that had welcomed the avant-garde in the 1920s, and it embraced Bowie and Iggy Pop. They were reminders of the Weimar culture in Germany in 1918–1933, where artists and intellectuals were free to explore and create in a variety of fields. Gay culture and strong women were welcome in Weimar Berlin. Bauhaus design, the Dada art movement, Fritz Lang, Marlene Dietrich, Anita Berber, Bertolt Brecht, Christopher Isherwood, Thomas Mann, Arnold Schoenberg, and Albert Einstein are all associated with this period before the Nazi nightmare.

Bowie and Iggy Pop (whose real name is James Osterberg) came to Berlin partly to clean up from drugs: Bowie from cocaine and Iggy from heroin. They had no idea that Berlin was the heroin capital of the world. They didn't get completely clean, but their drug problems dissipated in Berlin.

The city was divided in two, and Bowie fit perfectly in West Berlin. He was soon one of them—a friend and neighbor. He enjoyed a relationship with Romy Haag, an entertainer who ran a cabaret club. Berlin had many warehouse spaces and art galleries for him to explore, and Bowie painted often. Berliners were polite and left the superstar alone. He appreciated the freedom they gave him. Yet he was also going through personal issues during his time there, including difficulties in his marriage and a contentious legal battle with his ex-manager.

Still, Bowie's problems never affected his focus on his art and music. *"Heroes"* recording sessions often went all night long, and Iggy Pop said Bowie was always organized, no matter what he was going through.

"I was very lucky to be there at that time, mainly because it was undergoing artistically its greatest renaissance since the Weimar days of the 1920s," Bowie remarked, "when it was definitely the cultural gateway to Europe. When I was there, the whole new German expressionist period had started, and all of the German electronic bands were coming down to Berlin to work."[30]

Meanwhile East Germany was centrally controlled, without fair elections, freedom of speech, or freedom to create or move about. Life in East Berlin was characterized as impoverished and polluted. It was difficult to listen to subversive music like Bowie or punk rock, although it could be heard through West Berlin radio.

A remarkably talented group of musicians played on Bowie's Berlin Trilogy albums: *Low*, *"Heroes"*, and *Lodger*. Tony Visconti produced all three albums with Bowie and played on them along with Dennis Davis, George Murray, Brian Eno, Carlos Alomar, Robert Fripp, Ricky Gardiner, Roy Young, Adrian Belew, and other talented musicians.

Of the three albums in the trilogy, *"Heroes"* was the only one fully recorded in Berlin. *Lodger* wasn't recorded in Berlin at all. *Low* was mostly recorded in France but was completed and mixed in Berlin. *Low* and *"Heroes"*, both released in 1977, were infused with content related to Berlin and the Berlin Wall. *Lodger* came out in 1979 and does not suggest Berlin much, if at all. The label Berlin Trilogy might have been a marketing ploy to link the albums and sales, but Bowie himself referred to the three albums as a trilogy.

"I liked the idea of the Berlin Wall because, at that time, I felt that it was always necessary to be in a place where there was tension," he said. "And you couldn't find a place with more tension than…West Berlin [with its] factional elements, both musically and artistically. There was also a very strong socialist, left-wing element there, which gave it this kind of anarchistic vibe. I can see why, throughout the 20th century, it was the city [that] writers continually returned to, because both the negative and positive aspects of whatever's going to happen in Europe always emanate at some point, right back to the 1920s, from Berlin."[31]

Bowie's past—glam rock, Ziggy, *Aladdin Sane*, Los Angeles, the Thin White Duke—didn't make the trip to Berlin. At least, it is not present on *Low*. *Low* is reality. Bowie was coming clean on *Low*, with its chilling, isolated sound and raw lyrics that synced with Berlin, a city and culture that had been laid low, evidenced most clearly by the Berlin Wall.

Low has two distinct sides. The first contains short, emotional, innovative songs that deal with a variety of difficulties and traumas. "Breaking Glass" suggests psychological drama and dark conflict. Three songs, "Breaking Glass," "What in the World," and "Sound and Vision" mention being in a room, suggesting an isolated or imaginary world. "Speed of Life" contains no lyrics because Bowie couldn't think of any. In "What in the World," a young woman yearns for freedom, like Christa Wolf's protagonist in *Christa T.*

"Always Crashing in the Same Car" refers to Bowie ramming his Mercedes into a drug dealer's car after something went wrong in Berlin. No one said anything, and no one stopped him. In a hotel parking lot, Bowie drove in circles at over ninety miles per hour before he ran out of gas, saving him and Iggy Pop.[32] The song also has the meaning of making the same mistake again and again.

"Be My Wife" speaks to his loneliness and rootlessness. "A New Car in a New Town" has no lyrics and a positive energy that refers to starting over in Berlin.

It took more than words to capture the grayness, isolation, alienation, and fear of the city, the Wall, and the Cold War. The second side of *Low* is almost entirely instrumental; the songs are electronic, inspired by Eno and German Krautrock (for example, Kraftwerk and Neu!), and these influences appear for the first time on a Bowie album.

"Berlin has the strange ability to make you write only the important things," Bowie said. "Anything else, you don't mention—and in the end, you produce *Low*."[33]

"Warszawa" refers to the bleakness of the Cold War and Warsaw, where Bowie had recently traveled. The song includes a made-up language, perhaps a play on Thomas Jerome Newton's album *The Visitor* in the Anthean language. "Art Decade" refers to art decay and the lost German cultural renaissance during the Weimar Republic. "Weeping Wall" is about the Berlin Wall and the misery in East Berlin. "Subterraneans" captures Thomas Jerome Newton's lost family in Anthea and those similarly forgotten in East Berlin.

Bowie also said this about making *Low*: "It was a dangerous period for me. I was at the end of my tether physically and emotionally and had serious doubts about my sanity. But this was in France. Overall, I get a sense of real optimism through the veils of despair from *Low*. I can hear myself really struggling to get well."[34]

The *"Heroes"* album was Bowie's emergence from the *Low* period, conquering his drug habit. *"Heroes"* was recorded at Hansa Studios in Berlin near the Wall. The pillars on the studio's exterior were still pockmarked with bullet holes from the war.

Carlos Alomar talked about recording in Berlin: "It was not foreboding, just that the air was thick with a darker vibe. You have got to remember, we're painting a picture based on our emotional disposition and you're thinking: Germans, Nazis, the Wall, oppression. These things are hanging in the air, and when things get darker physically, you kind of think of darker themes too. Berlin was a rather dark, industrial place to work. There was one point when we wanted to see a bit of light and we asked them to open the curtains. There were these gigantic, heavy curtains and when they did that, we saw the walk where the gunner is and that was a rather rude awakening. Although it gave us a cold slap in the face as to where we were, it also gave us a heavier resolve about the intensity of what we were doing."[35]

Side one of *"Heroes"* is energetic and edgy, perhaps influenced by punk and the fact that Berlin was a dangerous place. "Beauty and the Beast," though, might connote the good as well as the evil in Berlin. "Joe the Lion" is partially a tribute to Los Angeles artist Chris Burden, who nailed himself to a car and had someone shoot him in the arm. "Sons of the Silent Age" was recorded before Bowie came to Berlin and describes a silent generation, which could easily refer to East Germans. "Blackout" may refer to real blackouts, internal and external. Its experimental sonic confusion is driven by a remarkable performance by an artist at the height of his power.

The second side of *"Heroes"* is primarily a return to instrumental or ambient music. "V-2 Schneider" is a bow to Florian Schneider, a founding member of the German band Kraftwerk. "Sense of Doubt" is a foreboding piece that fits right in with the darkest moments of the 1981 German film *Christiane F,* the true story of an alienated and attractive Berlin teen falling in love with a heroin addict and becoming addicted to heroin herself. The film touched a nerve for the young people of Berlin and around the world.

Bowie appears in the film playing himself, and the soundtrack is entirely his music. Three songs originally appeared on the *Station to Station* album, though it's the singles version of "Stay" and a live rendition of "Station to Station" from Bowie's 1978 live album *Stage.* The remaining seven songs are from *Low,* *"Heroes",* and *Lodger.*

In her sensational memoir on which the film was based, the real Christiane Vera Felscherinow wrote that Bowie was her idol. *Christiane F.,* both the film and the book, still maintain a powerful cult following on social media. The film is now considered an essential part of German cinema.

"Moss Garden" is said to be about a Zen garden, but it contains a mystery that isn't completely serene. "Neuköln" is a moody jaunt through a district in Berlin where Turkish "guest workers" lived near the Wall. "The Secret Life of Arabia" refers to Middle East influences and is the forerunner of a new direction and his next album, *Lodger.*

While Berlin bleeds through both *Low* and *"Heroes",* *Lodger* is an experimental album that has gained more respect as it has aged. *Lodger* travels outside of Berlin to Turkey, Africa, and beyond. The song "Move On" suggests Bowie was ready to go to the next station in his life, but he wasn't only traveling; he was looking back. He'd done as much as he could in Berlin. At that point in his life, Bowie never stayed too long in the same place literally or artistically.

"Nothing else sounded like those albums," Bowie said. "Nothing else came close. If I never made another album, it really wouldn't matter now, my complete being is within those three. They are my DNA."[36]

Bowie's most important song to come out of Berlin, was, of course, the sublime "Heroes." It was not a big hit when it was released, but it became the soundtrack of the Berlin Wall.

His vocal performance of "Heroes" was one of the most extraordinary of his career, his tense passion and edgy plea capturing the imagery and the emotions of the Wall. The lyrics about swimming like dolphins had special meaning for Germans because of those who died trying to swim across the Spree River to the West. In 1977, the same year Bowie recorded *Low* and *"Heroes"*, East German border guards killed eighteen-year-old Dietmar Schwietzer when he attempted to escape. That same year, Henri Weise, a twenty-two-year-old East German, drowned trying to swim across the Spree River.

The two lovers at the Wall who inspired Bowie's lyrics were his producer, Tony Visconti, and singer Antonia Maass. Bowie happened to spot them at the Wall kissing.

Berlin mayor Michael Müller stated after Bowie died that "Heroes" became "the hymn of our then-divided city, and its longing for freedom."[37]

V

IN THE 1970S, BOWIE'S MUSIC WAS CENSORED by the Kremlin—it was considered subversive—but there was a black market, so he was known to some Russian music lovers in cities like St. Petersburg and Leningrad. An underground network called samizdat created cassettes of his music for distribution.[38] Later, in the 1980s, Bowie became a cult figure in Russia when technology made it easier to copy his work. His music went viral among new Russian fans.

On Bowie's first trip to Russia in 1973, he took the Trans-Siberian Express from Japan to Moscow with his childhood friend, Geoff MacCormack, where they were given communist propaganda: the book *Marx, Engels and Lenin on Scientific Communism*, which contained information about what they could and couldn't photograph, and a bizarre flyer about the destructive influence of the classic American cartoon *Tom and Jerry*.

Describing their travels through Siberia for the teen magazine *Mirabelle*, Bowie said, "I could never have imagined such expanses of unspoiled, natural country without actually seeing it myself. It was like a glimpse into another age, another world, and it made a very strong impression on me. It was strange to be sitting on a train, which is the product of technology—the invention of mankind, and traveling through land so untouched and unspoiled by man and his inventions."[39]

Bowie made friends with two young women who worked on the train, Danya and Nadya. They hung out with him when they were not working. In his *Mirabelle* interview, Bowie recalled that "they sat with big smiles on their faces, sometimes for hours on end, listening to my music, and at the end of each song, they would applaud and cheer!"

Danya and Nadya saved Bowie from being arrested after he took photos and refused to turn them over to a man who they believed was a plainclothes police officer. Danya and Nadya did not allow the man to board before the train left that station.

On that trip Bowie was also interrogated by two men who tried to speak with American accents and suspiciously did not know who he was, which was highly unlikely if they had been Americans. The men started a "friendly" conversation and eventually asked about his politics. Bowie and MacCormack suspected them of being KGB.

When Bowie finally arrived in Moscow, Russians stared disapprovingly at his spiked red hair, platform boots, and colorful wardrobe.

After receiving a lukewarm reception after one of his few concerts in Russia, he vowed to never play there again.[40]

In 1976 Bowie, Iggy Pop, photographer Andrew Kent (author of *Bowie: Behind the Curtain*), and others traveled to Moscow by train between concert venues. Though there were restrictions on traveling through the Soviet Union, especially if you were from a Western or NATO country, Bowie knew one could get a transit visa from Zurich to Helsinki, passing through Poland and Moscow.

Kent recalled, "We were ghosts until we got to Brest, Poland, where an albino KGB agent took us off the train and interrogated us. They took a *Playboy* magazine and some books of David's and let us go, saying someone would meet us in Moscow, but no one did."[41]

At the border, Bowie and Iggy Pop were strip-searched before they were permitted to leave. They radiated individuality and freedom, two qualities the Kremlin could not tolerate.

VI

IN 1987 BOWIE PLAYED THE CONCERT FOR BERLIN, a three-day event on a stage erected right in front of the Reichstag, the former Parliament building, on the West German side of the Berlin Wall. The Reichstag had been destroyed by the 1933 arson that Hitler used to suspend civil rights and grant himself dictatorial powers to arrest and mass-detain the Left. Hitler blamed the Communists for the fire, but it was more likely his own Nazi party was the culprit. After the blaze, with many of the elected Left arrested, Germany became a one-party, fascist state.[42]

Bowie performed the second night, and the West piped in the concert to East German radio. Bowie had heard rumors that East Berliners might congregate on the other side of the Wall, so he addressed them right before launching into "Heroes": "We send our best wishes to all of our friends who are on the other side of the Wall."[43]

Bowie gave a powerful and dramatic performance of "Heroes," in which he broke out of shackles on stage while those on both sides of the Wall sang along.

"So it was like a double concert where the Wall was the division," Bowie explained, "and we would hear them cheering and singing along from the other side. God, even now I get choked up. It was breaking my heart. I'd never done anything like that in my life, and I guess I never will again." He added that singing "Heroes" felt "anthemic, almost like a prayer."[44]

The East German authorities had seen and heard enough, and the next night they arrested and beat those who attempted to listen to the concert. When a minor riot occurred, unruly East Berliners shouted, "The Wall must fall!" and "Gorby, get us out!"

East German security reacted with too much force, pummeling those in attendance with billy clubs, causing a severe backlash in East Berlin.

The week after Bowie's concert, President Reagan gave his famous Berlin speech near the Reichstag building and in front of the Brandenburg Gate, behind two panes of bulletproof glass: "General Secretary Gorbachev, if you seek peace, if you seek prosperity for the Soviet Union and Eastern Europe, if you seek liberalization: Come here to this gate! Mr. Gorbachev, open this gate!" Reagan paused because of the cheers, then said, "Mr. Gorbachev, tear down this wall!"[45]

Reagan drew a crowd of forty-five thousand to his speech. Heavy security surrounded his visit because twenty-four thousand anti-Reagan protesters, who were not allowed to attend the speech, had gathered in West Berlin the day before he arrived.[46]

The speech received little media coverage at the time and landed on the back pages of major American and European newspapers. It was only in retrospect that it gained significance, at least in the West.[47]

The Soviet news agency TASS called the speech "openly provocative" and "war-mongering." But CBS White House correspondent Bill Plante, who was in Berlin for the speech, said, "The audience was exhilarated. And, so were most of us who covered the event."[48]

German Chancellor Helmut Kohl said, "He [Reagan] was a stroke of luck for the world, especially for Europe."[49]

Gorbachev commented much later: "We really were not impressed. We knew that Mr. Reagan's original profession was actor."[50]

More important than Reagan's speech were his diplomatic efforts and ability to compromise in his second term. He built trust and improved relations with Gorbachev. Before Reagan left office, he and Gorbachev signed the Intermediate-Range Nuclear Forces (INF) Treaty, which eliminated medium- and short-range missiles capable of carrying nuclear weapons.

"I think, frankly, [that] President Gorbachev and I discovered a sort of a bond," Reagan said in Moscow in 1990, "a friendship between us, that we thought could become such a bond between all the people."[51]

Another powerful force in the effort to free the Eastern Bloc from Soviet domination was Pope John Paul II, who visited and said mass in his native Poland in 1979. Millions came out to see him, and his message of freedom was a huge injection of faith and courage for Solidarity, a Polish anti-communist trade union of more than nine million members that began in 1980, led by shipyard electrician and future president Lech Wałęsa.

Solidarity espoused nonviolence, freedom, justice, and democracy, and they had the pope's unwavering support. In 1989 Solidarity formed a coalition with two smaller parties to become the first non-communist government in a Soviet-run country.

When the pope met with Gorbachev in late 1989, after the Wall had fallen, he criticized communism and capitalism. "I don't serve any political parties, I serve God," the pope told

Gorbachev, "so I'm after the same things that you are trying to achieve...."[52] The two expressed their admiration for each other, and Gorbachev later said that the collapse of the Iron Curtain would have been impossible without John Paul II.

The single person most responsible for the Wall coming down was, of course, Gorbachev. Reagan stated, "Mr. Gorbachev deserves most of the credit, as the leader of this country."[53]

Gorbachev sought better relations with the West for economic reasons and created strong bonds with Western leaders. In 1985 he implemented glasnost, a policy of "openness and transparency" in the Soviet government, and perestroika, or restructuring, decentralizing economic decision-making. Glasnost made it possible for citizens to point out problems and propose solutions in the government, and promoted freedom of information, giving the media more access to information.

Perhaps the most important change Gorbachev made was ending the Brezhnev Doctrine, which justified intervention and the use of military force in threatened Soviet-aligned socialist states. The loosening of totalitarian control gave the Eastern Bloc countries more freedom to revolt against Soviet oppression, and it put pressure on East German authorities to be more open as well.

Gorbachev's glasnost era opened the door to major rock concerts in East Germany, including Bruce Springsteen's influential concert in 1988. Springsteen played a rocking set for four hours to more than three hundred thousand eager fans in East Berlin. The event wasn't near the Wall because the East German authorities feared that the excitement might cause a mass exodus across the border.

During the concert, Springsteen spoke to the attendees in rudimentary German: "I'm not here for any government. I've come to play rock 'n' roll for you in the hope that one day, all the barriers will be torn down."[54]

"Once in a while you play a place, you play a show that ends up staying inside of you, living with you for the rest of your life. East Berlin in 1988 was certainly one of them," Springsteen reminisced.

After Springsteen's epic concert, East Germans wanted more openness, not less, something their leaders had not expected. They had thought the concert would keep people in check, but their strategy backfired. Springsteen's concert contributed to the sense that real change was coming.

On November 4, 1989, the largest demonstration ever in East Germany took place at Alexanderplatz in East Berlin, where half a million citizens protested for political reform. The Alexanderplatz demonstration came about when a frustrated group of actors and fellow travelers with the Deutsches Theater in East Berlin had the idea of organizing a state-sanctioned demonstration to discuss "the context" of the state's existing constitution. To their surprise, the East Berlin authorities agreed to their application for a demonstration, amazing everyone because it was the first demonstration organized by citizens rather than the government.

"It's as if someone has thrown open the windows after all these years of stagnation, after years of dullness and mustiness, of phrase-mongering and bureaucratic despotism," said one of the day's speakers, novelist Stefan Heym.[55]

Before the Alexanderplatz demonstration there had been important October protests in Dresden and Leipzig. The Soviet grip on East Germany was crumbling.

On November 9, 1989, Günter Schabowski, an official of the

ruling Socialist Unity Party of Germany, announced a new visa and travel policy: "Permanent relocations can be done through all border checkpoints between the GDR into the FRG or West Berlin." He emphasized that the policy referred to more than just tourism, and when a reporter at the press conference asked when the policy would begin, Schabowski said, "As far as I know, it takes effect immediately, without delay."

That wasn't correct. Schabowski had learned of the new policy on the way to the news conference and was not familiar with the details. The East German authorities had no intention of opening the border. The policy was meant to make it easier for East Germans to travel outside the country and even leave permanently; however, they were required to obtain a visa, which involved a lot of red tape, something Schabowski failed to mention.[56]

On the news that evening, West German anchorman Hanns Joachim Friedrichs restated Schabowski's interpretation of the policy, adding, "This 9 November is a historic day. The GDR has announced that, starting immediately, its borders are open to everyone. The gates in the Wall stand open wide."[57]

Thousands of people swarmed the border, wanting to cross. The border guards were confused; the new rules had not been communicated to them, and they were receiving no guidance from their superiors. But no one in the East German government wanted to be responsible for violence, and eventually the commander of the border guards opened the checkpoints despite there being no explicit order or mandate to do so.

The dam had broken wide open, and there was no going back unless the GDR wanted to use excessive force to rein East Germans in. That weekend more than two million East Germans passed over to West Berlin.

Bowie and the Berlin Wall

In the end the Wall came down because of a misunderstanding, an accident, or perhaps fate.

VII

IT TOOK THIS LOOSE COALITION of people from divergent backgrounds, beliefs, and professions to bring down the Wall through peaceful means.

The debt-ridden economies of the Soviet Union and its satellites played a role in the collapse of East Germany, as did increasing dissent and demand for freedoms in Eastern Bloc nations. Other factors included pressure and support from multiple United States administrations, Pope John Paul II's pacifist outreach and strength, Gorbachev's brave leadership and policies, and the restrained Soviet and East German governments that did not resort to violence.

Gorbachev eventually accepted, without conditions, Chancellor Kohl and President Bush's plan to reunify Germany and end the Cold War. Gorbachev became a hero in the West. *Time* magazine named him Man of the Year in 1988 and Man of the Decade in 1989, and he was awarded the Nobel Peace Prize in 1990.

By 1991, the Soviet Union no longer existed, and Gorbachev, not popular in Russia, resigned the same year. He ran for office again in 1996 and received less than one percent of the vote.

In the end, the people who protested, who were beaten, who lost their jobs, who lived in fear, and who remained resolute and hopeful that a new day would come, were perhaps the most important factor.

Among the heroes who contributed to bringing down the Wall was David Bowie. His impact on Berlin began fourteen years before the Wall fell. He recorded and lived near the Wall. He was an insider and an outsider who was inspired by the city to produce his greatest works of art, albums that he believed were at the core of his being.

But Bowie was more than a tremendous artist in Berlin. He was a part of Berlin's Zeitgeist, exploring neighborhoods, restaurants, museums, nightclubs, cafés, bars, and concerts. He went on bike rides and even did his own grocery shopping. His daily presence lifted the city's spirits, and he became a beacon of hope. His 1987 concert at the Reichstag near the Wall was another key moment before the Wall fell two years later.

Even after Bowie departed, his music remained the most important soundtrack for Cold War Berlin in the 1970s and 1980s, communicating the lows as well as the courage so many exhibited in opposing the Wall and protesting to bring it down. His work in one of the most iconic films in German cinema history, *Christiane F.*, still resonates with young people today, more than forty years after it premiered to glowing reviews in 1981.

In 2002 Bowie played "Heroes" in Berlin again. "This time," he said, "what was so fantastic…is that half the audience had been in East Berlin that time way before. So now I was face to face with the people I had been singing it to all those years ago. And we were all singing it together. Again, it was powerful. Things like that really give you a sense of what a song and performance can do."[58]

VENICE TO VENICE

I

THE HALF-BURNED-OUT BUILDINGS were riddled with bullets. Random gunfire interrupted the silence. A toxic orange glow polluted the sky above the city.

A pathetically skinny dog with sores mapping its body wandered about, searching for food. It stopped on the road to smell a corpse, then began to lick it.

In one of the buildings, Brian—an intelligence officer embedded with the troops—winced with a sour expression. The soldiers didn't react to the dog, watching with a deadness in their eyes as if they saw something like this every day.

What a mess, Brian thought. By 2006 there was no way the Bush administration could spin this as anything but a disaster. Brian had known it would come to this before the eighty-eight thousand tons of bombs were dropped. He had been outspoken, warning they would not be greeted as liberators. They would be an occupying force, and a civil war between the Shiites and Sunnis would do more damage than the bombs. What he emphasized most was that thousands of Americans would be wounded or killed.

The dog's head exploded. The shot could have come from any of the buildings, but the troops began shooting up an already bullet-ridden structure.

"They're out there," a soldier said.

A small, trembling dark-haired girl crept out of a door. Her tangled hair resembled dreadlocks. She was covered in dust and appeared to be on her own.

Brian studied her bare feet edging forward; she was so frightened she could barely move.

The two soldiers closest to him were focused on her too. Brian shut his eyes for a moment, and when he opened them, he believed she was staring at him.

A burly sergeant appeared alongside him. "Jesus."

"It could be a trap," a second soldier said.

"What is she doing here?" Brian asked.

"What the hell are we doing here?"

"What are you doing here?" the sergeant said, leaning into Brian.

"Just doing my job."

"And what is your job?"

"Intelligence gathering."

The sergeant laughed. "I don't see a whole lot of intelligence around here."

"That's what I'll report back."

The sergeant slapped Brian's shoulder.

A truck appeared from around the corner, driving slowly.

"Vehicle!"

Brian could see a teenage boy who appeared to be tied to the steering wheel. A man jumped out of the passenger side and raced behind the truck. The truck veered to the right now and sped up to where the girl quivered.

"We have to get her out of there," Brian shouted.

"Down," the sergeant said, yanking him to the ground.

The truck detonated, Brian covering himself, feeling the heat from the fiery explosion.

II

THE EARLY-AFTERNOON CLOUDS and lazy blue skies descended upon the condominium. Brian watched Michael spread his arms out and hover above the pool, hanging there for several long seconds before he stretched straight and knifed into the water between two oblivious kids.

Michael rose and then waded in the pool up to his slim waist. His flawless wet skin glistened in the sunlight.

A man in a tracksuit and huge glasses appeared next to Brian.

"The pool was eco-cleaned without chemicals or chlorine. Clear, isn't it?" the man said.

The sun reflected off the phosphorescent water. It did seem unusually clear.

Brian watched Michael again when the man moved on. He was climbing out of the pool now and was tossed a towel by Brian's nineteen-year-old daughter, Emily, before they made their way over to him.

Michael must have been at least six foot one. Brian felt old and a little beat up near Michael, a feeling he didn't have with the other kids. When Michael put his arm around Emily, Brian was surprised. She had not mentioned that she was dating anyone.

It was February 2017, and Brian had officially been living and working in Venice, California, for about a year. He watched Michael and Emily laughing and talking about something. She had been attending UCLA since 2016, and he had been going to yoga with her about twice a month since he moved to Venice. Brian had landed a job he was passionate about, but he was even happier to be living near his daughter.

After some back and forth, they decided to drive to Abbot Kinney to listen to a jazz trio that was playing at Hank's, a popular and classic Venice restaurant. Inside they joined a mixed, eclectic audience of African Americans who had been coming to Hank's for years and the white Westside crowd.

"Where are you from, Michael?" Brian asked after they were seated.

"I'm from the other Venice."

"Venice, Italy? Now you're in Venice again."

"Yes, Venice to Venice."

"Venice is my favorite city. Emily's mother and I honeymooned there."

Emily frowned and focused on the trio. His divorce from her mother lingered in the air for a moment.

"Venice connects the East and the West, but it's in danger," Michael said. "There are now one hundred and fifty tourists to one Venetian. We are turning into a sort of Disneyland. If this doesn't destroy Venice, climate change will sink us."

Brian glanced at Emily, but she didn't seem to be listening. Why was she uninterested? Maybe she had heard it before.

Michael gestured, cupping his hands in front of his chest. "But today we have a new enemy that's more potent than past battles. Venetians are selling their property to those who have no memory of Venice and what it means to be a Venetian. We are being dismantled and sold piece by piece."

When Michael stopped talking, Brian took a long drink of water and watched Emily lean into Michael. He had never seen her this affectionate with a boy before.

After they finished lunch, he and Emily embraced outside while Michael stood back and watched. Brian felt buoyant; Emily was smiling and held him for a few seconds longer than usual. She was normally so stiff around him, but today she was relaxed, and he believed he had connected with her.

"It was great to see you, honey," he said.

"Yeah."

Fire trucks streaked down Venice Boulevard, sirens blaring. A huge plume of smoke polluted the sky near the Venice canals.

Brian watched Emily and Michael hold hands and stroll away down Abbot Kinney. Then he peered at the smoke.

When Brian arrived, the fire was out, but the street looked as if a bomb had gone off; two homes were in cinders. The smoke reminded him of the smells and destruction he'd experienced in Iraq. The police had sealed the area off, while firefighters were studying the ashes. Brian flashed his ID, and a Venice police officer examined it, then lifted the police tape.

"Come on in. Not much to see."

Brian spotted a gray-haired firefighter who appeared to be important. The man's hairline was drenched in sweat. Despite all the man's gear, Brian could see he was in tremendous shape.

"Any idea how a row of homes like this went up in flames?" Brian asked, holding up his ID.

"FBI?" The firefighter focused his sharp eyes on him. "Off the record, it might be a gas line or something in the homes that exploded, and we can't rule out arson. We're not sure yet."

"That's a hell of a gas line."

"You got here awfully fast." The firefighter raised his eyebrows, perhaps believing Brian was there for a reason.

"I was in the area. Anyone hurt?"

"Four people and some cats were killed."

"Cats?"

"A bunch of them." The man gave him a look and returned to work.

It turned out the firefighter was correct; eleven cats had been torched in the fire. They had been huddled together as if trapped.

That afternoon Brian, eager to exercise, jogged down Venice side streets to the beach. He gained extra energy when he thought about the enjoyable lunch with Emily and her friend Michael.

The boardwalk was mellow with most of the tourists gone. A man hawked medical marijuana with a huge sign displaying a bud. A few homeless people milled about. The cafés on the boardwalk were a quarter full, and he made eye contact with a rock star sitting in a coffee shop with a young man in dreadlocks.

Brian veered off onto the sand toward the water's edge and the pier. A large set of waves had come on suddenly, and surfers, who had been lounging on the sand, were now rushing out, cradling surfboards.

Brian scanned the area and noticed a man standing on the pier, wearing a dark suit and a fedora. The man was pivoted away from the surfers. He appeared to be staring at Brian, but the man was just far enough away that he wasn't sure. Brian peered back and had started to walk toward the man when probing fingers massaged his shoulders. Firm breasts pressed against his back.

It was Nirvana, a friend and schoolmate of Emily's. She wrapped her arms around him and gave him a hug from behind.

Nirvana was a yoga instructor and attended UCLA. She was majoring in love, she had told him when he asked her what she was studying, but Emily had told him Nirvana was working on a B.S. in economics. Nirvana played rock 'n' roll in her power yoga class. Sometimes it was contemporary music he had not heard before, or classic bands such as Bowie, Blondie, and, of course, Nirvana.

"What's going on up here, Mr. Tight Shoulders? You're made of cement." Nirvana leaped on him piggyback-style and held him close.

"No, Nirvana, you have to get off me."

"Come on, let me ride you down the beach."

He waited. "Nirvana?"

She slid off him.

The last of the sun splashed across her lovely hair. A big smile eclipsed her face. She was wearing a tank top and short shorts. A rolled-up yoga mat was strapped to her back.

"What are you doing out here?" she asked.

"Just enjoying the weekend." Brian glanced back to the pier, but the man was nowhere to be seen.

When he turned back, she had walked ahead of him. "You seem like you're carrying the weight of the world," she said, whirling around to see his reaction.

He gazed out at the sea. "Have you spoken to Emily?"

"I just left a message for her to come to Heidi's class. You should come too. She's the teacher all the yoga instructors go to. Emily loves her."

He smiled. "I'd love to come."

In the yoga studio, the twilight permeated the skylights and fell across the blond hardwood floors.

He searched for Emily among the packed group of forty or

so yogis warming up, probably twenty-five women of all ages and about fifteen guys, several with impressive six-pack abs and tattoos. Brian followed Nirvana to the front of the room, where he did not want to be but where the only two empty spaces were available. Emily wasn't there.

When Heidi entered the room, a ripple of applause broke out. She was extraordinarily fit and around his age. She smiled and told everyone she was glad to be home, and the students clapped again.

Brian immediately became more comfortable; Heidi offered every level of yogi an option for each pose. It became quiet in the class, almost like a church, as her passion and expertise dominated the experience.

Later, in the dimly lit yoga studio, she placed a block beneath him and aligned his hips. "Try and soften," she said.

After class the lights appeared too bright. As the students scurried to roll up their mats and leave, Brian caught Heidi's eye, and when he smiled too eagerly, she turned away to several students waiting to speak with her.

Outside he thanked Nirvana for the class recommendation, and they went in different directions.

Oddly, it had rained while they were in class—a welcome relief, considering the drought in California. The rain, enhanced by the balmy ocean spray, had cleared out much of the smoke lingering from the fire. The class had made him feel ten years younger.

A lumbering fog was rolling in, and water rippled nearby in the canals as if a kayaker or a small rowboat was out there in the darkness. He increased his pace and almost stepped on a dead cat. The cat's eyes were open, as if it had had a heart attack or come to a sudden death. There were neither visible marks on the body nor blood.

Candlelight emanated from homes as he continued, and

outside one shed-like house he spotted a wooden Star of David on the door. He felt lost in this run-down neighborhood—ghetto, even.

Ahead of him, he recognized the man in the suit at the beach. The man was watching him, which put Brian on the defensive.

"Who are you? Why were you staring at me on the pier?" Brian asked.

"We've worked together."

The man flashed a charming, knowing smile, then strolled on. He was more than twice Brian's width, and his head was gigantic, as were the ears protruding from below his fedora. His nose was huge but seemed normal on his colossal head. He had to be in his mid-to-late seventies, though the man kept a nimble pace despite his size.

Brian followed.

The man stopped in an inlet protected by a peeling blue wooden guardrail with "Venice" carved into it. A row of lights populated the jagged coast.

An old man in ragged clothing—a gown of some kind and bundles of cloth wrapped around his feet in place of shoes—limped past them. Another man, carrying a rolled-up blanket, scowled and kept moving.

"Where did we work together?" Brian asked.

"In Venice."

"In Venice?"

"It was a long time ago." The man smiled out at the nebulous sea.

Brian had no memory of working with this man. He would have remembered him. "I didn't get your name."

The man considered the question, then said, almost cheerfully, "Giuseppe Rossellini."

Brian eyed him. "I don't remember working with you, Mr. Rossellini."

"I remember you well; you're an honest man."

Rossellini extended his huge hand. His grip was powerful. "The Iraq War sin has opened up the world to chaos and totalitarianism," he said. "The West will require redemption and renewal to stop it."

Why would he say this? It was interesting, but Brian suspected the man might be delusional. "Iraq was a long time ago," he replied.

"It's an infinitesimal amount of time. And there are consequences when you unjustly kill hundreds of thousands. The repercussions are just beginning."

That captured Brian's full attention.

He had been adamant about his opposition to the Iraq War. Later he realized the agency had used him and had set him up to take the fall. They wanted to be on record as opposing the invasion of Iraq in case it went poorly. Plenty of agency insiders knew the intelligence used to justify war was weak or not credible. No official reason was ever given for Brian's firing; he only knew it came from up high in the White House.

At home, Brian plopped on his belly on the sofa. He and Rossellini had spoken for more than fifteen minutes. The man had a deep understanding of what happened in Iraq. He seemed fixated on the repercussions he believed were coming in some form or another.

Out of the corner of his eye, Brian saw something move on the hardwood floor. At first he thought it was a cat, but this was no cat; it was a giant black rat.

He dashed into the kitchen and came out with a broom.

The rat scurried toward him, so he jumped onto the sofa,

then flung and poked the broom head at the rat. The rat hissed and faced him with its little feet, big black body, and fearless head. Brian leaped off the couch and slipped to the floor with a heavy thud that sent the rat bolting into the kitchen.

He escaped into his bedroom and slammed the door. He loaded his Glock and flipped the safety off, then creaked the door ajar and tiptoed out with the broom in one hand and the Glock in the other.

Standing as far back as possible from the kitchen entrance, he peeked in. The rat was scratching the walls and the cupboards, but it squeaked out a war cry and leaped toward him. He scrambled back, jumped up onto the sofa again, and smacked the beast with the broom. The rat screeched and slid on its side before twisting upright. Bang. The shot stopped the rat on the dark wood. It struggled to move. Another shot, right in the head.

Brian used the broom to flip the rat into a clear plastic trash bag that he sealed and set outside the door in an empty Amazon box. For a moment he lingered above it, examining the brute; it was the size of a cat or even a small dog.

Brian called his colleague, Hayward, who had about a year to go before he retired from a stellar but unheralded FBI career. "Hayward, you have to see this."

While he waited, Brian wiped up the mess, then disinfected the floors. Changed into boots, denim, a heavy coat, and gloves, he used the broom—without the broom head now—to poke under the bed and any area he couldn't see. He moved furniture and examined the walls and flooring. There was no way a rat that size could have entered the place, he thought.

Brian heard a whistle come from outside the kitchen door. He saw Hayward examining the rat. "This was inside here?" Hayward asked.

"Yeah."

Hayward was of average height and in his mid-sixties. He still had hair left, but what you noticed about him was his eyes. They contained a reserve that said he'd seen it all before. Brian had tremendous respect for his competence, experience, and intelligence.

"That is one huge rat." Hayward puffed out his cheeks and exhaled. "There's something going on with these dead cats and a guy showing up at the office tonight shouting about death cults."

"I ran across a dead cat today."

"Yeah, they're turning up all over Venice, I hear."

"Who was he?"

"A homeless guy, and he was scared of something."

"How did he get into the office?"

Hayward shrugged. "Same way the rat got into your place." He kneeled near the rat. "So, you had to shoot it?"

"Yeah." Brian took a deep breath and rubbed his forehead.

"It really shook you up?"

"I'm fine."

"I have some Jack in the car."

"Go get it."

When Brian went to bed, he couldn't sleep. Strange noises, cracks, and footsteps that could possibly be a rat or something worse kept his mind racing. How could a rat that size have entered his place?

His thoughts eventually drifted to Rossellini. He had said, "the Iraq War sin." That's what Brian thought too. Bush and Cheney had never shown remorse or even a sense of the enormous mistake they'd made. His heart pumped furiously as he remembered their arrogance.

Rossellini was right—unnecessary wars did have a way of

crippling a country. Brian had already seen the loss of respect for the United States among its allies, not to mention a more aggressive Russia.

He daydreamed back to the Berlin Wall falling and what a magnificent moment and success that had been. So many forces, left and right, had come together to make it happen.

He'd been at a David Bowie concert at the Wall in 1987, when East Berliners risked getting beaten or tossed in jail to sing along to the song "Heroes," the anthem of divided Berlin. Thinking of those days, when he was a junior analyst at the agency, made him nostalgic. He had been so optimistic then, so different from the dark pessimism he felt now, particularly after Trump was elected. He had never thought that would happen in the United States; it was only corrupt countries that elected outright criminals.

The Iraq War sin, he thought, the Iraq War sin.

In the morning, Brian jogged down to the canals, where he ran right into the charcoal-colored emptiness where the fire had taken place. Brian had learned that the victims of the fire were burned beyond recognition. In fact, nothing was known about these people except their approximate ages and genders. Area locals had no idea who they were. No businesses or schools reported anyone missing. No utilities or TV or internet bills were associated with the homes that had been destroyed. The original homeowners had passed away in the 1980s.

He stopped to examine the charred outlines before he wandered over to the inlet and the peeling blue guardrail with "Venice" carved into it. It faced a house across the canals, not the sea.

Before Brian left for work, his bungalow was draped over with a blue and white fumigation tent. When he approached a CDC representative, who was wearing a scarf, she stepped back and held a hand out to tell him not to come any closer.

"Is this protocol?" he asked.

"No," the CDC rep said.

He tried to get her to elaborate, but she stated several times that it wasn't her place to give him information.

"You're being unusually tight-lipped about this."

Brian never made it to work because the bureau called to tell him they had scheduled him an immediate appointment with a doctor, who checked him for certain symptoms and took lab tests.

"Do you have a fever? Are your lymph nodes swollen? Any chills?" the doctor rattled off. Before Brian left, the doctor said, "I want you to call and come in immediately if these symptoms show up. And you're going to have to quarantine until we get the tests back."

The doctor would not mention the obvious, that there was something contagious about the rat or whatever it carried. But why all the secrecy? When the moment was right, he would appeal for more information.

Three days later he was cleared to return to work and immediately entered Hayward's office, where he found Assistant Director Patterson, an imposing African American man and head of the LA FBI, and Hayward leaning into a desktop computer.

"Play it again," Patterson said.

Hayward rewound the video.

"Stop right there."

On the screen was a close-up of a handsome man, an imam with a scraggly gray beard and sharp eyes. The imam glanced around the small group sitting in a circle, which included another bearded man.

Brian had not known they were spying on the mosque. Hayward explained there were several radicalized members that they had received clearance to monitor. The imam had not fallen under any suspicion.

"Where are all these dead cats coming from?" the imam asked.

The group seemed puzzled, except for the bearded man. "It's ominous. I think we can all feel it," he said.

"I've invited the FBI here to discuss," the imam said.

"Why?" the bearded man blurted. His face puffed as he glared at the imam.

"I don't want any violence blamed on us."

Patterson ordered them to see the imam as soon as possible, then walked out of the room.

A banner in Arabic that read "Mosque of Peace" was strung across the nondescript building—flat roof, long, bricked façade. It was the only clue that this was the Islamic Center of Venice. Brian had never met the imam, but Hayward had established a trusting relationship with him over the past ten years.

At the front desk, a woman with long black hair greeted them. "Good morning."

When Brian displayed his FBI credentials, she didn't seem surprised.

"He's in his office. Let me take you there," she said, smiling.

They followed her through an exit they hadn't realized was a door to a hallway. Papered over with calendars, photos, cards, and lists, the door merged into the wall. The woman led them to an office where the imam was kneeling on a rug.

He rose when they entered. "Thank you for coming," he said.

"It's good to see you," Hayward said.

Brian saw respect between the two men as the imam and Hayward grasped each other's hands for several seconds.

"I thought it was imperative to talk to you about, how should I put it, a potential danger that has appeared in Venice."

Hayward nodded and bowed. "Thank you."

"Will this danger take the form of terrorism?" Brian asked.

"Yes, anything to create chaos and division, particularly violence," the imam replied calmly.

"Are you aware of anyone or any group capable of or interested in terrorist activity?"

"No, not really."

"Not really?"

"There was a man I kicked out of the mosque recently. I think you should look into him."

"Did he make a specific threat?"

"No, but we could feel it."

Hayward handed him a card. "Give this number a call, and someone will follow up."

The FBI received so many leads that they couldn't follow up on all of them. Brian thought Hayward had done the right thing by handing it off to someone else to investigate.

"Another concern are the dead cats," the imam said. "Cats see their evil and kill the rats that carry their disease. It hasn't happened in contemporary times."

Brian stiffened until the imam spoke again.

"I know it doesn't make sense, but even though I might appear crazy to your logical minds, I felt you needed to hear this. I hope I'm wrong. There is evil in the world, and that evil takes many forms." The imam's eyes gleamed with intensity as he looked at Brian, then Hayward. "It could be any religion or faith or culture," he said. "It could be conservative or anarchist, and it's alive in Venice."

After work, the sun nearing the horizon sprayed out golden

particles, making the land appear small and the sky ever expanding. Sand on the beach wriggled between Brian's toes. He had become golden brown. Surfers paddled into waves that rose and crashed down, but the pros caught the waves and rode perpendicular to the beach.

Brian strolled along the Venice pier, searching for Rossellini. The beach was crowded and noisy, with surf lovers cheering on a tall blond on a paddleboard who cut right through the pier's pillars.

He thought for sure Rossellini would show up after the crowd died down, so he sat in a Venice Boardwalk restaurant and had dinner and waited until well after dark before he gave up.

Brian checked into a hotel because his house was still tented. In the hotel room, he lay on his back and switched on CNN. A fifty-something military man with obviously dyed hair was blabbing about how the Iraq War had been won. "The surge won the Iraq War. It was ours to lose after that."

Brian flipped off the television and flung the remote into the chair in the corner. Of all the liars spewing propaganda before, during, and after the Iraq War, the colonel annoyed him the most, and not just because the colonel was dating his ex-wife.

He and Kathy's wedding had been at an old farmhouse in Arlington, Virginia. Horses roamed outside the fences and kids petted them during the reception. Their marriage was a happy one, particularly after Emily's birth.

Everything changed with 9/11. Kathy became indignant, resentful, and dishonest, mimicking right-wing radio constantly. They had never seen eye to eye on politics, but he could no longer ignore her because it was constantly being thrown in his face.

She quoted the moronic generals and colonels who predicted quick victory. She argued with and alienated their friends. She became angry with anyone who didn't agree with her.

"You're either for me or against me," she told him one night.

When Barack Obama won the 2008 election, Kathy was insulted and furious. She claimed that the president, who was born in Hawaii, was born in Kenya. They divorced a month after Obama's inauguration.

She was still in their house in Virginia, and he had not seen her in five years. They only spoke if it had to do with Emily. He had never met the colonel and, to his annoyance, had heard about his ex dating him from former colleagues.

Brian did not regret his marriage, because it had produced Emily. But he was remorseful he had worked and traveled so much that he'd missed much of her late teen years.

Back at work the next day, Brian found Hayward in his office eating a donut. Lining the walls were photos of a "Most Wanted" list that Hayward had put together based on his own algorithms.

Brian studied it. "You wanted to talk to me?" he asked.

Hayward shut the door to his office. "You know that gigantic rat?"

"Which one?"

Hayward ignored him. "The CDC was out combing the neighborhood for more of them. They're concerned the rat is carrying some kind of disease."

"They find any?"

"Not that I've heard."

They both considered that for a moment.

"How in the hell does a giant rat show up at my place in Venice, California?"

When Hayward laughed, Brian had to smile as well.

"It doesn't appear to be a break-in," Hayward said. "And it's not indigenous to the United States. Not Mexican or Central or South American either."

"It couldn't have come by plane."

"Had to be by boat. It's like a dinosaur has shown up." Hayward wiped his perspiring brow. His eyes darted about as if he were rejuvenated by the news, and he paced around his desk.

"I don't even know where to go with this," Brian said.

"It's still hush-hush in here while the CDC canvasses the area as a free pest control service," Hayward added.

Brian's phone buzzed. He looked at it—Patterson's assistant.

As he entered Patterson's office, he tried to ignore the new portrait of Donald J. Trump hanging on the wall.

"Assistant Director."

"Brian, you're going to be taking a trip."

"Okay."

"You'll land in Aviano and proceed to an undisclosed location."

"The LA FBI is involved in something overseas?"

Patterson sat back with the sly smile of someone who knows something you don't. "No, you are."

Brian didn't react, waiting for more. Finally, he asked, "Anything specific you can tell me?"

"You'll be updated in Aviano."

Why wouldn't Patterson give him an idea of what was going on? It was unlikely he had no information. Brian wondered if this had something to do with the rat. It was clear Patterson was not going to tell him anything and even seemed to enjoy holding it over him. "When?" Brian asked.

"Thanksgiving week."

After Emily texted him to meet her and Michael at Tom's

Shoes on Abbot Kinney, he left work and found them sipping coffee in the back on the deck, where young people congregated with their laptops and coffee from Tom's coffee bar. They eagerly waved him over.

"Sorry I'm late."

Michael handed him a latte.

"You tell him," Emily said.

"No, you tell him," Michael said.

A big smile burst onto Emily's face. "I'm going to Venice, Italy, during the Thanksgiving break."

"That's fantastic."

"I'm beyond excited," Emily said, hopping up and back down with a big smile.

Michael reached out and held her hand. "It's all free except for the plane ticket," he said. "And we want you to come too. I have a free place for you to stay."

Brian gazed at Emily. "Really? I'm not sure what to say."

"Say yes," she said.

"I won't be intruding on your fun?"

"We want you to come."

Brian smiled. "Okay, let me confirm at work. I think I can get away for a day or two." For security reasons, he didn't mention he would be in Italy anyway.

"Tell my dad what you said about Venice," Emily said to Michael.

Michael's expression became deadly serious. "Venice is a city of half water and half land, a city that believes in Homer, Ovid, the Virgin Mary, and the collective and the individual, and it is filled with sea mist, seaweed, glassblowing, purple flowers, secret doors to alternate universes, and spies everywhere."

"Wow," Brian said to Emily.

"I can't wait," she said.

III

AT AVIANO AIR BASE, Brian was ushered to a secure room, where the tall, lean General Clark was waiting for him. The general wanted to talk about the Middle East.

"Nothing's changed; it's still a mess," Clark said.

"It's appalling how the news media and politicians still don't know what the hell is going on in that part of the world." Brian remembered all the claims that Iraq had been won. But all they had won was trouble.

An intelligence officer and the regional station chief entered, and Brian shook hands with them.

"You're probably wondering why we asked you here," the chief said.

"I'm curious what the connection is to me."

"During a rendition, you were mentioned by name. Abu al-Asiri. Ring a bell?"

"No."

"An operative in ISIS," the intelligence officer said. "Active in Iraq and Syria. Near the top of the food chain."

The regional station chief shook his head, though Brian wasn't sure why. "He said you know what's coming," the chief said. "He's a bit apocalyptic. Heaven, hell, and damnation. That sort of thing."

"We had a hard time believing it, except everything we've been able to corroborate has turned out to be true," the intelligence officer added.

An hour later, Brian was on a flight to an East European country with the three men. Excitement flowed through him. He lived for these moments that might shed light on darkness or perhaps reveal a truth that many were in denial of accepting.

They landed on a small airstrip. Outside, Brian saw only dried-out bushes and tangled, shrunken limbs without foliage. The wind howled and whipped around them.

A military vehicle took them down a rough dirt road to a remote farmhouse with a perimeter of barbed wire, speed bumps, and stone walls to protect the building from a suicide bomber in a vehicle.

Inside, the rooms reeked of something sinister. The walls used to be blue, a cheery blue, but now they were ravaged by time. A dead feeling hovered in the air.

The regional station chief gestured for Brian to sit at a small table with two chairs. The intelligence officer, General Clark, and chief sat in a row of chairs facing the table.

A clean-shaven Middle Eastern man with salt-and-pepper hair cropped short shuffled in with his feet shackled. His eyes were black, and his gaze fixated on Brian. Two tall soldiers stood by his side.

Al-Asiri pointed his short index finger at Brian. "He knows."

Brian sensed everyone's attention on him.

"He knows they've entered through the death and destruction and chaos in Iraq."

Brian tried to appear weary and not only skeptical but a little contemptuous. His heart was skipping because he believed what the man was saying.

"You see them because they are now inside you." Al-Asiri lifted his shirt, and though not threatening, the soldiers faced him, but he was just displaying a scar that ran across his belly up to his neck. "I see them too. It starts small. Dead cats or an outbreak of disease carried by fleas on rodents. Cats recognize their evil and conspire against them and expose their hiding places. Cats kill the vermin they use to unleash their sickness. It's unresolved. There's no future or past in this world. How it works? I don't know. But I renounce killing and give my life to god, like your Christ, though I only can redeem my own sins—if I can even do that. It's up to you to stop it there. I don't know how you do it, but you've seen it firsthand."

The rat. This was about the rat, and that sent a chill down Brian's spine. "How do you know that?" he asked.

Abu al-Asiri nodded as if it was a good question. "I thought I was a good Muslim, but after witnessing the crucifixion of Christians and my fellow Muslims by ISIS, I lost my religion. But something opened in me, and I see things now. I've been traveling to Venice, California, and I have seen you. They are there. It's a small fire that seeks to spread."

"This is bullshit," Clark said loudly to everyone. He fidgeted in his chair, like he was ready to move on.

Abu al-Asiri smiled as if he understood.

"Do you have intelligence on American or foreign operatives in the US or anywhere else?" Brian asked.

"They know that you are an enemy. They are watching you and your family."

A burning sensation swarmed Brian's expanding chest. "Don't ever talk about my family."

Al-Asiri tilted his head quizzically.

Brian glanced at General Clark.

"I think he's lost his mind," the general said.

It was still dark out when Brian arrived in Venice. Despite the dim light, the boatman expertly navigated and skimmed easily across the choppy Adriatic. Brian sat in the back, taking it all in. He was still puzzled by the conversation with al-Asiri. Was it a conspiracy of some kind? Or a group attempting to confuse and attack? That was the only thing that made sense. Either way, he couldn't pretend it did not bother him.

The pensione that Michael had arranged was simple and charming, located in Santa Croce. A dour older woman with beautiful white hair escorted him to his room.

"Thank you." He offered her a tip that she declined before she broke into a radiant smile.

Brian thought he might catch a couple hours of sleep, but he wasn't tired, so he ventured out, where the sound of the swishing canal followed him as he explored the empty city. He stopped to watch a group of men wearing dark clothing and little hats unloading something—salt.

"We meet again."

Brian recognized the voice immediately. He spun around, and there was Rossellini in the same suit he was wearing when Brian last spoke with him.

They walked in silence to a café bar that Rossellini knew. The waiter didn't say a word; he brought them two cappuccinos and stepped into the kitchen. Rossellini angled his head back as if he was resonating in the aroma of bread and coffee that filled the place.

"What are you doing here?"

The man sipped his cappuccino. "I'm searching for someone I've pursued for a long time."

"And what will you do when you find him or her?"

"Silence him," Rossellini said with cold firmness.

That jumped out at him. Brian understood Rossellini was not just a jovial mystery man. "I'm going to have you investigated, Mr. Rossellini."

Rossellini smiled.

"Your showing up in Venice, Italy, is a serious matter."

Rossellini gazed at an ancient fresco of Venus that dominated the ceiling. "Your time is particularly serious: weapons of mass destruction, the pillaging of the natural world. Now the deaths in Iraq have allowed arrogant extremists to win elections all around the world."

Brian glanced outside at the glimmer of light hazily dawning on the streets.

"It's time for me to go," Rossellini said, looking off into the distance.

"We're not done." He gripped Rossellini's arm but immediately let go, regretting the disrespect.

"You're right; there's much to do," Rossellini said.

Back at the pensione, Brian examined himself in the mirror and rubbed his face. He didn't need a shave; he appeared remarkably clean and refreshed.

When he met Emily and Michael six hours later near San Giorgio's, Venice was already becoming too crowded.

"I'll show you the hidden Venice," Michael said with a small smile that suggested he was proud of his city.

They crossed tiny bridges and canals and ventured down labyrinthian streets where sometimes the walkway was so narrow that they had to pass through single file. They wandered first through book, art, and glassblowing shops in Dorsoduro; then they explored the cemetery on San Michele where Pound, Diaghilev, and Stravinsky were buried.

On Lazzaretto Vecchio, Michael guided them to where thousands of Venetians, victims of the bubonic plague, were buried in a mass grave between the fifteenth and seventeenth centuries. He told them the plague had killed fifty thousand in Venice. "They had no idea it was caused by fleas," Michael said, his eyes focused on the mass grave. "Some believed it was retribution for Venice's arrogance and greed, the Crusades, and sins against god. But wars and the plagues could not bring down Venice, and we found a happy medium between the religious and the secular. What bonded us was a hatred of dictators."

In a water taxi they passed a gigantic cruise ship that hovered above them as if it were an alien invading force. Brian felt tiny next to the hideous ocean liner.

Michael gazed uneasily up at the ship. "We are being invaded by monster ships filled with barbarians."

On the way to Piazza San Marco, they ran across a row of itinerant Middle Eastern or African sellers of handbags. Emily wanted to examine the fake Gucci, Prada, Coach, and Louis Vuitton for sale.

"They look and feel identical to the real thing," she said.

Brian made eye contact with several of the sellers. Something told him he was being watched—vulnerability gnawed at his stomach, and for a moment the randomness and complexity of the world dragged him through equations and calculations that his brain could not keep up with. It was over so fast that he was convinced it was a unique moment of clarity and clairvoyance—or else maybe he was losing his mind.

Brian zeroed in on one seller, recognizing him from Hayward's most wanted list. He believed it was Hasan Mostafa, a shadowy figure they believed to be a skilled bomb maker and recruiter, who had carried out multiple terrorist attacks in Iraq.

Mostafa wheeled his goods to a vendor.

Brian speed-dialed Hayward, who picked up immediately.

"Buongiorno," Hayward said into the phone.

"Send me your top terrorist list: number seven, Hasan Mostafa, his photos."

"Okay."

He could hear Hayward tapping at the keys.

"Done."

Brian smiled at Emily as she bargained with a vendor.

"Where are you?" Hayward asked.

"I believe Mostafa is here in Venice. Hold up."

Emily had purchased the bag and wanted to move on.

"I'm really sorry," he said to Emily, "but I have to take this call. Can I catch up to you in twenty minutes?"

"You're on vacation." She sounded upset. He didn't blame her. He glanced at Michael, who was observing him with concerned interest.

"It's important, or he wouldn't ask," Michael said. "I know a place for us to have an espresso."

Emily marched off, Michael chasing after her.

"I'm sorry, they can't do anything without me in LA," Brian shouted after them.

"I heard that," Hayward said.

Mostafa had started to walk away too, but at a normal pace.

"What's going on?" Hayward asked.

Brian strolled in the same general direction as Mostafa, trying to appear focused away from him.

"I'm in pursuit."

"Jesus Christ," Hayward said. "Are you sure about this?"

Brian examined the photos Hayward had sent—images of Mostafa with a beard and without. It was him. "I'm certain. Can you GPS my location?"

"Already done."

"Maybe it's an immigration issue he's worried about? The Italians aren't going to like this."

"I'll want them to take over. Bring in the AISI," Brian said, referencing the Italian FBI.

"This will go to the top, and I don't mean Patterson."

Mostafa rounded a corner, Brian jogging to catch up, and when he reached the corner, he saw that Mostafa had begun to run. Brian broke into a sprint after him.

Mostafa knew the streets and area, but Brian was faster. People yelled at them both as they weaved through the crowded, narrow streets. For a moment Brian believed he'd lost him, and then Mostafa bolted out in front of him through a garden. Several offended Italians gave them an upturned hand.

Brian stopped, out of breath, in an isolated square, circled by homes.

Mostafa had vanished. Perhaps he had gotten away or entered one of the three doors in the square.

The quiet surroundings disturbed Brian. His mobile connection had dropped.

One door was ajar, so he pushed it open. Inside, it was dark, and he groped for a light, but he couldn't find a switch. He waited for his eyes to become acclimated, then felt something at his feet.

Near his shoes was a long black rat. Brian jumped back and out, scrambling toward the center of the square. The rat followed but seemed confused by the daylight, as if it was blind. It scampered off and bumped into the building.

Brian's phone rang—Hayward.

"AISI are on their way."

A shot ricocheted off stones near Brian, and he spotted Mostafa on the roof with a handgun. Brian frantically zigzagged to the wall below and pressed his back against the building.

He saw Mostafa's shadow moving. Brian moved in the same direction so he wouldn't give Mostafa an angle to shoot him.

Another shot went off, barely audible, but Brian didn't see a bullet hit anything near him. He glanced up, and before he could take another step, Mostafa's body cracked against the square five feet from Brian. He had been shot in the head.

A massive figure with a revolver peered down at them. It was Rossellini with the sun behind him. Then Italian law enforcement roared in.

Brian raised his hands when the police drew their weapons. He could hear Hayward's voice chirp from the phone, "Are you all right? Brian, can you hear me? Brian?" He looked up again, but Rossellini was gone.

Brian was handcuffed but was soon released and brought to the AISI office after they confirmed that he hadn't killed anyone and that he was an American FBI special agent.

The AISI were hostile toward him, but he remained cool, knowing they had a right to be upset at a foreign intelligence agent who had acted on a terrorist without their knowledge in their country.

Later Patterson and Hayward joined a video conference with Brian and several Italian AISI, including the AISI director, a handsome, balding man.

"I called in the AISI because it's not my jurisdiction, and I knew they would need to handle this," Brian said for the third time.

"You recognized Mostafa?" the AISI director asked him.

"Yes."

"And called the Venice, California, FBI first."

"I thought it would be best if they called the AISI."

The AISI director studied him. "Let's talk about this person who gunned down Mostafa in cold blood in Venice."

"He calls himself Giuseppe Rossellini. I don't believe that's his real name."

Mostafa was wanted internationally but had nothing to do with Italy, and it was a big surprise that he was in Venice. Rossellini was not known to the AISI. They weren't sure he was Italian at all.

The meeting went on all day, with Brian repeating multiple times what he'd already told them. Patterson confirmed that Brian had received approval to visit Venice after his mission was complete. There was no connection between the two trips was the official word, but Brian no longer believed that.

Late that evening, back on the street, Brian eyed everyone with suspicion. He was certain he was under surveillance by the AISI. He wondered if that was true of the FBI or Rossellini as well. He didn't believe anyone connected with Mostafa would know who he was, but he was worried about them too.

Unable to reach Emily, he wandered closer to St. Mark's Basilica and admired the cupolas, statues, gold, and Italo-Byzantine architecture. A man holding a beat-up hat gestured to him that he could enter.

Only a few nuns were inside. Emptiness filled him, despite the mosaics, marble, and spiritual atmosphere. Rossellini had assassinated someone, and whether that person was a terrorist or not, Brian felt betrayed.

He barely slept that night and arrived early to meet Emily and Michael in the morning at a café.

Pigeons and doves fluttered around Brian's table when they arrived.

"I'm so sorry about yesterday. It was an emergency," he said before they sat down.

Michael gestured as if he understood, but Emily wasn't having it.

"All day?" she asked in a snide tone.

Brian could see she was wound tight. She crossed her legs and wrapped her arms around her waist, then turned away from him.

"There's nothing I would have rather done than spend the day with you," Brian said.

"I've heard that before."

"Emily, I'm sorry."

"In Venice nothing is as it seems," Michael said.

"What does that mean?" Emily snapped.

"Venice is a mystery, and people here guard that mystery," Michael said, oblivious to the tension around him.

Brian could see that Emily was exasperated with Michael too. Finally, she rolled her eyes, then got up and walked off without a word.

IV

THERE WERE SEVERAL DELAYS on the flight back to the US. Brian wanted to sleep but instead sat with his eyes closed, picturing Mostafa hitting the stones and Rossellini on the roof with the sun shining behind him after he'd assassinated the man.

What a disaster the trip had been. Emily had remained aloof the rest of their time in Venice. Brian almost forgot about al-Asiri and all of his strangeness; it seemed a long time ago.

Back in Venice, California, when Brian trudged into the FBI office, his co-workers were waiting for him and gave him a standing ovation. He forced a smile, but it did make him feel a little better.

Later Hayward entered his office, biting into a sandwich made with cheap white bread. "We should have all went on vacation to Venice," Hayward said through a mouthful.

Brian scanned some briefing papers on his desk.

"Nothing going on here," Hayward said.

"Well, that's a good thing."

They were discussing the events in Italy when a tall FBI agent popped his head in. "There's been a shooting, potential terrorism."

By the time Brian arrived, the police had taped off the perimeter. A large crowd was watching a photographer take shots of the scene.

After a preliminary investigation, Brian and Hayward approached Patterson when he showed up thirty minutes later. Eyewitnesses said two men with AR-15s had had a confrontation. The dead man, Peter Ramsey, lay on the ground with an assault rifle next to him.

"Any intelligence on them?" Patterson asked.

"We know who Ramsey is," Hayward said. "He was the homeless man who broke into FBI headquarters a couple weeks ago shouting about a cult of death. He's well known in Venice. Not known to be a troublemaker."

"And the shooter?" Patterson asked.

"A Terry Narlo—he drove his own truck to the scene, but it's murky from there," Brian said. "If it was Narlo, he is divorced and estranged from his wife and daughter. Unemployed, with money problems. But the ex-wife said Narlo had never owned a gun as far as she knew. We're headed over to his place now."

Hayward's playful and unconventional self had disappeared. His expression was flat and serious, the lines on his face were much more pronounced than Brian had noticed before.

"We believe Narlo was going to the festival to commit a terrorist attack," Hayward said without emotion. "Eyewitnesses say he had multiple weapons. Ramsey had ammo that you would expect to kill one person. He likely delayed and exposed Narlo, so he had to flee."

"We don't goddamn know, do we? They could have just gotten into an argument," Patterson said.

"With AR-15s," Hayward countered, then stepped back when Patterson glared at him.

A team of FBI agents searched Narlo's house, a run-down tract home in Chatsworth. Brian and Hayward wandered through the house, getting a feel for the occupant. It was messy and dirty, with old furniture, drapes, and appliances.

"There was a sophistication in the shooting," Hayward said. "Narlo purchased state-of-the-art equipment but had no military training and no previous history of owning a gun."

"And where did Ramsey learn to use a weapon? What's his story? He's not a veteran?" Brian asked.

"And why did he show up and confront Narlo in Venice?" Hayward tossed a handful of nuts into his mouth. "Unless it was a message to Narlo."

"What message?"

"To show that they're capable of extremes, and they're here to protect Venice."

Who would be protecting Venice? Brian had no idea. He didn't think Hayward did either, but might have suspected it to be the truth. Hayward often started with a theory that he would discard or explore, depending on the evidence and what his partner thought of it.

"Why didn't he come to the police or the FBI if he knew Narlo was on the loose?" Brian asked.

"He did show up at the FBI office," Hayward said.

"That's right."

"And nothing he said made any sense."

Brian watched Hayward lower his head, probably thinking about what he would say next. "I think there's something dangerous and strange going on out there," Hayward said.

"What do you base that on?"

"I have no reason not to believe it. The pieces need to fit together, and that fits. The imam's comments. The rat and cats, the fire, Rossellini, al-Asiri. I just can't pull it all together," Hayward said.

A special agent kneeling in front of a closet filled with old jackets and trucker hats called out to Brian and Hayward. "Supervisor."

She opened a duffel bag filled with cash, then began to take photos of it. Large bills that they would try to trace.

"He sold something," Brian said.

"Maybe his soul?"

"I wouldn't mention that to the assistant director."

Hayward nodded. "You know what's interesting about this house?"

"Nothing."

"Yeah."

"Something changed him recently."

They discussed this for close to an hour. There was nothing in Narlo's history that would suggest he would kill a homeless man or even own an assault weapon.

Brian glanced at his watch. He wanted to make Heidi's yoga class and meet Emily there, even though she had not responded to his text.

He arrived on time to the studio, and ninety minutes later, the lights were dim. He could barely hear people breathing, as he, Nirvana, and thirty-eight other yogis lay on their backs in Savasana.

After yoga class Nirvana clung to him as they strolled out in the crisp, clear night. "You have to come to dinner," she said.

"I have to get back to the office."

"But a friend of ours will be there. She texted me that she's coming."

"Well, in that case I'm starved and would love to go to dinner. I was hoping she would be at yoga. That's the reason I'm here."

"I want to hear all about Venice. I'm so jealous."

At Gjelina, a restaurant on Abbot Kinney, Nirvana maneu-vered him so he had to sit with his back against the wall. She faced him, her back to everyone else. The other diners—talk-ative, young, attractive people—energized the stylish and pop-ular New American dining spot.

Brian glanced at his watch. "Did she say what time she's coming?" he asked.

"She just texted and said she'll be here in a few minutes," Nirvana said, before leaning over the table toward him. "Okay, so what happened?" She seemed eager to hear some gossip.

"What do you mean?"

"In Venice, why did they break up?"

"They broke up?"

"You didn't know? Michael was really upset."

"I didn't know." He wasn't surprised. Teenagers broke up all the time.

"Something happened in Italy," Nirvana said. "Emily texted me that she was having the best time—then nothing. And when she got home, she said she wanted to date other people."

He laid the napkin on his lap. "She's upset at me too."

"I told her it wasn't your fault."

"Thanks. Is she on her way?"

"She's studying for a final."

Exasperated, Brian tossed his crumpled napkin on the table and blurted, "Didn't she just text you saying she was coming?"

"No, I was talking about someone else."

He thumbed his phone. "I have to go. I'd love to have dinner with you, but let's do it another night when Emily can join us."

He stopped talking when he spotted Heidi, who had just entered and was surveying the room. Nirvana spun around and waved Heidi over. She appeared to be as surprised to see Brian as he was to see her. Nirvana must have planned for him and

Heidi to sit next to each other. Brian didn't think she was unhappy about it.

"You two know each other, right?" Nirvana asked.

"Not officially," Heidi said.

"Brian."

"Heidi."

They smiled and shook hands.

"I love your classes. Honestly, they're life-changing," he said.

"Thank you."

"Brian has a motorcycle and works for the state department," Nirvana said.

"Nirvana?"

"He's cool," Nirvana added.

"You do yoga, that's cool," Heidi replied.

"I don't have a motorcycle. And I don't work for the state
department anymore."

"I see," Heidi said.

"Heidi speaks French," Nirvana said.

He smiled. "Très bien."

"Merci beaucoup."

Heidi unzipped her jacket, showing off her lovely lean body
in yoga pants and top.

"Brian's daughter, Emily, is my best friend at UCLA. You
know Emily," Nirvana said.

Brian and Heidi exchanged smiles, amused by Nirvana's
matchmaking.

"I know Emily. How old is she?"

"Nineteen," he said.

"She and I are both economics majors," Nirvana said.

Heidi and Brian caught each other's eye again. Nirvana kept
looking back and forth at them like she was trying to see if this
could be the beginning of a romance.

"Economics," Heidi said. "I'm impressed. My son is twenty. He's going to UC Santa Barbara and majoring in biology."

"I've never been to Santa Barbara. But I've been wanting to visit the wine country," Brian said, turning his attention solely to Heidi.

"It's very romantic," Nirvana said.

Heidi eyed him. He didn't often feel embarrassed, but for a moment he was.

After dinner, Nirvana wandered off down Abbot Kinney with friends to hang out at a bar. "Don't wait up for me!" she shouted back at them.

"She's a character," Brian said to Heidi.

"So much energy."

He fidgeted before focusing on Heidi. "Is there a number or email where I can reach you?"

Heidi dug into her purse.

"My memory is excellent," he said.

She handed him her card. "Let's not take any chances."

Before Brian pulled into his driveway, his phone vibrated wildly. "Terrorist attack. Dozens killed," the text message said.

He drove in a determined daze, and when he arrived, a local newsperson was speaking into a microphone. A country and western bar's neon sign glowed behind her in the distance. "The suspected shooter in the killing of a man just last week in Venice, California, Terrence Carl Narlo, has allegedly struck again," she said. "He opened fire with an assault weapon in a country and western bar and dance club just north of Los Angeles."

Outside the bar, Brian hurried up to Hayward and Patterson, who were huddled together. He was still wearing his yoga sweatpants but now with the ubiquitous FBI jacket.

Reporters and grieving onlookers were roped off from the scene.

"I got here as soon as I could. How many people?" Brian asked.

"Forty-plus dead or wounded," Hayward replied curtly.

"Suspects?"

"Narlo," Patterson said in his deep baritone.

A swarm of people, probably family members, began yelling and shoving their way inside the perimeter until the police rushed in and deescalated the situation.

"Is Narlo dead or alive?" Brian asked.

"He pulled away in a red pickup truck," Hayward said, shaking his head.

"How did the son of a bitch just drive off?" Patterson said to no one.

"And why a country and western bar?" Hayward asked.

Veins bulged in Patterson's forehead. "We're going to find out."

The next morning Brian and Hayward learned that Narlo had donated to the Islamic Center of Venice. They immediately drove to question the imam. They found him in a blooming garden behind the center.

"I've been expecting you," the imam said, strolling with his hands behind his back.

"You knew Terry Narlo? He attended the mosque?" Brian asked.

The imam kept walking, then stopped. The dark bags under his eyes were severe. "Yes, but he was not a Muslim," the imam said.

Hayward had a sensitive expression on his face, like he wanted to show he understood the imam's struggle. "How do you know?"

"When he prayed, I knew. He was playing with us, mocking us." The imam flushed red, clearly angry at the disrespect and sacrilege.

"You didn't contact me about him?"

The imam gaped at them. "I did contact the FBI. I used the number you gave me. They said they would look into it."

Brian and Hayward regarded each other; this was likely true.

"It must have gotten lost among all the other incoming tips," Brian said.

"I'm going to tell you something that won't make sense," the imam said. "I believe the body was just a vessel."

"That vessel just murdered or wounded more than forty people," Brian said, his voice rising.

"I don't believe that was his body."

"What does that mean?" Brian retorted.

Hayward lifted his hands to calm him.

The imam focused on Brian as if to show he was not going to be intimidated. He spoke in a calm tone. "I realized he was different from the beginning, so I told him to leave because I believe this person was bought."

"Bought?"

"You can't take a body; it has to be given away or bought," the imam said.

Hayward was about to say something, but Brian interrupted. "Let's get back to reality," he said. "Did he speak of hatred of the United States or anyone?"

"He ranted on about the Iraq War."

"Anything else?" Narlo's social media was filled with racist rants about killings in the Middle East, blaming conservatives.

"Not that I'm aware."

"Nothing about ISIS or al-Qaeda?" Brian asked.

"No."

"Do you believe he is a lone wolf?"

"There will be others like him."

Brian and Hayward exchanged a glance.

"It's happening and growing bolder," the imam said. "I pray for you to be vigilant."

V

AT THE HOTEL CASA DEL MAR in Santa Monica, Brian and Hayward approached Patterson, who was spiffed up in a pinstriped suit and tie because he was attending an event there. Patterson was peering through the large windows at the purple sunset hovering over the ocean.

"Assistant Director," Hayward said.

Patterson kept his focus on the water. "What did the imam say?"

They hesitated.

"I can't hear you," Patterson said, facing them, his expression demanding an explanation.

"The imam seems to think that Narlo's body was switched," Brian said.

"Switched."

"Possessed," Hayward mumbled.

"Jesus fucking Christ," Patterson said. "And what do you think?"

Hayward imperceptibly shook his head, as if to say, "Don't go there."

"Not going to waste our time," Brian said.

"Right fucking answer," Patterson said.

Hayward cleared his throat. "We don't believe Narlo was a Muslim."

"That was always bullshit. Anything else?"

"Narlo has a brother in Topanga. We're trying to locate him," Brian said.

The TV above the bar showed families of the victims. Brian put his hand over his face.

"I'm sick of this shit. Another moron with an assault weapon," Patterson said.

Brian avoided eye contact and gravitated toward the rolling swells. "Let's look at it from a different angle," he said.

"Okay. What angle?" Patterson asked.

Brian couldn't think of one. "I don't know."

Patterson eyed him. "Hayward, could you excuse us for a couple of minutes."

When Hayward wandered away, Patterson focused on Brian, perhaps to make him feel uncomfortable. "I heard that you're in excellent health."

"So I'm told."

Patterson gazed out again at the ocean. "That rat you shot had a flea on it that was carrying Yersinia pestis."

He waited for his boss to elaborate.

"It's better known as the bubonic plague."

Brian wasn't surprised, but to hear that it was the bubonic plague was still a shock. "Has anyone contracted it?"

"It appears confined to your incident."

"There was a similar rat in Venice, Italy."

"Italians are aware of it, but they couldn't find the rat or any rats in that house." Patterson raised his eyebrows. "You've dodged a couple bullets."

Brian nodded.

"Now get home and get some rest, go see your family."

Brian finally reached Emily, who agreed to meet him for dinner the next evening. When he and Heidi arrived at the pizza place in Westwood, Emily was already there, sitting at a table with two boys in their early twenties whom Brian had not seen before. Both were wearing Rolex watches and preppy clothing. One had his elbow on the table and was smirking.

Emily's hair was stringy, and she wore a loose-fitting shirt with one too many buttons undone. Emily rose and hugged Heidi. She gave Brian a cursory embrace, then sat back down. Neither of the boys acknowledged him. They were too busy talking in heated tones about a fight they were having with their landlord.

"The landlord gave me some lip for playing my music too loud, so I just slapped him hard," one said.

"Boom," the other added. "Nice one, Karl."

"You should have seen his face," Karl said. He mocked the landlord's expression after he'd been smacked.

Emily seemed disengaged, almost not listening.

Brian sniffed; he smelled pot. "You doing all right, honey?" he asked.

"I'm fine," she said.

"How's school?"

"Fine."

A pitcher of beer was delivered. Karl filled his mug and smiled, a disturbing, wolfish smile that seemed to clench his entire face.

"You shouldn't eat pizza, you'll get fat," Karl said to Emily.

She pushed her plate away, sullen faced.

Karl focused on Brian. "You're FBI?"

Brian felt the blood surge to his face, but he studied Emily instead of responding.

Karl cocked his head with his mouth half full and said, "That terrorism attack. People need to understand that America has been killing Muslims every day and no one cares."

"Why don't we talk about something else?" Brian said. He had no interest in a political conversation with this punk kid.

"Have you been practicing yoga, Emily?" Heidi asked.

"No time."

"I don't practice yoga," Karl said.

"You should try it," Heidi said.

"It's for pussies," Karl said.

"You need to watch your mouth," Brian growled, pointing at Karl.

Karl glared at him, but he didn't say anything, then burst out of his chair and marched out with the other boy.

Brian turned to Emily. "You told him I was in the FBI?"

"I never told him that."

"What are you doing with this guy? And you smell like pot."

"I do whatever I want, and I don't need your permission. You can't just appear in my life and tell me what to do." She shoved off the table and hurried after Karl.

Heavy traffic made the ride back to Venice even more miserable for Brian. He thought he had gotten over the lost, alienated feeling of being an absent father. "Not the impression I was hoping to give you," he said, grimacing at Heidi.

"It's okay." She squeezed his hand.

They didn't speak for a couple of blocks.

"I haven't felt this down since Iraq," he said.

"You were in Iraq?"

"A total nightmare." He merged into the left lane. "I was embedded with the troops a couple times. If people didn't accept the administration's beliefs, they were out, so it was all nonexpert true believers in the beginning."

"I thought it was crazy at the time."

"Everyone should have known they were lying."

He took a shortcut above Main Street to avoid the traffic on Pico. "I remember a little girl over there," he said. "Black hair. I thought she was staring at me. She looked so innocent and scared."

"Was there a reason she was staring at you?"

"I don't know. A vehicle exploded, and then it was...." He couldn't complete the sentence.

"Oh no."

Brian could feel her facing him with what he imagined was an appalled expression. He tightened his grip on the wheel and stared straight ahead. "A couple of months later I was fired," he went on, "supposedly pressured by someone in the vice president's office. I got a divorce soon after that, but always on my mind was that little girl. It remains fresh in my mind."

A car cut him off, forcing him to brake suddenly. "Jesus." He took a deep breath and angrily watched the car speed away.

Heidi laid a hand on his arm.

"I can't help thinking it was a sign," he said as he settled down.

"A sign for what?"

"I don't know, but it felt personal, and tonight it was personal too. I was so wrapped up in work that I disappeared on my daughter. I won't let that happen again."

After dropping Heidi off, Brian had pulled into his garage, when he spotted a person in the driveway, someone wearing a hoodie.

Brian slipped his Glock out of its inside holster. The slight figure moved forward beneath the porch light, so Brian shifted the SUV into reverse, ready to gun it, then rolled down the window. "Who the hell are you?"

The man pulled back the hoodie. It was Michael, slouching and squinting in what Brian thought was pain.

"Michael?"

Inside, Michael sat distraught on the sofa. Brian turned on the heater, which lit with a boom that startled Michael.

"You should really call before you come over," Brian said.

"I didn't know your number."

"How did you know where I lived?"

"Emily showed me one time. We were going to come over, but she decided not to at the last moment."

Michael had shrunk, as if his body had been shriveled by enormous stress. He must have dropped ten pounds, and he was pale as a vampire. Michael's eyes seemed to search Brian for an answer.

"So, you're upset because you broke up, or is there more?" Brian asked, eyeing him with distrust.

This made Michael sit up. "I have no reason to live without her."

Brian sighed. "You want some port?"

Michael examined his open palms. "Yes, I think I do."

Brian retrieved a bottle of port and two whiskey glasses. He filled them and handed one to Michael.

"I don't drink," Michael said.

They clinked glasses.

Brian watched Michael drink the entire glass, then straighten.

"You looked like you enjoyed that," Brian said, pouring Michael another glass. "Sip this one."

Michael guzzled most of his second drink, and his gaze

drifted off before returning. "I really don't like this guy Emily is hanging out with. I don't think he's a good person."

"We're in agreement there," Brian said, wondering what she could be thinking.

Michael finished his glass and licked his lips. "She's the reason I'm in Venice. Now that I'm here, I realize that."

"You're that in love with my daughter?"

Michael winced as if this were a stupid question. "Of course."

"Losing someone is an opportunity to grow as a person," Brian said to cheer him up. He knew that Michael will have forgotten all about Emily in a couple of months.

Michael's focus seemed riveted to the bullet holes in the hardwood floor. Then he said in Arabic, "The wound is the place where the light enters you."

"You speak Arabic?"

"I just picked that up."

Brian knew Michael was lying. "You said it perfectly."

"We had a Syrian nanny."

"You had a nanny?"

"Yes, she was a refugee and my mom wanted to help her out." Michael wrung his hands. "I should go," he said. "I'm keeping you up."

"I'm not tired." Brian tried to push another glass of port on him.

Michael stood and shuffled his way to the door.

Brian followed. "Who are you?"

"I'm a Venetian."

Brian watched Michael open the door and exit. He thought of going after Michael, but for what? Brian had no specific information to back him up, and he didn't want to do that to someone Emily knew personally.

Agitated, he paced for ten minutes inside the bungalow. Finally, he grabbed a bottle of wine and his coat and drove to Heidi's.

It took her a few minutes to answer the door.

"I thought you might like company," he said.

After some small talk about Michael, Heidi unbuttoned his shirt, and he leaned down and pecked her lips, neck, and cheeks.

"I had two classes and three personal sessions today and just finished checking my messages," she said.

"You must be tired."

"I'm rejuvenated, but I could use a shower."

He smiled.

Inside the shower, they pressed close. His rigid cock poked into her hip, and she began to fondle him.

Heidi contemplated his face. "It's the yoga."

"It's you."

They began a long, slow kiss, and he stroked her lean back. "So beautiful," he said.

"You too," she said after a couple minutes. Her gaze went down to the water beating on their feet, then back up to him.

When he massaged her body with a bar of soap, she turned away and put both hands on the tile. He pointed the shower head all over her and rinsed her off, then held her with the hot water pouring down around them.

On her bed, Heidi's rangy fingers guided him inside her. Her smile beamed up at him as she gripped his back and moaned. He tried to slow down and hold off while she wrapped her legs around him. She was huffing and oohing when he exploded inside her, and they held each other tighter.

"Thank you," he whispered.

They made love several more times, then lay entangled before drifting off to sleep.

At five in the morning, Brian's cell phone buzzed him awake. Hayward's high-pitched voice greeted him. "Narlo was caught on a surveillance camera speaking with a young man the week prior to the massacre."

"Describe the young man."

"Black hair. White skin. Hard to say what nationality. In his late teens or early twenties, we think. He looks young. Not ugly like the rest of them."

Brian's chin fell to his chest. Why had he known this was coming? It was Michael. It had to be Michael.

His mind was all over the place as he sped down Venice Boulevard, weaving in and out of traffic. It stung, the thought that Michael was one of them, that the kid had been playing him the entire time. Then he considered Michael's oddness and intelligence. He thought of Michael speaking Arabic. Michael had appeared stricken last night, and Brian had sensed it was more than the breakup with Emily. Maybe he had gotten pulled into it and then didn't want to go through with the violence. If it was him, Brian's number-one concern was the safety of his daughter.

At the bureau, Brian, Hayward, and Patterson sat in a dark office watching the surveillance camera footage the FBI had obtained from various businesses in the area. Narlo entered Intelligentsia Coffee on Abbot Kinney, and a few minutes later Michael ambled out with him. Then without warning Narlo flung his finger in Michael's face and stalked off.

Hayward flipped the lights on. "He might be a foreign student, so maybe he's here on a school visa."

"I know who he is," Brian said, his jaw clenching. "He's a student at UCLA named Michael Nikos from Venice, Italy, or at least that's who he said he was."

Patterson's and Hayward's expressions were blank.

"Is that verified?"

"No. I also saw him in Venice, Italy."

"Jesus. Anything else?" Patterson asked.

"He dated my daughter, but they broke up."

"And?"

Brian shrugged. "That's it, except I saw him last night," he said, and described the previous night's details.

"Let's focus on bringing him in. Now." Patterson gripped his shoulder for a moment, likely a show of support, before he walked out. "We'll talk."

"Son of a bitch," Hayward said.

"I have no idea who this kid is or what he knows."

"No clues from him?"

"He said something to me in Arabic that sounded perfect to my ear."

"What do you make of that?"

"I thought he might be hiding something." He wondered if Michael had come over to tell him what was going on, then lost courage.

Brian and Hayward parked in the street outside Michael's small standalone studio near Venice Beach. They slipped on gloves as the gray-haired landlord unlocked the door.

Brian knocked on Michael's door. "Michael, open up."

There was no answer.

"He's not here," the landlord said. "Like I said."

The interior was wood with a large beam across the ceiling. A yoga swing for inversions hung on it. In the corner, blankets were folded neatly with a pillow on top. A mini fridge, a couch, and a coffee table were in the room as well. A yoga mat lay in the middle of the studio. The place was clean, and nothing appeared to be out of place.

Brian opened the shutters and peeked out at the ocean view.

"What was he? A monk?" Hayward asked.

"He slept on the floor."

"This is prime real estate, so close to the beach. Someone must have been funding him."

"He didn't have a job," Brian said, opening the fridge. A lone container of water stood inside.

"And he's not from Venice. He showed up in the database search in Venice, but when we attempted to verify, it fell apart."

"He fooled everyone," Brian said.

Inside the closet was a dresser that held neatly folded underwear, socks, shorts, and T-shirts. A couple pairs of pants and two white shirts hung above it.

Seeing his minimal, organized place, Brian believed Michael was here in Venice for a purpose. He was not here for school or a good time. There was some other reason.

"It isn't easy to set someone up with a fake birth certificate, school records, baptism records. It's all there. Photos too. Him as a little kid," Hayward said.

"Photos?"

"They just came in." Hayward handed his tablet to Brian.

The first photo showed Michael as a little boy with thick, straight black hair. A beautiful woman rested her hand on Michael's shoulder. Her light-brown hair was parted in the middle, and she had a slightly round face, her lips closed and smiling as if she held a secret. Michael wore the lopsided smile of a happy boy. The large man behind him had wavy hair combed straight back. His thick hand held a fedora. It was him. The glint in his eyes said he was having fun with this photograph.

Brian sniffed. "Goddamn. That's Rossellini," he said.

Hayward snatched the tablet from him. "What? Interviewing him is my reason for living."

"He's unique."

"I'll get it up on Interpol."

Brian's phone rang, a FaceTime request from Emily. He accepted. "Hi, honey."

"It's Nirvana. Emily needs you to come over now," she whispered.

"Why are you calling on her phone?"

"She's upset. I've never seen her this upset."

"Tell me what's going on."

"It's important."

"Okay, we're wrapping up."

"Hurry."

Brian had a dinner date with Heidi scheduled, so he called her on the way and asked her to meet him at Emily's Westside apartment. Heidi was there when Brian arrived. They rushed up the stairs to Emily's apartment, and there they all were: his ex-wife Kathy, the colonel, Nirvana, Emily, and Karl.

Emily's eyes were huge and moist, and she appeared to be in agony when she gave Brian a look. The colonel was speaking with Karl, who leaned forward with eager interest. Kathy was listening intently to them.

"There were some dead-enders and al-Qaeda, but we had Iraq won," the colonel said, reclining on the sofa with his legs spread. "They voted for freedom. It should have revolutionized the Middle East."

The colonel's hair was perfectly combed, jet black, and sprayed. He had on new khaki pants and a polo shirt. Kathy was attired in a similar outfit, as if there had been a two-for-one special at J.Crew.

Kathy glared at Brian with a mixture of hatred and defensiveness. When Kathy interlocked her arm with the colonel's, Emily rushed out of the room, Nirvana right behind her.

"Look at Egypt and Syria," Karl said. "Freedom is difficult. George W. Bush will go down in history as a great hero to the Muslim world."

"Jesus Christ," Brian said to no one.

Kathy sneered at him.

"And there were weapons of mass destruction," the colonel said.

"I know," Karl said, gesturing with his hands. "He used them before. He supported al-Qaeda, and it was a haven for terrorists."

"It was a massive operation. Some mistakes, but urban combat is the most difficult terrain." The colonel stood and shook Brian's hand.

Brian pressed himself into the handshake, then jerked the colonel's hand down and away. The colonel did the same.

"A pleasure. Rick."

"Brian," Kathy said, crossing her legs and folding her arms.

"You're a colonel. That's impressive, but you should be a general," Karl said.

"This is my girlfriend, Heidi."

The colonel clasped both of Heidi's hands. "It's an honor to meet you, Heidi." He held her hands a little too long, then turned to Brian. "You have a wonderful daughter."

Brian gazed past him. "Yeah, and where is my daughter? Emily?" He led Heidi down the hall and found Emily, visibly upset, in her bedroom with Nirvana, who had her arm around her.

"They're why Nirvana called me?" Brian asked.

"What do you think?" Emily said testily. "I can't deal with them alone."

"I hate that guy," Nirvana said.

Heidi stood off to the side, but Nirvana jumped up and hugged her.

"Emily, we have to talk," Brian said, even though he knew he couldn't talk to her about Michael there.

She leaned back and put her head in her hands. "I can't talk about it."

"Not about this. Let's just get through this. Be polite. How long are they staying?"

"A couple of days."

Nirvana waved her hands to get everyone's attention. "Let's go somewhere where there's a game on. Then we don't have to talk to anyone."

"The colonel's been talking to me all morning, and he and Karl love each other," Emily said.

Silence spoke loudly in the room.

"None of you like Karl? I know, you hate him." Emily's voice was sharp.

"Karl doesn't seem like your type," Nirvana said, then avoided her eyes.

Emily wiped her nose; she was about to cry again. "What do you think, Heidi?"

Heidi seemed hesitant but finally said, "I—I think we learn from every relationship."

Emily began to cry. "I know, I know. I'm dumping him. I can't wait to never see him again. Oh my god. What was I thinking? It was an experiment."

Kathy's heels clicked against the hardwood floors. Emily stood and wiped the tears from her eyes.

"Oh, here you are," Kathy said, her eyes searching the room.

"Sorry. We were just coming back." Emily turned to Nirvana. "Nirvana, you're okay?"

"I'm okay."

"Nirvana had some boy trouble."

Nirvana hurried out, Emily following. Kathy marched out behind them.

Brian exhaled. "Do I have to go back?"

Heidi pushed him toward the door. "Yes."

In the front room, Karl and the colonel were discussing war again.

"It's military men who hate war the most," the colonel was saying.

"Hey, didn't you say you wanted to watch the game, Dad?" Emily said.

"I hate to miss it."

"What game?" Kathy asked.

No one responded until Brian said, "The basketball game."

Nirvana suggested they go out to eat where the game would be on, and Brian was surprised that Kathy agreed so quickly.

"The colonel's book is on the bestseller list," Kathy said. "He's buying."

At a spacious pizza place on Westwood Boulevard, they all crammed around a long table. Emily maneuvered so Brian sat between her and Karl, who gave her a confused look. "What's going on?"

"Thank god for Trump," Kathy said for no reason, stopping all conversation. She was staring with a sour expression at former President Obama, who was on the news on one of the multiple TVs. "What Obama did was scary," she said.

Nirvana offered Kathy a disbelieving smile. "You mean, bring the economy back after the Republicans wrecked it?"

"I like Obama, but let's not talk politics," Emily said firmly.

Kathy flushed, but she held her tongue.

"He was a dictator, like Hitler," Karl spewed.

Emily sniffed at him. "You're an idiot."

Karl jolted up to confront her, but Brian blocked him.

"You can't talk to me like that, you bitch," Karl said.

Brian slapped Karl hard across the face. "Don't ever speak like that to my daughter."

The slap drew everyone's attention in the restaurant. Rage flickered in Karl's eyes as he jumped away from the bench. Brian smirked, ready to beat the living crap out of him.

The colonel slid between them and put his arm around Karl. "That was uncalled for," the colonel said.

Kathy was on her feet. "He deserved it." She glared at Karl and pointed to the door. "I want you out of my daughter's life, out forever."

"I thought you were my friend?" Karl whined.

"Get out!" Kathy shouted.

"You don't know who I am." Karl marched away and flung open the door. Karl's sidekick, who evidently was sitting at another table, followed.

Emily's hands fluttered over her face with her eyes peeking out between her fingers. Heidi and Nirvana sandwiched her in a group hug.

"That guy is bad news," Brian said, turning toward his daughter to comfort her. The colonel grabbed his arm.

"What he said was wrong, I admit," the colonel said.

Brian belted the colonel in the face, sending the man crashing to the floor. "That was wrong too, I admit," Brian said.

The colonel scrambled to his feet, but Kathy jumped between them.

"Come on, fight me like a man," the colonel said. Although his fists were up, the colonel, who possibly could kick his ass, seemed unwilling to fight through Kathy.

She pushed him back. "You need to leave."

"Wait, I wasn't condoning what he said," the colonel stuttered. "And he's a goddamn liberal," he said, nodding to Brian. "You said it yourself."

"Oh, shut up!" Kathy said.

There was panic in the colonel's eyes. "We're on the same team."

"Not anymore. I'll call you at the hotel."

The restaurant crew watched, probably waiting for more fireworks. Brian noticed mobile phones pointed their way, taking photos or video. "Well, we'll be on Facebook or some blog tonight," he said.

"We should go," Heidi said.

"No man has ever hit me without me hitting him back," the colonel said.

Emily exploded, twisting her body in anger. "God, go away."

Her outburst took everyone by surprise, especially the colonel, who looked around for perhaps support. Brian held in a satisfied smile.

"This isn't the end of this, pal," the colonel said to him before strutting out.

"That's for all the soldiers you guys got killed and wounded," Brian said loudly to the colonel's back.

Nirvana stepped forward. She had boxed up the pizza. "Shall we go?"

He took a box and put his arm around Emily. "I think you should stay at my place tonight."

Emily agreed, and at his bungalow, she appeared to be in reasonably good spirits when they were finally alone and feasting on pizza and drinking kombucha.

"I want you to call your mother tonight."

"Okay."

"She made us proud."

"She did. I've been so stupid since Michael. I don't know

why I went with such an opposite type of person."

"I need to talk to you about Michael." He ran his hand through his hair. "This is going to be complicated and messy. I don't know how to keep you out of it."

Emily stopped eating. "What do you mean?"

"We have videotape of Michael speaking with Terry Narlo."

"The man who killed all those people?" The words rushed out of her mouth.

"We don't know the facts, but we have to explore all possibilities. This is incredibly important," he said in a calm voice.

"I don't believe Michael would hurt anyone," she said, lowering her gaze.

Brian thought she seemed a little dazed taking this all in.

"Is that where you shot the rat?" she asked, examining the bullet hole.

"Yeah." He wanted to get back to the subject. "Michael's not who he says he is. He may not even be from Venice, Italy. We don't know."

"How else could he know the Venice streets the way he did?"

Brian nodded. "He might have been involved, then came to his senses and tried to stop it. We don't know." He watched Emily. She seemed to be holding up well. "Did you meet any of his relatives or friends?"

"Once I saw him with a big man in a suit, an older man, and they spoke without looking at each other. Michael listened, mostly. Then they stopped and glanced in my direction, as if they realized I was watching them. It was spooky." She spoke with a syncopated slowness. Brian thought she was thinking through every word she said.

"Jesus. Okay. What did this man look like?"

She shrugged. "Dark-gray suit, big and stocky. Older."

"Older than me?"

"Much older than you."

"Italian?"

"Maybe."

"Anything else? Anything odd?"

Emily sipped her drink. "Michael could speak a lot of languages."

"Fluently?"

"I don't know; he just said things in Chinese, Russian, African languages. He sounded like a native speaker to me, but I don't know."

"Did he know what he was saying?"

"He would translate it sometimes."

Brian pondered this. "I'm sorry, but the bureau will want to interview you."

Emily nodded.

Emotion overcame him. "I know I was gone a lot and the divorce tore up our family, but I'm here now and I am not going away."

VI

UNABLE TO CONTACT TERRY NARLO'S BROTHER, Brian and Hayward decided to drive up a woodsy road in Topanga to his large, well-kept, rustic home surrounded by trees.

When they exited the SUV, it was oddly silent, and the only sound Brian heard was the pine needles he stepped across. No one appeared to be home.

"Narlo's brother looks like he did well for himself," Hayward said.

Brian knocked on the front door, but no one answered, as they had expected.

Hayward peeked inside the picture windows. "Nothing."

They walked across the deck to the side of the house and the carport, where a brown canvas covered up a large vehicle. With some difficulty, Brian lifted the cover and saw that it was a red pickup truck. "How did that get overlooked?"

Hayward had his phone out. "I'll get the team out here and a warrant." Then he flicked Brian's shoulder and nodded toward Narlo aiming an AR-15 at them.

Narlo vibrated with a speed-fueled, chaotic energy. His hair was disheveled, and his clothes looked like they hadn't been changed in days.

"Lower the weapon, Terry," Brian said.

Narlo seemed to consider Hayward, who was behind Brian.
"There's no going back," Narlo said.

"Terry, you killed twenty-one-year-old girls." Brian didn't
know if this was the right thing to say, but he couldn't show any
doubt.

"I didn't have a choice."

"You have a twenty-year-old daughter, Terry," Brian said.

Narlo jittered about, distracted by a sudden gust of wind,
before he seemed to remember that he was pointing the assault
weapon at Brian. "You have a daughter too," Narlo said, as if
that was important.

"How do you know that?" Brian asked, trying to keep Narlo
talking and distracted. He thought he would bring up Michael
too.

Narlo gave him a tortured smile before the shots rang out.
Narlo collapsed, his AR-15 falling to the side. Hayward had hit
him in the head and twice in the chest. Brian swung around,
and Hayward, still with the Glock in his left hand, speed-dialed
the bureau.

"The alleged mass murderer Terry Narlo has been shot and
seriously wounded," Hayward said. "We need a team out here
now. We're off State 27, Topanga Canyon Boulevard. GPS me."

In less than thirty minutes, medics and a swarm of FBI
agents were investigating the scene. Patterson appeared behind
Brian. "Let's take a little walk and talk off the record."

Patterson led him to the edge of the property, where they
had a magnificent view of the Pacific.

"Hayward was well within his rights," Brian said.

Patterson nodded, but he didn't seem interested. "How long
were you at the agency, Brian? And then the bureau? Twenty
years?"

"More than twenty."

"You've been one of the best. You're someone who deserves their big pension."

Brian peered out at the sea. It was rough today, with lots of white swells.

Patterson pivoted away from Brian to the ocean as well. "Narlo's dead, but there are too many loose ends hanging out there."

"There are." Brian began to say something else, but Patterson held up a hand to stop him.

"So, this Michael kid happened to be dating your daughter, and you met him?"

"Yeah, I considered requesting a background check on him if it could be justified."

"So, you saw red flags. Why?"

"When I look back, I believe he was always hiding something. I'm thinking now he's been trained since he was a boy."

"Nothing else? No acquaintances? No paper trails. Nothing your daughter said? Nothing you saw?"

"He was unusual, but I never suspected him of being a terrorist."

"So, you were shocked when you saw him speaking with Narlo?"

"Stunned."

"He's like the mystery man, Rossellini."

Brian faced Patterson, who positioned his hands halfway into his pockets. "Yeah, have you heard the news?"

"Good news?"

"Rossellini and Michael are connected."

"Go on."

"Among Michael's photos was one that made it appear

Rossellini was Michael's father or guardian. And my daughter said she saw Michael speak with a man who matched Rossellini's description."

"You believed Rossellini was harmless—before he killed an armed and experienced terrorist."

"It's not illegal to know a helluva lot about Venice and history. He seemed to be on our side."

"He's definitely on our side, but who the hell is he?" Patterson flashed a conspiratorial smile. "This is the most unusual case I've encountered in my career."

"Yeah," Brian said, "and it's revolving around me. This Michael kid is incredibly well educated. I think he was specifically recruited for a cause and targeted my daughter." He turned to the house, where agents were carrying out evidence. "I have no idea why."

Patterson paused before asking, "What about Rossellini?"

"He claimed that Venice in Los Angeles is a continuation of the Italian Venice."

"Jesus Christ. What about Heidi? Who is she?"

"A yoga teacher. That's it. She has nothing to do with any of this."

"But she has something to do with you?"

"Yes, she's my girlfriend."

"Sorry, we have to know everything about you in this situation."

Hayward hurried over to them. "Michael was spotted in Santa Monica."

About twenty cops and FBI agents surrounded the eighteen-story hotel blocks from the beach. A helicopter hovered above the hotel as a SWAT team prepared to rope down to the roof.

Across the street from the hotel, Brian, Patterson, and

Hayward watched the situation unfold on FBI live video on a tablet. Michael was sitting on the roof with his feet dangling over the side of the building. Then he rose and strolled across the roof, taking slow, measured steps, almost as if he was scared or disheartened. He hesitated before disappearing into the small enclosure that housed the stairs coming up and down from the roof. He would be in custody soon.

"Be prepared, we'll be the first to interrogate him," Patterson said, then walked toward the hotel.

Two hours later Hayward was sitting in the back seat of the SUV, playing a game on his tablet. Brian leaned against the SUV and spoke into his phone. "Emily, it's your dad. Give me a call as soon as you can." He slid his Samsung into his pocket. He had been trying to reach her all day.

"If he was injured, an ambulance would have been here by now," Hayward said out the window.

"Maybe someone else is interrogating him."

"Here comes the assistant director. He's not happy."

Patterson marched toward them from the hotel. "He's not in the building," he said when he reached them.

Hayward got out of the backseat. "What do you mean?"

"They've torn the place apart. He's not there."

"The press is going to kill us. We all saw him, right?" Patterson said.

"There has got to be an explanation," Hayward said.

Patterson shot Hayward a dirty look. "Explain it to me when you figure it out." He got in the front passenger side of the SUV and slammed the door.

"There are several dimensions to what's going on," Brian said quietly to Hayward.

"I was thinking the same thing."

They eyed each other for a moment.

"Of course, this conversation is off the record."

"What conversation?"

Brian opened the driver's side door. Hayward hopped in the back.

Later that evening Brian sipped a glass of red wine, lounging with Heidi on her expansive sofa. Along with his splitting headache had come the sober realization he was up against something he did not understand.

"You're somewhere else tonight," Heidi said, running her hand through his hair.

"I'm sorry. It's this case. I've never been this personally invested." It was unprecedented that he would have a personal relationship with suspects, and he had felt doubly deflated when they didn't bring Michael in. The connection between Rossellini and Michael would open the doors to everything that was happening in Venice—and even with Narlo gone, it wasn't over. This wasn't just about stopping it but understanding so they could prevent something like it in the future.

Brian's phone rang. "It's Hayward," he said to Heidi. "Hey," he said, answering the phone.

"Brian, I need to show you something," Hayward said softly.

"Now?"

"I'm out front."

"What do you mean?"

"I'm out front of Heidi's house."

Brian sat up and glanced at Heidi. "Okay."

"What is it?" Heidi asked.

"Hayward is here."

"Here?"

They heard knocks on the door, and Brian let him in.

Hayward entered with his head bowed. "I'm sorry to intrude," he said, nodding to Heidi.

"Do you want to be alone?" Heidi asked.

"No. You should hear this as well." Hayward's voice cracked, and his face became ashen.

"What the hell is going on?"

Hayward had his tablet in hand. "Emily has been abducted."

Heidi covered her mouth with both hands.

Hayward handed him the tablet. It was a photo of Emily blindfolded and Karl behind her. "I'm sorry."

Brian was incapable of speaking. He wanted to act immediately, but what was the plan? What could he do? He recovered some composure and asked, "What steps have you taken?"

"Patterson has authorized the full power of the FBI to find her."

After six hours of discussions with Hayward as well as conference calls with Patterson and other department leaders, Brian tried to catch a couple of hours of sleep at four in the morning, but his mind raced, so he got up and sat on the sofa in the dark and went over the possibilities in his mind. Karl, Michael, Rossellini, Narlo. What had brought this disparate group to Venice? What was Karl's connection? Narlo was a mass murderer, but Brian couldn't understand how Michael could be connected to him.

What he couldn't get out of his head was both al-Asiri and Rossellini speaking about the death and destruction in Iraq as the impetus for the current violence and conflict. It was something he'd seen before in his career: violence and killing and unjust wars or conflicts often sparked revenge and hatred for hundreds of years. Sometimes a new event would open the door to all kinds of forces seeking to right a wrong or fuel rage at an

Venice to Venice

enemy, real or perceived. It was he, one of the many who had opposed the Iraq War from the beginning, who had to protect his family now, while those who had caused it were sleeping easily tonight.

Heidi appeared at his side. "It's four o'clock. Why don't you try to get some sleep? It's going to be a long day."

"I can't sleep. I'm going into the office."

She put an arm around his shoulders. "Okay, will you call me when you hear anything?"

"I want you to be careful," he said, stroking her cheek. "Keep everything locked and your home alarm on. Call me if anything, no matter how small, concerns you."

"I'm scared. I admit it," she said, gripping his hand.

His stomach sank when he saw the fear shimmering in her eyes.

He was scared too.

The Venice streets were deserted as he drove down Abbot Kinney. Brian barely noticed the huge figure leaning inconspicuously against the building. He thought it was a mirage or trick of the mind, but standing in front of the restaurant with the lion of St. Mark flag was Rossellini in his suit.

Brian pulled over and opened the door after Rossellini walked to the curb and raised his hands as if surrendering. "Are you armed?"

"No."

"You're a wanted man."

"Some things never change."

Rossellini barely managed to squeeze his body into the front seat. Brian texted the bureau and Hayward that he was bringing Rossellini in. He felt no fear from Rossellini, and he wanted a chance to speak to him before all hell broke loose. Rossellini

112

appeared calm, but he did not smile like he usually did.

"What's happened to my daughter?" Brian asked with a barely concealed animosity.

Rossellini appeared surprised. This was the first time Brian had seen any uncertainty in the man. "Your daughter?"

He shouted in Rossellini's ear, "Did you know she's been abducted?"

"Abducted? No." Rossellini went catatonic for a moment. "No," he repeated.

"What do you know about Karl?"

Rossellini's voice rose and cracked with emotion. "He's a petty fool. A low-level halfwit who can be manipulated to do anything."

"Is he dangerous?"

"Yes."

"He's kidnapped my daughter," Brian roared.

"He's just taking orders."

"From who?"

"I don't know everything."

"Jesus."

Rossellini's breath started to make a wheezing sound.

"And where the hell is Michael?"

"Michael is preparing himself."

"For what?"

"For what's coming."

"You need to come clean with me, Rossellini, today! You need to tell us what you do know."

A grim melancholy flattened Rossellini's face. "Venice requires sacrifice and redemption. Michael is the only one capable of that."

"What does that mean?"

"It means Michael is the only one who can save Emily."

FBI SUVs appeared behind and alongside them. Rossellini cleared his throat as Brian ran a red light.

"We're going to interrogate you, Mr. Rossellini, and we're going to learn the truth and find out who you really are. Transparency is a requirement here."

Rossellini closed his eyes for a moment, and his chin fell. "I see."

"You can call your lawyer inside. Someone will read you your rights."

"Venice is fragile. Trust Michael," Rossellini said softly.

Brian pulled into the FBI parking garage and flashed his card. "He's not resisting," Brian said.

Special agents were already waiting. When Brian hopped out of the SUV, his phone rang. It was Hayward. "I have Rossellini with me in the garage," Brian told him.

"Almost there."

Brian got out and opened the passenger-side door. When Rossellini didn't change position, he placed his hand on Rossellini's shoulder. No movement. He leaned in. "Rossellini? Rossellini? Talk to me."

Rossellini's head was tilted back, and his massive fingers seemed unable to fold into each other. Brian checked the pulse on Rossellini's neck. He already knew that the man was dead.

"We need a medic and an ambulance. He doesn't have a pulse."

Hayward appeared at his side. "Didn't you just pick him up? What happened?"

"Heart attack, I'm thinking."

"No, no, no." Hayward's shoulders slumped. "It was my dream to interrogate him."

"I have no idea how this looks."

"It looks weird. It all looks weird."

"That's because it is."

The medic was there in minutes and could not revive him. When the ambulance arrived, Brian watched as they attempted to extract Rossellini from the SUV. The medic slipped, and Rossellini teetered and toppled onto the man, crushing him. Four or five men were finally able to raise Rossellini onto a transport. Brian could almost hear Rossellini laugh—that chuckle that resonated from deep within him, as if there were reservoirs of a fantastic opera bellowing inside. In fact, now that he thought about it, Rossellini always seemed to be laughing. Mirth dominated his pleasant face unless he turned deadly serious about something, like the time he said he was going to silence someone.

Brian sat alone in his office for the next hour until he was summoned to Patterson's office. Brian couldn't meet his gaze. Hayward sat mute next to him.

"He croaks in the parking garage," Patterson finally said, tapping his fingers on his desk.

"Yeah." Brian raised his hands in a futile gesture.

"Did he mention Emily?"

"He connected Michael to Emily. He said he's the only one who can save her, whatever that means."

"You believe him?"

"I don't disbelieve him."

The phone rang, and Patterson picked it up, making guttural sounds to acknowledge whatever was being said. "He didn't die of heart failure," he said, slamming down the phone. "His heart was as healthy as a horse."

"What happened?"

"They don't know. No one knows a damn thing. He doesn't have an ID or money." Patterson banged his fist on the desk. "So, you're driving around, and there he was."

"Like he was waiting for me. It happened that way every time."

"And why in hell is someone like Rossellini floating around in the background?" Patterson asked.

"Why is Michael floating around in the background?" Hayward added.

Brian now believed that Rossellini and Michael had come to Venice to resist the forces the imam and Rossellini were concerned about—that amorphous group bent on revenge for the unjust killings in the Iraq War. Al-Asiri had brought up Brian's family. Narlo must have been part of the terrorist group that sought to seek revenge and cause fear. Perhaps that's all the rat and cats had to do with it, sow chaos. There was no other group like this that he was aware of. They were secretive, cunning, and capable.

"Michael is the key," Brian said.

But he had no idea what that key would unlock.

VII

BRIAN USED HIS KEY TO ENTER Emily's apartment. It felt desolate inside, and he sensed each step or movement he made, as if he were trapped inside himself. "Emily?"

There were a couple of dishes in the sink that had been there for a while, but nothing seemed to be out of place.

In Emily's bedroom, Brian lay on her bed, which was cool to his touch. She was all that mattered now. His career, his life, nothing would mean anything if he lost her. He had tried to do the right thing throughout his life, he thought. He questioned whether the world was amoral, but his core belief was that he could act too. He would remain in the fight as long as he was alive.

Early the next morning, he and Heidi went for a walk on the pier. Fog blanketed the view, and few people were out.

"This is where I first saw Rossellini," he told her, leaning on the rails. They peered down at where the invisible small waves were crashing in. "I keep thinking that Emily and I were chosen for some reason."

Heidi placed her hand on his back. "Why do you think that?"

"Because we were vulnerable."

"It's because you can handle it."

"I'm nothing special."

"I think you're a strong person who will stand up to do the right thing no matter the consequences," she said. "Like telling the truth in the run-up to the Iraq War."

"And look where it's gotten me."

"If more people told the truth like you, it would have saved thousands of lives as well as American prestige."

Not to mention trillions of dollars, he thought.

In the distance Brian made out the figures of three men in suits and fedoras. He had the sense they weren't walking but somehow moving through the fog.

Suddenly the fog lifted around one of the men, and Brian could see a face that suggested something sinister in its handsomeness. The man turned toward him with a slight smile.

Brian stood straight as the three men faded back into the mist. He was certain these three were part of the conspiracy and violence. Perhaps they controlled Karl and Narlo. He also knew there was no basis for assuming that. "I should get back to work," he said.

Karl's rental was identified that afternoon.

Brian, Patterson, and Hayward watched from a distance and out of line of possible fire as five armed special agents in bulletproof vests approached the Craftsman home. Three police units waited behind their black-and-whites, parked on the tree-lined street.

Two agents went around the side to the backyard so no one could escape from the rear of the house. Brian noticed a blond cat walk past them. The cat ambled across the front lawn and sat on the porch.

"We're certain this is the place?" Patterson asked.

"It's the place," Hayward replied.

"But no one has seen Emily here?"

"No, just the boys, Karl and the one with no name."

The stress had caused Brian to stop eating, but the lack of food seemed to increase his energy and clear his head.

A muscular special agent knocked on the door. No one answered. One of the agents on the porch peeked through the window. He signaled that he saw no one in the house.

A brown cat appeared on the roof.

The agent rang the doorbell and pounded on the door again. "FBI. Open up. We have a search warrant. FBI. We want to make this as easy as possible for you," he shouted.

No response. The agent turned to Patterson, who nodded.

Two police officers with a battering ram charged the door, almost breaking it open. It collapsed inward on the second charge.

The agents entered the house slowly, weapons raised. "FBI, please identify yourself." They disappeared into the house.

Brian moved to the right of Hayward so he could be one of the first to enter. When the agents signaled the all clear, Brian rushed to the front door. "Any sign of a young woman?"

"No."

Brian hurried past the man to search for clues. Inside, trash and junk lay everywhere. He entered the kitchen, where it appeared no one had cleaned the dishes in months. Flies buzzed around a half-eaten pizza. Ants were everywhere.

Brian hurried out of the kitchen and down the hall. Hayward was in the back bedroom, standing six feet from the carcass of a big dead rat.

"Not killed that long ago. I would guess by a cat, judging by the markings," Hayward said.

Brian guided Hayward out of the room. "We need to get out of here and have the house quarantined," he said.

He and Hayward ordered everyone out and exited onto the porch. The blond cat had been joined by a second cat.

"They got into an argument with their landlord a week or so ago, and they were given a thirty-day notice," Hayward said.

Patterson placed a hand on Brian's shoulder. "There's no sign that Emily's been here. We'll check for fingerprints when it's safe."

He nodded. "Thank you, Assistant Director."

"Let's go back to the office and brainstorm. They'll report directly to me if they find anything. I'm personally involved in every aspect of this case."

Brian turned back and discovered that there were more than twelve cats on the roof. Two more cats had joined those on the porch. When he stopped walking and stared at them, Hayward and Patterson did too.

Brian's phone buzzed. He read the text that had come in, then handed his phone to Patterson without a word.

Patterson read the text aloud: "We only want him. He surrenders or you will never see her alive again."

"Karl sent this?" Hayward asked.

Brian focused on the cats. "According to the text."

"You said you had a confrontation with Karl?"

"He called my daughter a bitch," Brian said, trying to hold in his fraying nerves.

"First thing we need to confirm is that Emily is safe," Patterson said. "Then we'll find out specifically who they want, so there is no confusion."

"That's what the experts recommend?" Hayward asked.

Patterson waved an arm. "They don't know shit."

Brian and Hayward were huddled in Brian's office, trying to outline different scenarios, when Kathy appeared in the doorway. After Hayward excused himself, Kathy fell into his arms. "Our baby."

He embraced her, their tears flowing.

"Why have they taken her? To get back at you? Revenge because she broke up with him?"

"We don't know."

She stepped back, and they stood only a foot from each other. "You don't know, or you can't tell me?"

"I would tell you. But it's more than Karl. I'm sure of that."

"What do they want?" she asked, holding his hand.

"They might want me," he said, trying not to sound worried.

"Why?"

"Information? Kill me? Revenge?"

"They're going to be caught. They can't get away."

"They can't."

Her eyes were red and enveloped him. "I know I made mistakes. You're either with me or against me—that sort of thing."

"I feel that way with this case. And I'm sorry I slapped that boy."

"He deserved it." Kathy sniffed a few tears and blew her nose into a handkerchief she had yanked out of her purse. "Are you in love with the yoga teacher?"

"I am."

"You look younger. I feel old."

"Yoga." He shrugged.

"Emily loves yoga. I need to start, just to be closer to her if nothing else."

"That's how I started."

Kathy began to cry again but coughed the tears back in. "Why our family? I don't understand what's happening."

That evening Brian lay feverish on Heidi's couch while Heidi worked in the other room. When he heard something thump lightly outside, he slipped on a coat and tucked his Glock in the pocket before he stepped out the door.

Heidi's ivy grew across the entire fence along the patio. The backyard appeared to be a living organism, with succulents, vines, and shrubbery flourishing everywhere; bird feeders and statues of angels and Buddhas were mixed in. Brian sensed someone was out there too.

Brian glanced back at the house, and kneeling on the roof was Michael, his eyes full of fear, but perhaps not as fearful as Brian's. Michael was a skeleton, as if he had been starving himself.

Brian alerted the bureau on his phone, then shouted at Michael to come down. Michael didn't move.

"What do you know about Emily's abduction?" Brian was furious, and if he got a hold of Michael, he was going to shove him around.

"It's my fault. If I hadn't lost my courage at the hotel, they wouldn't have taken her." Michael tilted his head as if he heard something or someone nearby.

Brian pulled out his Glock. "You're coming in today. No more games."

"I'm giving myself up to them."

"You're giving yourself up now."

"I'm sorry," Michael said in a matter-of-fact tone. "I have to drink from this cup."

"Why do they care about you?"

"Rossellini is gone, so it's up to me."

Brian continued to aim the gun at him. "Michael," he warned.

Michael appeared oblivious to the gun. "Emily is going to be okay, I promise. I won't let them harm her."

"Michael!"

Michael jumped and hit the ground on the other side of the fence, his footsteps rapidly fading.

A moment later law enforcement roared up to the front of the house.

Brian lowered the gun.

Brian felt more isolated than ever under the piercing glares and harsh questioning that followed. Even Patterson seemed to doubt him. They all appeared to think that he wasn't telling them everything. He was called in to face a team of special agents assembled in a conference room, including Patterson and Hayward.

"The troops think you or the bureau are hiding something," an agent said.

"Am I on trial here?" Brian asked.

"You're in the middle of everything."

"And everyone conveniently gets away," another agent added.

After an hour of badgering, with Brian repeating his experiences with Michael, he'd had enough. "All right, you want to know everything I know?" he said, challenging them. "The war in Iraq opened the door to the forces of darkness, and now there's a war between them and the freedom of the West. The West was represented by Venice, Italy, but ceded that role to the United States. Rossellini was some kind of mystery man who worked with fellows like me who he thought had good judgment and were honest. I think Michael is part of his group. I don't believe either of them were or are terrorists. But this Karl and his crew are, and they want the kid Michael. I don't know why, but he's the prize they're after. And they have my daughter!"

Brian knew he sounded insane, but he didn't care. The other six in the room either tiptoed around him as if he were the

crazy uncle in the family or seemed to hold him in some es-
teem. The fact that his daughter had been taken gave him license to say things no one else would.

Everyone was silent for a few seconds as Brian hid his face
in his hands, overcome with fury. "Goddamn it. Am I a suspect
now?" he asked.

"Get Brian something," Patterson said. "Water, a soda."

"Water."

A special agent tossed him a bottle.

He drank most of it in one swig. "Now you know everything
I know. And you know where I learned that? Rossellini."

"And he's dead," Patterson said.

"Yeah. You think I should have written that up and briefed
everyone?" Brian asked.

"Who could they be working for?" an agent asked. "They
have to be working for someone."

"It's groups that are fighting among themselves," Hayward
said.

No clues. No chatter. Brian and Hayward were growing concerned that Emily was no longer in LA or maybe even in the
country. Brian broke down several times. His heart seized up on
him, and he had to curl up in his office or run outside to catch
his breath.

He woke after sleeping on the floor in his office. Overcome
with exhaustion, he managed to pull himself up and trudge out.

On his way to Heidi's, his phone rang, a FaceTime request
that he accepted as he pulled to the side of the road.

"It's Michael. I'm at the Marina. It will happen here."

Brian could see boats below Michael. He knew where this
was. "What will happen?"

"Goodbye. I love you and Emily."

"Michael!" Brian hit the gas and screeched right toward the Marina.

When he reached the docks, he rang Patterson. "Michael called. Something's going down at the Marina."

"We're on our way. Recommendation on how we proceed?" Patterson asked.

"I don't know. Michael just said meet him at the Marina."

"Don't get out of the car until we arrive," Patterson barked.

Brian got out and jogged, then walked alongside the boats. Everything swirled around him; he felt outside himself.

A large boat entered the harbor, and one was going out. The sky was sunny, cloudless. The cool, glassy water reflected his panic back to him.

"Brian." The voice came from near a fleet of yachts that took up the premium slips. He turned in a circle before he located Michael on top of an apartment building close to the water.

He waved, but Michael didn't respond. He heard Michael say, "I love you"—not necessarily directed at him but at the world—and then Michael disappeared from the edge of the roof.

"Michael!"

Michael was plunging down, arms spread wide, no drama in his face or body. It was completely natural, as if he were diving into a pool. Brian watched Michael plummet headfirst until he was impaled by a piece of steel on a yacht. The thud brought Brian back to earth.

Blood was everywhere, streaking the white boat with red that washed across the deck.

Not thinking straight, Brian hopped on the yacht and tried to get below deck, hoping Emily could be there, which didn't make sense, but he kicked the door open anyway and stumbled down the stairs. "Emily?"

As soon as he was inside the cabin, he saw the weapons. Enough roadside bombs and bomb material to take out huge chunks of Venice.

The special agents arrived, and police cars and ambulance sirens flew in from multiple directions.

Brian came back up and flagged Hayward. "It's a cache of weapons, maybe even weapons of mass destruction."

"Everyone off," Hayward ordered. "Now. We need to check for booby traps."

Brian got off the boat and realized he had received a text. It was a photo of Emily and an address close by in Venice. He hailed Hayward, who drove him down a street of beachside homes.

"There it is," Hayward said, pointing to a white two-story house right on the water.

Hayward drove across all lanes right up to the home, where Brian jumped out. Two cops and several special agents joined them with their guns ready. Brian frantically called Emily's name. The front door was unlocked, and they cautiously made their way into this remarkably clean house that appeared to be a vacation rental, not a home anyone lived in.

Brian rushed up the stairs. "Emily!"

Down the hall he heard banging on the door in a back room. Emily was leaning against the door when he tried to open it. Her hands and feet were bound. When he and Hayward untied her, Emily hugged him so tightly that he was unable to loosen her grip. Her hot tears wet his cheek.

"Thank god. Thank god. I love you," he repeated over and over.

They kept their arms wrapped around each other until Brian stepped back and examined her. She was pale and had no make-up on. He beamed into her eyes, then began to cry.

Hayward approached. "Do you want me to take you to the hospital?"

Emily shook her head. "No, I'm okay. I want to be out in the sun."

"Physically you're okay?" Brian asked, looking her in the eye.

"Nothing happened."

Several more agents and cops had entered the house.

"Can you answer any questions?"

She nodded that she could.

"Let's go to the bureau, and we'll call your mother and Heidi."

Outside, Brian helped Emily into the SUV and shut the door.

"They got what they wanted, and that's the Michael kid?" Hayward asked.

"I don't know anything anymore."

"Me either."

Two days later Brian and Hayward visited the coroner, a pleas-ant-looking fellow who wore large glasses. They had worked with him on several occasions.

"Two crazy killings in one day," the coroner said.

"What do you mean, two?" Hayward asked.

"We had a head come in. No body."

"Jesus. What happened?"

"All I know is someone found a fresh head."

"Can we see it?" Hayward asked.

"You really want to?"

"No, but it's that kind of week."

The coroner led them to a table with a plastic cover, which he pulled back. It was Karl. Brian and Hayward exchanged a glance.

"Know him?" the coroner asked.

"Yeah," Brian said.

"That is a hell of a way to go."

They couldn't take their eyes off the head.

"I have some good news," Brian said. "The CDC cleared his house of any potential disease."

Hayward squinted at Karl. "He doesn't look happy."

The coroner covered the head back up.

"Let's see the kid's body and get this over with," Hayward said.

"He wasn't beaten up much."

Hayward gaped at the coroner. "What are you talking about? He was impaled."

"That's not what was brought in."

The coroner pulled out the gurney where Michael was kept. No Michael and only a white sheet. "What the hell?" The coroner checked his chart. "There must be a mix-up of some kind."

Brian and Hayward eyed each other.

"Yeah, a mix-up," Brian said.

VIII

NINE MONTHS LATER at Intelligentsia Coffee on Abbot
Kinney, Brian sipped a latte, reading the Los Angeles Times on
his iPad, when he felt someone near him and realized a petite
women dressed in light blue stood across from him. Her face
was acne scarred, and she had warm, penetrating brown eyes.

"I'm a friend of Giuseppe's. Do you mind?" She extended
her hand, a wry smile dominating her face. "Dina."

"Brian." He couldn't think for a moment, then gestured toward the empty chair for her to sit. "Please."

"Giuseppe was a fascinating character," she said.

"Yes," Brian said, setting down his iPad.

Her eyes narrowed. "Losing Michael was devastating, but
others have been inspired by him and have become his disci-
ples, so to speak. The martyr becomes thousands."

"I regret how I treated them both. I was wrong."

You were a rock," Dina said. "A rock we could depend on.
That's why I'm here." She sipped her coffee. "I have an issue
I am hoping you can assist with."

THE *MYSTERIES*
OF *GAME THEORY*

I

IN LOS ANGELES, IT WAS THE VIRUS that concerned
him the most, and it kept him underground. James spent much
of the time on his bed reading or listening to books. When he
tired of reading, he lay numb to the violence outside. Books
were strewn about the house.

After the first year, the bombs, gunfire, and sound of crashing buildings dissipated, then disappeared. The heavy crush of
silence outside felt as if it were inside him.

A few times in the beginning, he heard steps or voices outside and peeked out at the small groups or individuals passing
by. Once someone shook his door handle, but when he shouted
that he had a gun, they scampered off.

After eighteen months, he'd begun to leap up because he
would see someone or something moving around him, even
though he had secured the house, sealing the door shut with a
steel latch, installing bars outside each window like he was in
prison. He would scan the rooms, and there was never anything
there, but he frantically searched for whoever was in the house.

Where the hell had his sister Cleo gone? At her condo, he'd
seen the windows shot out and the sheets covering the dead

people on the sidewalk outside her place. Why hadn't she met him at his house? That was the plan.

The constant pressure in his abdomen was his sister Cleo. He had done everything he could to find her. He had dashed out through dark streets, avoiding warring factions who were attempting to escape on the freeway. It was never going to happen. Even he could see that the 101 was a parking lot and nothing was moving, especially the cars and the mass of people whose only hope was to leave the city on foot.

One of the last scenes he had seen streaming online was mobs of people trying to escape LA and rich people willing to pay a million dollars for a short helicopter ride out, but there was nothing anyone could do.

Around the world, military and barbed wire walls kept desperate, infected, and starving people from entering their borders in country after country. Quarantines or safe havens sentenced those on the outside to certain death from the pandemic. But no country could protect itself from a lethal, highly contagious virus that didn't recognize boundaries and devastated entire armies.

Now, after more than two years underground, James ripped into one of the last freeze-dried meals, absorbing the entire flavor and keeping the stringy texture in his mouth. If Cleo had been there, they would have run out of food a year earlier. They wouldn't have made it without scavenging outside for more food. Still, he had eaten as little as possible, thinking Cleo might appear.

Some of the food fell on the wild beard he had grown.

Every website had disappeared long ago, and so had his Wi-Fi service, but a new satellite service had popped up just days before. He'd received a notification saying it was safe to go out.

James wasn't sure whether to believe it, but he heard the faint rumble of what he thought was transportation. Something was happening outside.

II

HIS NEIGHBORHOOD WAS A GHOST TOWN. He wandered down Westwood and spotted a few people who were so skinny, they appeared to be skeletons. They were walking slowly, and he could see they were wary of him. He crossed the street to avoid getting any closer. Everyone seemed cautious and paranoid. Everyone was wearing a face mask.

A sparsely filled shuttle passed him; the passengers' heads were bowed, and no one looked out. They were like apparitions, he thought. His own clothes were ready to fall off his thin frame.

Later he took a shuttle that passed a massive military installation. It dropped him off at a long line going around the block. People stayed more than six feet apart. No one spoke unless it was in a whisper.

He felt as if he had gotten out of a prison camp where he had been beaten and starved for two years. All he had now were memories of the devastation. His previous life was lost.

He had to wait for more than two hours to enter the warehouse to receive food and supplies. The inventory of large retailers such as Home Depot, Walmart, Costco, and Nordstrom, and even of boutique stores, had been confiscated by the military, and products were now available for free if you needed them.

A military woman and man took his name and personal information and entered it into a computer.

"He doesn't look too bad," the woman said.

The man eyed him. "Are you ill or do you have a fever?"

"No."

"Anything you want to tell us?"

"No."

The man and woman glanced at each other.

"How did you survive?" the man asked.

"I read books."

"That's a new one," the woman said with surprise.

"You'll be vaccinated in the next hour," the man said.

"Okay."

"You'll also be issued a card that allows you to receive health care, meals, and water each month," the woman said. "Medical clinics are all over the city. You'll need to see one as soon as possible. It's mandatory."

"After you're vaccinated, we'll want to speak with you about how you survived. They'll help you get cleaned up," the man added.

The woman handed him a paper. "Here's your number. Head straight back."

Their anxious and sympathetic eyes felt intrusive, even though he knew they were trying to help.

In the back were hundreds of long tables with military personnel interviewing citizens who had just come up. James opened up to a stone-faced military liaison, who questioned him about his employment history. The questions seemed harmless.

"Can you give me more detail about what you did at Facebook?"

"It was all about making money and how they could target

ads more profitably and more efficiently. That's all my depart-ment cared about," he said.

"For example?"

"Facebook had so much information on its users that they could reach them on a micro level, and it was my job to figure it out, so if I identified a certain movie you liked, we would feed you ads that people who also liked that movie interacted with. It could be more complex, but it made Facebook millions of dollars."

The military liaison furiously typed notes on a laptop.

The fact that he had been a data scientist at Facebook inter-ested the liaison a great deal. It was why, he was told, he was hired by the government the following week. They also spent a lot of time on his sister Cleo.

"I need to find her," James said again and again.

"Yes, we can help you do that."

"I'll tell you everything I know."

III

JAMES CAUGHT ONE OF THE now ubiquitous electric shuttles that transported everyone around what was left of Los Angeles. His hair had been cut short, and he was clean shaven, though he was still drastically underweight.

The city streets were clean, with most buildings boarded up. There were no homeless, and only a fraction of the citizens remained compared to West LA's population two years earlier, but there was an edge in the air, partly because of the armed vehicles and troops in constant view, as if they were worried about an attack from the outside—or the inside.

When he arrived at work, James didn't speak to anyone. He pored over data from military databases and imported it into Excel, then created a pivot table to help him understand the distribution of food groups and medical supplies.

His boss, Jens Ensley, had taken an interest in him. At sixty-one, Jens looked ten years younger. He wore glasses and maintained an air of competence and intelligence.

James believed Jens led many departments and thousands of employees, but he didn't know, just as he had no idea who was in charge. He didn't want to ask questions. He'd take a wait-and-see approach before he said too much.

"I've created a predictive analytics worksheet," he told Jens as he opened the file. "If we change the hours, it will estimate how much we produce. If we change the number of products, it will update the number of hours to create. We can add more fields anytime we want."

"Brilliant," Jens said. He clasped his hands and raised them to his mouth for a moment. "We need to be thinking about the future. How do we make our world sustainable? What resources are available to manufacture goods? How much fertile farmland do we have? How much can we continue to farm or create?"

Jens seemed to care about making things better. James wanted to know more about Jens's background, but he hadn't found the right moment to ask him. It was difficult to know anyone's background because all major server farms had been knocked out, and search engines like Google no longer existed. Only limited local-government-controlled servers and a restricted internet were live and accessible.

He wondered how long before the internet would be open to everyone, but concern crept into his mind as he recalled the last gang of politicians in charge. The president and his refusal to lock down or do anything about the pandemic, even when it became clear that the virus killed almost everyone who contracted it. The incompetent and corrupt fools who supported him, then escalated internal conflict and eliminated everyone's rights. His heart pounded at their arrogance and criminality.

Jens appeared to be the opposite; he was a man who believed in science and data and was one of the obviously competent leadership that had organized a civilized world after the pandemic. But who was Jens and who were his bosses? It was impossible to trust anyone with so little information.

That afternoon he entered Jens's office and found him staring out the window at the construction and the transportation flowing in the new Westside downtown.

"Life has returned to men and women," Jens said, keeping his back to him.

"It feels like coming out of Plato's cave. We've all been studying shadows for two years, and now we're confused by the sunlight."

Jens turned from the window to study him. "You surprised?"

"I didn't expect it."

"What did you expect?"

"Violence, a toxic environment, the pandemic still a threat." Jens looked back out the window.

"I remember watching the pandemic panic in LA on the internet before it went offline," James said. "The streets filled with gangs and militias. The raiding, the lawlessness. Dead people everywhere. Now, two years later, nothing."

"The virus is dead. It will not return," Jens said. "Forced isolation made the difference. You stayed in or you died."

James thought he might cry for a moment, thinking of all the death.

"Were you alone?"

"I had my books." He smiled, then felt the tears welling up again. "My sister was supposed to join me."

Jens became more alert. "You read a lot of books while underground?" he asked.

"Hundreds of them."

"You used your time wisely," Jens said. "It's tragic that most people did not prepare. We all knew it was coming."

"I stocked up on survival food, air filters, generators, bars for the windows, ultra-secure doors, and lots of books. I prepared a year in advance using the Survivor's Handbook." James's neck felt long and vulnerable. He was so thin that he sometimes felt like he was living in a teenager's body. "Everything seems different now."

"Everything is new and designed so there are no losers," Jens said.

"So, it's a nonzero-sum game?"

"There are no zeros, James. Think of it like that."

The afternoon light sifted through the wide window, as if the sun was just outside the third-story office. Jens's thin lips slid into a smile. He closed the blinds halfway.

Two-plus years was a long time to be in seclusion; it was an adjustment to be above ground. And James had been broken. He thought they all were, even Jens. With so much death, a sense of lost souls floating about surrounded him. He had believed religion would play a larger role, and perhaps it did privately with people, but the world seemed to have lost its faith in anything.

When he wasn't at work, James liked to walk alone—walk anywhere, searching for something. He didn't know what it was, except for his sister. The thought that she had been killed ripped through him, but he had not given up hope. Still, there was no record of her anywhere. He would always be trying to find her. That's what he thought about on his walks. He never sensed any trouble or danger on these long jaunts.

The wind howling through the world's silence made him feel barren. The new wide-open sky crushed him, intensifying his smallness and insignificance.

Everything had gone smoothly since he'd been up, not only for him, but as far as he could tell, for everyone. However, something about the data he saw daily troubled him. How did the government, whoever they were, have this data so quickly?

How was food production available so soon and in proportion to the number of people needing to be fed? And most of all, how and when had they produced so many vaccines? It had to be the military in charge, and perhaps it hadn't occurred to them yet to be transparent.

He hoofed it along the plains, wishing he could hike in the hills and take in the surrounding area from a bird's-eye view. What was left of the diversity that was Los Angeles? Where were the boundaries now? He wandered west, believing he would run into the 405 Freeway. It might still be in use, though only sporadically, because he heard no traffic. Maybe it was used to transport goods in from other regions in those shiny new metal trucks he frequently saw heading out of town.

Outside downtown, the silence grew alienating. Where were the animals? Cats? Dogs? Birds? Were they out in the wild? It must have been too hard to feed an animal while underground. And there were legitimate concerns pets were spreading the virus. The thought of all the pets dying made his teeth clench.

His left calf cramped for a moment, and he considered turning back when he came to a street surrounded by barbed wire. It was impossible to move forward, but he limped along it instead.

Hotels and luxury apartments had been hollowed out. He climbed over the huge blocks of concrete that had been part of a building or parking structure. James had ventured far enough that he must be past UCLA, and this long street might have been Wilshire, he thought.

Many of his friends and coworkers had lived in Santa Monica, Venice, West LA, Marina Del Ray, Playa, Malibu, and Topanga, and now those areas were empty and isolated.

He choked back his emotion and whiffed in the humid air. He ached for a connection with someone, anyone.

James traced his fingers along the cold wire fence. He would have climbed it, but the extra layers of barbwire at the top were not something he could maneuver over. He had done yoga and resistance training while he was caved up, but he had little endurance. Though his diet was better now that he was able to eat real fruit and vegetables, his muscles were still weakened from the years of malnutrition and the lack of sun and cardio.

He turned south, and the fence ended. By now it was almost dark. He needed to head back. There wasn't a curfew, but he rarely saw people out at night, at least not in his part of town.

During the hike back, reflections from inside wrecked homes, hotels, and condos flashed him. The idea that someone could be watching him with night vision glasses popped into his head. Or it could be his paranoid imagination. Once you'd been through a civil conflict and government hegemony, it was difficult to lose the reflexive paranoia.

He had no reason to care much. He had nothing to lose.

Loneliness crawled through his hips up to his abdomen and made him walk slightly bent over as he trudged on. Nothing. Nothing. Zero. The words pulsated in his chest. At least there was no anarchy in the streets, no bombs crushing down on impact as if they were mountains hitting the ground.

He wondered what had happened to all the bodies. There must have been hundreds of thousands of dead people. And this was Los Angeles, once a sprawling metropolis. Now the Westside had plenty of empty real estate, and the population was perhaps ten to fifteen percent of what it had been before, at least empirically. He didn't have the full picture because Jens or someone didn't allow it, but he could make an educated guess with the data points he had. If what happened in LA had happened to the entire world, billions of people had been wiped off the earth by the pandemic. Jens had hinted at that. It wasn't merely a physical fact; you felt it all around you. It lay just below the surface in your mind.

His senses had not fully adapted to being outside and active, and he stumbled off balance sometimes, as if the earth had shifted and was not as stable as it was before. A wave of guilt flooded him. If Cleo wasn't in LA, where could she have gone? He had tried several government agencies and pasted her photo up wherever he could, but with no luck. He had thought about her every day while in hiding. They should have stayed together.

James shivered as the temperature plummeted with the early evening. A crescent moon settled into the landscape. He rested for a few minutes near the construction site of a large building or complex. The government was drilling and nailing and hammering and renovating real estate all over town. An initiative for everyone to clean up their areas was in place.

It occurred to him that he should confide more in Jens. Yes, Jens might help.

IV

THREE WEEKS LATER, A SENSE OF NORMALCY had developed in James's spirit. His steps had become lighter. He wasn't always looking down. And for the first time, he'd started to feel that everything would be okay, and that maybe, just maybe, he would find his sister or at least some resolution and peace.

As he sauntered down the street after work, a tall woman, only a few inches shorter than he, jogged from across the street toward him. He didn't want to gawk at her, but he couldn't help following her long, lean legs accentuated by tight-fitting black yoga pants.

"Hey," she said, swinging her strawberry-blond hair.

He gestured to himself.

"I've seen you," she said.

A large smile burst onto his face in spite of himself. "You're referring to me?"

"Yeah." She tilted her head, and her hair layered her right cheek as she extended her hand. "I'm Sheilah."

Her hand was delicate. It had been so long since he had touched a woman that his pulse raced, and he felt himself escaping from inside his head. She smiled fervently at him.

"I work in the same building as you sometimes," she said.

He had no memory of seeing her there. "What do you do?"

"I'm an HR director. The goal is to have full employment or at least have people working part time. I hate the paperwork, but it's a fun job. I'm good at chatting with everyone and scheduling meetings and helping new people become acclimated."

Most women's hair hung limp and plain, but Sheilah's hair was bouncy and rich and streaked with highlights. Her eyes gleamed with dreamy anticipation.

"Where are you going?" he asked.

"Just walking. We were underground so long that I like to be under this strange big sky."

She turned her head slightly as if to invite him to walk with her.

"Why don't we go together?" he said in a rushed voice.

They walked. She led the way because she apparently knew this part of town. He didn't try to make small talk; she was a speed walker, swaying her arms with a smile etched on her face. He kept up with her by jogging at times, but after a couple of miles, he had to stop to rest.

"That's the fastest I've walked," he said. "My body is still gaining strength. I think it's the more balanced diet too."

She didn't seem fatigued at all; in fact, she jogged in place, though her cheeks appeared sunken from the exercise. He sensed she was a few years older than he, but not too much.

"You could use a drink," she said.

"Sure, the Superstore?" he asked, referring to the chain of stores where you could buy food, housing goods, clothes, or whatever the government put up for sale from their warehouses. It wasn't exactly a "super" store, though, but the only store, and it was stocked with a daily ration of vegetables and fruit. Some days of the week it was out of most items.

All goods were rationed. Most basic medication, even aspirin, was impossible to find unless you had a prescription from the government doctors.

"No, I know a bar nearby," Sheilah said.

He thought she meant one of the makeshift filtered water stands he had seen around the city when he first came up.

An electronic shuttle ride and twelve blocks away was a sprawling two-story building with tinted windows. Sheilah flashed an ID, and they were allowed in.

Inside, there were more people working than were frequenting the place. A group of military men and several women were leaving, allowing James and Sheilah to take their spot, an L-shaped corner sofa on the second floor. They gazed out at the long horizon that led to the ocean; it looked as if the land ran on into eternity, becoming whiter and whiter.

"I have credits," he said, referring to his government stipend card. It wasn't a lot, but he had not yet run out each month, though it felt odd to not exactly waste his money, but to spend it on a luxury and not a necessity.

Sheilah smiled. "It's free."

"For anyone?"

"For members," she said.

"How do you become a member?"

"I don't know. It's like a private country club sort of thing, I think."

When he ordered an iced tea, she said that sounded fine to her as well. He didn't want to be too nosy, so he didn't ask how she'd become a member.

The waiter was a small man who did everything in a hurry, scampering across the bar and hopping around. He brought their drinks immediately.

They clinked glasses.

"To our health," James said.

They both drank more than half the glass, then laughed.

"We were thirsty," Sheilah said.

He liked the way she brushed back her hair and crossed her legs. She seemed to be attracted to him too.

A woman with a small child crossed the street east of the bar.

"There are hardly any children," James said, turning to watch them pass by the building. "It must have been a nightmare to have a child the past two years."

Sheilah sat up and observed them. "It's too sad to think about," she said.

"And God help you if you got pregnant underground."

"I would think more would have had children. There was nothing to do." She lifted her glass and dropped an ice cube in and out of her mouth. "It's uplifting to be out after being cooped up for so long." Her voice trailed off, as if she were far away from her own comment.

"We adapt, don't we? I wonder who will write this history so we all can understand what happened."

"I only know that I'm alive and we're at peace and we're living again," she said with a sudden flash of enthusiasm.

"I don't even think about dying anymore."

"Why think about dying?" she asked. Her knee brushed against his, and she kept it there.

"A lot of people died," he said.

She frowned, and he worried he was being too negative.

"I wonder if the internet will be up again?" he said to change the subject.

"I never go online."

"Or when new media outlets will appear?"

"You are such a worrier." She laughed. "How about right now?"

He smiled, a little embarrassed. "You're right," he said. "I do worry too much." His brain was full of calculations and the past, but Sheilah drew him out.

She laid a hand on his knee. "Shall we have a real drink?"

"They have those here?"

"They have everything."

He ordered a martini, but the bitter taste of alcohol made him scrunch up his face. He set the martini down. "That was terrible. I've lost the taste for drink."

Sheilah sipped her gimlet. "Mine's great," she said.

His second and third drinks tasted much better. He hadn't felt this relaxed since he'd come up.

She finished her drink, then tossed her hair again so it was no longer in her eyes. Perhaps this was a flirtatious move? She was steadily focused on him now and once eyed him up and down with what he imagined was approval.

Later, outside the bar, a light, cool breeze swept off the mugginess.

"Thank you. I enjoyed that," he said.

They embraced and did not let go of each other.

They entered her luxury condo thirty minutes later. It had been freshly painted, and the fixtures and hardwood floors were new. A large window overlooked a patch of trees.

"This is a nice place," he said.

"Yeah, I'm lucky."

"So many were not," he said, "including pets."

He regretted saying something so gloomy, but she seemed interested in the subject.

"They fumigated the entire city while we were underground. That's why we don't see any cats, dogs, or bugs. Now and then I see a bird," she said.

"I thought the virus killed everything?"

"That too."

Her hand gripped his, and her fine, stark face moved close to his before they kissed, an open-mouthed kiss, wet and warm. Her tongue moved frenetically back and forth. She pulled him to the sofa and rolled onto her side, and they kissed again, the insane kissing with her tongue darting everywhere. They began unbuttoning their clothes and flinging it off, and when they were half undressed, she led him into the bedroom, where they made love for the next two hours.

When he woke up, he was spooning with her. He got up and poured them each a glass of water, and she perched herself on her elbow when he slid the glass along her back. She finished her water in a couple of gulps.

"Are you hungry?" he asked.

She shook her head and lay back. She didn't seem particularly joyful, only a little spaced out.

"You're beautiful. I'm so glad we met," he said.

As he stroked her hips, she twisted toward him. "You're a really nice guy."

He moved on top of her and entered, and they rocked on and on, and then it was so wow, wow, and he lost himself again and erupted. He remained inside her, pressing his loins against hers and gently kissing her.

"You're amazing," he said.

In the background, eerie, compelling electronic music infused the condo with a complex ambience he recognized. Music had been playing, but he hadn't paid attention to it earlier. Sheilah's eyes were closed.

"What is this music?" he asked.

"David Bowie," she said, opening her eyes.

"I like it."

"That's all I listened to while underground. My roommate loved Bowie and had all his albums, so I got to know about him and his music. He's a true artist," she said.

He loved that she had tapped into a great artist. He had gone through a Bowie period but hadn't listened to him in a while, preferring the contemporary or local bands that were on his iPhone—which now only functioned as a music player.

"I think it's amazing that you spent your time discovering a brilliant artist like Bowie." He wanted to know whom she had been underground with, but he wasn't going to bring it up at that moment.

"What are you thinking?" he asked instead after a prolonged silence.

She closed her eyes.

After his incredible night with Sheilah, James arrived at work early and in a happy mood. He ventured to Jens's office and rapped lightly on the door. Few people were in the office at this hour.

"James," Jens said, looking up, then back down. Jens always had neat piles of papers organized on his desk. His shirts and pants were crisp, as if they had been dry-cleaned.

"Do you have a minute?"

"I do."

James shut the door behind him. "I'm sorry to bother you, but I'd like to ask you a personal question—advice, really."

Jens sat back.

James thought it signaled he was interested. "My sister is missing," he said. "I've tried everywhere but haven't had any luck. She was supposed to meet me before we had to go underground, and she never showed up. Unless something happened to her, she would have been there."

Jens nodded as if he understood. "Happy to do what I can. Let me see if I can put someone on this," he said.

"I appreciate it." He reached out his hand, but Jens declined to shake it. "Right, I'm sorry," James said, remembering that shaking hands was discouraged because of the pandemic.

"Do you have her photos, IDs, lists of friends and associates? Bring it in tomorrow and any information you think could be helpful."

James thanked his boss and started to leave, but Jens stopped him.

"Many people were displaced over the last two years, so don't lose heart," Jens said.

"So, you believe there is a chance?"

"There's a reasonable chance. Information is constantly coming in. We're working with other communities to create an open forum about these issues."

"Other communities?" He'd thought they were all under the same leadership.

Jens peered at him with a stern expression. "It's a work in progress. There's still the opposition and anarchist groups out there."

"Of course."

"We did our best to keep it together, but it was a split country and feelings ran deep."

James didn't want to have this conversation with his boss. He needed his job and feared alienating Jens by making a political statement.

Jens's smile eased his concerns. "We'll do what we can to find your sister. And remember, we were trying to survive like everyone else." Jens walked to the blinds and adjusted them. "I think we've done a fine job of it. This new reality has a chance to build on the American Founding Fathers, but I admit I didn't believe a more lethal pandemic would come on so fast and spiral out of control." He bowed his head.

James appreciated his honesty. "Don't you believe the worst is over?"

Jens's voice became energized as he focused intently on him. "We don't think anyone knows who is out there and what they can do. Do our enemies have biological capabilities? Look at us here, we're sitting ducks."

"We seem to have a large military presence. Are you saying we are susceptible to attack?"

"That's what I'm saying."

James stepped toward the door and paused. "I'd love to hear about the planning and organization and how we got to this point," he said.

"We'd been planning for a pandemic for many years, so we were ready to deal with it, but to see it unfold was unreal. Fortunately the infrastructure remained in decent shape. People could have come up six months ago, but we wanted to be sure it was feasible and the virus eliminated."

Who was Jens and why would he be involved in the planning for a potential pandemic? He had been somebody important before the virus. James wondered why more people didn't have a pent-up desire to talk or to demand answers. Gratitude that they were alive preceded everything. He recognized it in himself.

But Jens seemed to enjoy having him visit to discuss the past, and James felt they shared an odd rapport, which left him with a certain level of trust. Perhaps Jens had opened up to him because James confided in him about Cleo.

Back at his desk, James found his new office mate, Daniel, a young Hispanic man the same age as he, working on a spreadsheet. They acknowledged each other but didn't speak. James noticed books peeking out of Daniel's backpack. He wanted to say something, but Daniel seemed too focused to bother him with small talk.

On his shuttle ride home from work, a disturbance unfolded on the street near a Superstore. Three military types had subdued a shouting stocky man and slipped an elastic bag of some kind over the man's head. No more screams after that; the three soldiers secured the bag and flung him into a van. It took less than fifteen seconds. James was taken aback by their efficiency.

But he was not surprised by the act of rebellion or trouble. He had heard that many people had gone mad from solitary confinement, which he believed; he had lost his mind while underground.

That evening James lay naked with Sheilah, his eyes closed, her head snuggled up on his shoulder. He had been thinking about her all day. It was more than thinking, it was a gnawing loneliness, and he was thrilled that she'd embraced him affectionately when they met at her place. She had the same yearning for him in her eyes that he felt inside for her.

After some time Sheilah pulled away and lay on her back. "What do you want from this relationship? I really like you, I do, but I need to know," she said.

"I want you."

She seemed to be waiting for him to say something else, but he couldn't think of anything else to say. "I wish you wouldn't worry about things," she said.

He opened his eyes fully. "What do you mean?"

"About the government and the world. We're safe. We have

food and medicine and everything we need now. We could have children."

This was touching and serious, but he had always been a cautious person and rarely fell for someone so quickly. He had had few girlfriends. It hadn't occurred to him to think about children with her. The fact she had done this moved him, but all he could think to say was "Don't you want to know who is running this government?"

She sat up and shook out her hair. "I don't want this taken away from me."

"What are you talking about?"

"I don't want to lose everything. That's all I'm saying. Every night when I lay there in darkness, I prayed for this day."

"We're not going to lose anything."

She perched on the edge of the bed, her inviting back slumping. "I'm so sick of being used and alone," she said.

"I'm not using you," he said, sitting up. "I'm really into you."

"I'd like to believe that."

He put his arm around her. "We're boyfriend and girlfriend, right?"

"I guess, whatever that means."

"We don't go out with anyone else. We're in a committed relationship."

Sheilah eyed him as if she was unsure. Then she smiled, and they kissed.

V

"DAMN IT!" JAMES TOSSED HIS PADDLE onto the table. He and Daniel had played an intense game of ping pong in the game room, smashing the ball back and forth. "I thought I had you."

Daniel raised his arms, exultant. "You're getting better," he said. "Let's play again this afternoon."

James liked Daniel's energy. He was an easy office mate and had worked at Google Venice. Once they started speaking, they clicked.

"This is the best job I ever had," James said. "We play ping pong or read books fifty percent of the time."

It was true. There was not enough work to keep them busy all day, so sometimes they read in their office.

"Reading is what I did when I was in isolation," Daniel said.

"That's cool. Me too."

They spoke about their time at Facebook and Google, respectively, and agreed it was a good experience, but one thing bothered them both. There were not many artists or real book lovers, at least to their standards.

"What did you read while underground?" James asked.

Daniel rambled off a list of authors, titles, and subjects that were different from the books James had read, but still smart and literary works mixed with page-turning crime novels.

Reading books was the education James had always desired. Most people went to school to train for a job. Most never had the chance to read more than six books a month for several years. Now he felt like he had a college degree in the best sense, a classical sense, perhaps. He knew something elemental to life for the first time. Reading had kept him going while underground.

"I'm stoked that they put us in the same office," James said. "This situation is mind blowing."

"Do you buy what's happened?"

"What do you mean?" He knew exactly what Daniel meant. His surprise was that Daniel had said it.

"That there was this random pandemic that spread so quickly around the world, and a couple years later everything's cleaned up."

The cleanup crews had made great strides in fixing the sewage system and ensuring access to water. Solar grids were in place, so power was working for almost everyone all the time. Food was available.

"I don't know. I haven't seen anything to make me think otherwise."

"Don't get me wrong, it is great, but why can't anyone have a website and blog freely? I mean, how can we know anything?"

James had wondered the same thing.

"Who the hell put this together?" Daniel said.

James thought of Jens saying they had planned for a pandemic. He almost told Daniel but decided to wait for another time. He didn't know if it meant that Jens knew this pandemic was coming or that a pandemic was always a possibility, and the government wanted to be prepared.

"I don't trust them. Where the hell is everyone? Honestly, I'm afraid to ask," James said in a loud voice.

Daniel smiled, showing he agreed.

"We should hang out sometime."

"Absolutely."

"I have no friends except my girlfriend."

"You have a girlfriend. You're lucky."

"It was random."

"Nothing is random here."

Later James met Jens in the break room, and they took the stairs to the roof with their coffees. West LA appeared to be an island surrounded by neighborhoods where there were few signs of life except for the shuttles coming and going.

"There's so much gone."

"There are pockets everywhere that survived," Jens said.

They both stared south, where James could see convoys of military vehicles traveling both ways.

"I wanted to let you know that I've made inquiries," Jens said. "I'm sorry, but I haven't found any information on Cleo yet."

James glanced toward the ocean.

"Don't lose faith."

"You believe there is a chance?"

Jens gestured east. "There's a reasonable chance. We did our best to keep it together, but there's a lot of people out there."

James started to ask a question but stopped.

"She could be anywhere," Jens said. "People are reappearing every day."

That Saturday, James hiked out as far as he could go and way past signs that warned not to continue any farther. These were the "No lands," the barren strips that strangely still blew smoke from something smoldering in the earth.

He scanned the bombed-out landscape, suspecting that someone was following or watching him. It was probably his paranoia again.

A reflection darted out at him in the distance, so he roamed through broken-down cars and downed telephone poles toward it. After ten minutes, he began to think that perhaps it was nothing. Then someone driving a motorcycle pulled out from behind a structure and burst past him, popping a wheelie. The motorcycle rider was wearing camouflage pants and a dark jacket and helmet. And they could ride, zigzagging and skidding about as fast as possible through the obstacle course until they hit the straightaway and disappeared.

He watched the dark figure grow smaller and smaller. A gust of wind whipped his hair back. The world was silent again.

When he arrived home, it was still quiet—no sounds from TVs, radios, or cars outside. But the front door was ajar. He went around the back and tiptoed through the back door and into the kitchen, eyeing his knives. The front door creaked open.

He grabbed a medium-sized knife and tripped into the front room, then blew through the front door hanging open, but he didn't see or hear anyone. He crouched on the ground, not from fatigue but from stress, and stabbed the dirt and weeds.

That evening, before meeting Sheilah at her place, he wandered through the Superstore. This late everything was picked over. A sign read "No Hoarding" and warned that people were allowed to only buy "Three Meals Per Day Maximum."

Outside, he found a place to sit on the benches under the awnings, where he was delivered a plate of carrots and potatoes by a dark-haired girl.

"I didn't order this."

The girl ignored him.

He glanced at the plate and underneath found a piece of paper with a map drawn on it. It included one word, "Daniel," and directions.

He followed the directions, which led him to a cul-de-sac. He must have been at least fifteen miles from his place, and he was unsure what neighborhood he was in exactly. There were several larger homes where whoever made the map would have a view of anyone coming or going in any direction. There was also the opportunity for residents or visitors to disappear into a maze of dark alleyways and streets.

As he trekked quietly in, he noticed plastic edges around the houses; these homes had been tented recently.

He crouched down near a house for fifteen minutes, wondering if this meeting was going to happen, until a light flashed through a window of a home. It was a tiny pointer light, but he followed it to a boarded-up house.

The front door hadn't been fully shut. Inside, it was half lit.

A well-built man in his late twenties or early thirties greeted him—long hair, a scraggly beard, and a half-worried lopsided smile. "James."

"Who are you?"

"Duane. I'm a friend of Daniel's," the man said. "Daniel from your work?"

James didn't respond.

"You know Daniel?" Duane asked.

"Yeah. What is this all about?"

"Daniel is gone. They've taken him."

"Who has?"

"The secret police, whoever's in charge of security."

"What?"

"He was documenting the government's abuses."

James moved so Duane's light wasn't shining directly on him.

"You worked at Facebook?" Duane asked.

"Daniel tell you that?"

"No, I hacked into the government computers and looked at your profile. They have a lot of information on you. A lot more than normal. Work history. Family members. Education. Things you've purchased or subscribed to."

"Why would they do that? I'm a nobody."

Duane shrugged. "It's unusual."

He watched Duane, who looked as if he could handle himself in a bar fight.

"Daniel thought you could be trusted."

James grimaced. "Trusted how? I don't understand what's going on."

"Do you understand game theory?"

"The basics."

"Well, this is just game theory. It's a zero-sum game. This government believes there are winners and losers. Only they can win. Everyone else loses their freedom."

They examined one another, probably wondering the same thing: can I trust him?

"How do you know all this?" James asked.

"I'm a hacker. I know everything."

"How many others like you?"

"Lots."

James eyed him. This guy might be able to get things done, or he could bring disaster. "I lost my sister when the battle for LA was heating up. Can you help with that?"

"Okay. Let's start there and build some trust."

VI

IT HAD BEEN A WEEK, and there was no sign or word from Daniel. James swiveled in his office chair, eyeing Daniel's shutdown computer and empty chair.

He jumped up and strode to the human resources department, where a straightforward blond woman named Joan noticed him.

"Can I help you?" she asked. "James, correct?"

"Yes, I work here as an analyst."

Joan studied him with an expression that he thought meant she was concerned about something.

"Maybe you can help me," he said. "I share an office with another analyst named Daniel. He hasn't come in all week. I was wondering if he's all right."

Joan grew stone-faced. "He's no longer working here."

"Do you know where he went?"

"I'm afraid I can't share any personal information about him," she said, and shuffled away.

James returned past a conference room, where Jens was talking with a group of what appeared to be high-powered men. One of the men was a senior-ranking military officer who seemed to be angry about something and was speaking in an abusive tone.

He visited Sheilah every night for two weeks. Behind what he displayed to Sheilah, his internal and external lives were out of sync. He had been two people for so long that he barely noticed anymore. He sensed she was hiding something too, but maybe every relationship was like that. This unsettled him, because despite his split, she had touched his hidden self. She made him smile and laugh, and their sex was the best he had ever experienced. She had also saved him from the crushing isolation of this new world. But the person who read books and had always been highly sensitive remained uncertain and wary. He knew one thing was true. He was addicted to her, and maybe that was love. Maybe that was enough.

That evening he and Sheilah sat close, having a candlelit meal: potatoes, tomatoes, and bread.

"You seem far away," she said.

His mind was distant; he was thinking about Daniel and Duane. He didn't want to tell her. He wasn't sure why. "I have a lot on my mind," he said.

"Like what?"

"Like my sister."

"That's all you care about, isn't it?"

"No, it isn't," he said loudly. Why would she say that? "She's my sister. It has nothing to do with us."

She seemed to retreat into her own thoughts. "My brother hated me. I'm sure he could care less," she finally said. She sat stiff, half turned away. He leaned in closer to her to show he cared. Her face was ashen, and for a moment it appeared she wasn't breathing. When he held her hand, she did not respond.

"I'm sorry," he said. "I had no idea. I'm sorry I raised my voice."

"It's all right. I'm glad you care about your sister."

"I do. And I care about you."

"You always seem like you want to be alone. You're such a loner."

It was true. He was a loner. "Why do you say that?"

"You just want to read your books, even if you've read them before. I never know what you're thinking."

Her expression remained stern, rigid, which he wasn't sure how to handle. She seemed, for lack of a better word, pissed, not only at him, but perhaps at everything.

"Why don't we watch a movie together on my computer?" he said.

"I'm sick of watching movies, the same movies all the time." She pulled her hand away from his.

"What's wrong? Did I say something wrong?"

"Why don't we talk?"

His stomach ached. His face felt hot. "Okay. Let's talk."

"What are you hiding?"

"I'm not hiding anything."

"You're hiding something. I can tell."

"That's completely not true."

Sheilah blew out the candle, then took off running, leaving the back door swinging.

"Sheilah!" He ran outside and stopped, kicking at the ground and considering going after her, but he watched her sprint down the street instead.

On the way to work the next morning, James slouched in his seat, staring out the window. An older man with a cane plopped down next to him.

"Good morning."

James didn't intend to talk but managed a "Morning."

"Jim," the man said sprightly.

"James," he mumbled.

"It's a vacant world, isn't it, James?"

"Yeah, it is."

"You know what I miss the most? It's the Dodgers. My father read a comic book when he was nine about the Dodgers signing Jackie Robinson, and that's when he became a Dodger fan."

James almost smiled. "That's pretty cool."

"He's lucky he lived in his generation and not this one."

"Yeah, there's not much left that makes life worth living. Not even dogs."

"It's up to us to make it worth living."

"Yeah" was all James could bring himself to say.

The man didn't speak again.

At work, three hundred department workers sat quietly in a huge conference room. When Jens appeared at the podium, spontaneous heartfelt applause broke out.

"The United States has been through a pandemic and civil fighting, and we have survived and are building a new world," Jens said.

As Jens continued, emotion rose in James's chest. His right hand slapped at his thigh in a compulsive move as his body gently rocked back and forth. Some in the audience began to cry.

Jens went on. "We can never go back. The past is past, and we are stronger for it."

James spotted Sheilah in the crowd. Her eyes were intense, and she seemed to be tapping her hand, like he was tapping.

In the front row a mousy girl began screaming, "Together, together, together," shaking her fist. "Together. Together."

Soon the entire group in front was shouting until Jens raised and lowered his hands to cue them to stop. "Can we make our world and life better?" he asked.

Shouts of "Yes!" rippled through the audience.

"Yes, we can, with your help. We need to stay together," Jens said.

Pressure built up in James's chest. All those lonely nights in darkness, the days spent reading books and listening, afraid to go out, checking the down internet and radio hoping for news, finding nothing. It had yanked him inside out, and now tears welled up.

Yes, they must keep this together. They could never go back. The past was past, he thought.

When the meeting ended, he stalked Sheilah so he could run into her, but the mousy girl embraced her, and they left chatting together. He didn't want to intrude.

He thought Jens would be in a good mood after his rousing speech, but his boss appeared long faced and glum, retreating to his office, and later Jens was distracted at their weekly one-on-one meeting. James had good news on the distribution front, showing that production exceeded demand, but Jens didn't seem interested at all.

When James reached Sheilah's condo that afternoon, he knocked on her door, but she didn't answer. "Sheilah?"

He knocked again, but she wasn't home.

In some ways this was worse than being in isolation. The wrenching ache in his gut made eating impossible; he couldn't concentrate on anything. Had he ever been in love before? He had never suffered like this. In fact, once he had broken up with a girl and had to avoid her because of her depressing sadness. Now he regretted that.

Throughout the night, his mind raced with thoughts of when he would see her again. He tried to read, but he couldn't even get through one page. He took a shower. Afterward he lay in bed on top of the blankets, holding his stomach.

James was so caught up in his suffering that he did not realize Sheilah had entered his house in the middle of the night until she appeared in his bedroom. He jumped up and apologized several times. She said it was okay, then started to undress. In bed she reached around and stroked him, and he lay back, twisting his neck to kiss her.

"I have trust issues," she said.

"I love you," he said.

"I love you."

They kissed once more.

"Don't ever leave me again," he said.

"Okay."

James received another anonymous message requesting a meeting, probably from Duane, so the next week he stepped down a dark, quiet street, where his scraping footsteps were the only sound. At a small house a wooden cross hung sideways. He opened the gate and entered.

Inside, Duane sat with a MacBook on his lap. The empty room suggested that no one lived there.

"Thanks for coming," Duane said. He rose and reached out to shake James's hand, then seemed to realize what he was doing and dropped his arm back to his side.

"I don't think anyone followed me," James said.

"You passed several checkpoints. No one appeared to be."

Duane studied him with a curious, anxious frown, then picked up a manila folder and pulled out an 8 x 10 photograph.

Stamped on the photograph was a date. A woman with sandy hair was peering across a busy farmer's market. It was Cleo, her light-brown hair longer than usual. Perhaps she had lost weight too, but it was her intelligent eyes that he recognized most: she was deciding what to do next.

"Have you verified this?" he asked.

"Yes, as best we could."

"Can you take me to her?"

"Probably."

Duane worried him. His secretiveness suggested there might be repercussions if he was caught.

"Will I be safe if I go there?"

"If you get there, yes."

"What's going to stop me?"

"The government. You're not allowed to travel between sectors freely. Areas are partitioned now."

"So, the government isn't in control?"

"They're in control, but they don't go in unless they're heavily armed. They're not loved by large swaths of people."

"How do I get in?"

"You can't just travel around. You have to sneak in."

"I feel like I'm being set up."

"By who?"

James shrugged.

"I have to tell you that your friend Sheilah may not be who she says she is. We believe she has been recruited and paid to watch you. And I'm sure your place is bugged."

James gave Duane a sharp look, but his mind swirled. This couldn't be right. She wouldn't do that. "Why? Why would they do that?" was all he could stammer. "What's your evidence?"

"She lives in a luxury condo and has a senior position that has no staff or responsibility," Duane said.

"That's it?"

"Our network has seen authorities visit her condo multiple times."

"What do you mean?"

"I'm sorry. I don't want to bring you this news about her, but she's a plant."

James sat down. He'd thought she had friends in high places because she was beautiful.

"She must be a good actress," Duane said.

James ran his hand through his hair. "Has she had other boyfriends?"

Duane threw up his hands as if to say he didn't know.

"Are you fucking sure about this?" He barely listened to what Duane said next.

"A lot of people were in desperate situations, and they might have saved her life, then enlisted her services. This society was ripe for that, but we're sure she's an informant. I'm sorry," Duane said. "I can let you see the intelligence."

"I'll talk to her," James blurted.

"If you do, we can't help you find your sister."

He glared at Duane. "Why?"

"We can't compromise our people."

"I don't think Sheilah is a threat to you."

"You just met her."

He exhaled and paced the room. Panic lay just below the surface. "Does my sister know that I'm alive?"

"I don't know."

"I don't see how I can come back to work if I find her."

"You won't be coming back."

He watched as Duane typed something. "If you're bullshitting me about my sister, this is not going to go well."

"Why would I do that? What would be the point?"

"Are there more spies around?"

"Everywhere."

James hadn't known Sheilah long and knew nothing of her history. But he didn't know Duane either and had no idea if his people were better than the society they had now. Still, he had to find Cleo, and they both knew it. He wanted reassurances from Duane. He was not a traitor, but he was open to fighting for more freedom.

"What can I do to meet with my sister?" he said. "I need more."

Duane stared at the floor and made small movements with his hands. "Let's be clear, this is an oppressive regime. They started the wars within and outside the former United States of America. They don't allow dissent, and it's a state-run web with a firewall to prevent social media or unapproved content. The core issue, though, is that people disappear here."

When James didn't say anything, Duane sighed.

"Let me show some documents concerning Sheilah," Duane said. "I'm sorry, I truly am."

James scanned the screenshots on Duane's iPad. There it was, clearly saying that Sheilah had been "embedded" into his life.

There didn't seem to be anything underneath the world; it was a façade, with no meaning or texture. Maybe that's why James was always so anxious and apprehensive. He was on his own.

VII

JAMES WOKE BEFORE THE SUN was up and sat alone on the shuttle on his way to work. Maybe Sheilah was right, and he should settle down with her and not rock the boat, but he needed to find his sister; he couldn't escape that. Nor did he trust anyone. It was a zero-sum situation. If he lost Sheilah he found Cleo, and if he kept Sheilah he lost Cleo. Jens was wrong. There were losers in this society.

His other thought was to confront Sheilah with what he had learned from Duane. He remembered the times they'd made love and told each other, "I love you." If this was an act, what a messed-up person Sheilah was. But he couldn't work up hate or even dislike for her. It was the circumstances. She would never act that way in a normal world, he was certain of it.

As much as he tried to find another way, he realized he had accepted what Duane said. The documents had convinced him. There was no getting around that. He would break up with Sheilah and go back to her with the whole truth after he had reconnected with Cleo.

After work Sheilah met him at the Superstore. She wore a slim-fitting red skirt accentuating her toned body. Heads turned at her flowing hair and most of all at her energy. She kissed him on the lips.

"How was your day?" she asked.

The last of the sunset streamed across the tables.

"Same old stuff. A lot of number crunching."

A waitress brought them their food and water, and Sheilah sank her teeth into the avocado veggie sandwich that was featured that day. "What's wrong?" she asked.

His mouth was dry. He gulped down a glass of water. "I want to take a break in our relationship."

She gaped at him but seemed levelheaded. "Why? I don't understand. It feels perfect." She reached over and stroked his thigh.

"I'm just confused. And my sister. I have to focus on her." He winced at his words.

A fluttery anger trembled in her voice. "I thought you cared for me," she said. "You said you loved me, and all this time you've been wanting to break up with me? Are you a two-faced guy who pretended to like me for sex?"

"No, no, that's not true. Relationships are difficult under any circumstances. I'm not ready."

Sheilah peered intently into his eyes. "It's been hellish, but everything is okay now. I've changed as a person. I'm better."

He didn't know what to say; he tried to display a sincere and caring expression, as if that might help the situation.

"I don't want to talk about this here," she said.

They got on the first shuttle that stopped, which happened to be heading toward his place. They didn't look at each other or sit close enough to touch.

When they entered his kitchen, Sheilah gripped his shirt. "I don't understand. You said you loved me. Don't do this to me."

He didn't know what to say, so he said the same thing he'd said to the last person he'd broken up with. "I'm sorry. We don't connect as soulmates."

"Soulmates? Soulmates?" She repeated it louder and louder and swatted him with flailing arms that stung his face and head. He shielded himself and backed up against the kitchen counter. Tears rolled down her cheeks, but she swiped them away.

"You're a liar," she said, and bolted out the door.

In the middle of the night, he lay clammy on top of the blankets. Nothing soothed the awful sense of betraying Sheilah and himself.

He once lived near the freeway in Los Angeles and that roar of constant traffic was always there, and it had felt like it was not only outside, but inside him. That how Sheilah's absence felt to him.

Sheilah did not show up at work the next day, though she rarely was in his office building. After work, he loitered in the park outside her place and peered up at her condo window. What the hell had he been thinking? Loss and a deep sorrow welled up in him. Sharp slivers of pain shot through his heart.

At the Superstore, he spotted Sheilah's hair and legs. His gut ached at the vision of her gliding down one of the aisles. He followed her, oblivious to others in the store, and veered off down an adjacent aisle so he could bump into her as if it were an accident. He almost collided with her, but it was not Sheilah.

"Excuse me." He rushed away.

James met Duane at a pro-government rally taking place at a beat-up football stadium. A robust security presence patrolled inside and outside despite the small attendance. The speaker was dull and droned on: "We didn't choose conflict. We don't want conflict, but we need to be prepared."

The attendees seemed quiet, polite; most people were withdrawn, maybe not quite present in this world.

He sat a row above Duane in the bleachers. They did not acknowledge each other.

"Did you break up with her?" Duane asked after a ten-minute wait.

James swallowed hard before he spoke. "Yeah, and I'm not sure it was the right thing to do."

Duane tilted his head toward him, then stopped. "We talked about this," he said in an angry whisper.

James's face fell. "You're certain Cleo can be found?"

"One hundred percent." Duane got up to leave.

"I'm in," James said. "I can get time off in two weeks or anytime after, like you requested."

"There's one more thing," Duane said.

"Yeah?"

"Can you ride a motorcycle?"

VIII

JAMES CAREFULLY FILLED HIS BACKPACK with personal items: photos, papers, letters, books, and a change of clothes. Then he rode a shuttle to the outskirts of town and walked through an abandoned neighborhood.

Once he reached a dirt path, he used his flashlight to see what was ahead.

He heard what he thought was an animal, perhaps a coyote, but saw nothing, so he forged on.

After a couple of miles, he stepped onto crunchy rocks, almost like seashells. He pointed the flashlight around him: crushed human bones everywhere.

James stood still, no longer cold, but hot in his face; he stretched to his full height, taking in the stars in the sky. Another unspeakable event. He felt his spirit leave his body. He thought he would crack from the pressure, but then, like the last time he'd thought he might break, he didn't, and kept moving.

A helicopter buzzed in the distance, moving fast and beaming down a searchlight. He took a few strides, then slid flat onto the ground and yanked a dirt-colored blanket out of his backpack. The cold, hard ground bit into his back and shoulders. The helicopter light blinded him for a moment, then lingered, scanning to his right and left. He barely breathed until after it passed.

Even then James waited, watching the puffs of air from his exhalations, and sure enough, the helicopter returned and focused again where he lay. The light flashed across him several times before the chopper flew north.

With the helicopter no longer in sight, he jogged on a trail that weaved past the boneyard, only stopping when he saw the rapid pulsing of a light.

The stillness worried him, but then out of the darkness, he heard Duane.

"James."

"Duane?"

Duane tossed him a jacket. It was heavy and obviously real leather. In an inconspicuous shed behind him were tools and three motorcycles. James hadn't been on a bike in years.

"Have a nice hike?"

"What happened back there?"

"We think it's a mass grave where thousands of people were dumped and bulldozed over," Duane said.

A young woman wearing a black leather motorcycle outfit appeared out of the shadows and faced James. Resentment bristled in her face. "Hundreds of thousands," she said.

"You ready to ride?" Duane asked him.

"I'm ready."

"D'Arcy is our guide."

D'Arcy tossed James a helmet that he caught with his chest.

"If you see a helicopter again, get off the bike and run for it," Duane said.

"Don't follow us," D'Arcy added.

James started up the bike and lightly revved the engine.

"We're going the long way. It's too dangerous to take the direct route."

"Are the roads okay?"

D'Arcy smiled.

His bike's headlight lit up a narrow strip in front of him as they cut off across a lonely stretch where the wind whipped their bikes along, and James had to slow down not to crash. Duane turned around and rode alongside him, giving him the thumbs-up to go faster. James gave him a thumbs-down.

He had to stop several times to walk the bike around tires, broken-down cars, baskets, tumbleweed, chairs, and other debris in the pockmarked road. And the wind kept pressing on him so that he reduced his speed to a crawl as he drove through dark and desolate neighborhoods.

When they reached what James thought was the 110 Freeway near downtown, they followed D'Arcy into a garage, where they shut down their bikes and stretched.

"I want to be sure we aren't being tracked," D'Arcy said.

"Where are we?" James asked, but neither answered.

Three military helicopters appeared suddenly. They hovered near the garage for fifteen seconds, then turned around and headed back west.

"They must not have seen us," Duane said.

James watched D'Arcy stroll to the front of the garage. She seemed to be troubled by the helicopters. "Or didn't care," she said in a low voice.

They waited in silence for an hour before they headed out again. This time they drove slowly down eerie, abandoned side streets where graffiti tagged almost every building. Eventually a few lights in homes appeared, as well as bonfires with quiet figures sitting around them. Then came a straightaway that led into a bustling street with open bars and restaurants full of people, like a college town. Duane popped a wheelie that made several people turn to watch him.

There appeared to be no fear or security presence here. This was how people lived when they were on their own. Life did not look easy here, as buildings and streets were torn up and run down, but laughter burst out from the street several times. Several dogs were being walked by their owners.

Outside the popular area, D'Arcy led them to a dark and smoky bar, an indie hangout. As they entered, a Bowie song, "Five Years," was beginning, and James flashed back to Sheilah's place when they had first met. He wondered how she was coping. What was she doing, feeling, and thinking right now?

The crowded atmosphere was mellow except for a pool game in the middle of the room. A chalkboard with a long list of challengers leaned against the wall. Cleo could walk in here—it was the kind of place she would like.

"I want to go see my sister," he said.

"Tomorrow."

"Why don't we go now?"

"Trust me," Duane said.

James was surprised when D'Arcy placed her hand on his back before wandering away to talk with a dark-haired woman.

"Wine or beer?" Duane asked.

"Whatever you're having," James said, scanning the room for Cleo.

With a beer in hand, he followed Duane to an expansive back patio. Duane found a couple of chairs, where they sat facing the inside bar.

Duane sipped his beer and made a pleasant face. "Homemade," he said.

"Does my sister know I'm here?"

"Soon."

A girl with hair the same shade as Cleo's passed by him and joined a group of women. James lowered his head and tried not to cry, but he couldn't help it. He had enough self-control to stop and wiped his eyes on his sleeve. Duane maintained a blank expression.

D'Arcy appeared and retrieved her drink from Duane. She clinked her beer glass with James's. Her suddenly liking him was probably due to his trying to reconnect with his sister. She seemed to care about that.

"We're going to find her," she said. "I'm going to make sure of it." She pulled up a chair and flipped it backward, placing her arms on the backrest and facing James and Duane. "I lost my brother during the government fighting. He protected us until we got our act together."

James didn't sleep well, too excited about the prospect of seeing Cleo, and still suffering over a lingering sickness that pervaded his body. Its source was Sheilah. He couldn't shake this deep-seated angst embedded in his psyche.

The next morning, before they rode off through the foggy streets, Duane explained that for security reasons they would not be taking a straightforward route to Cleo's place. It was a process of elimination, he said.

"What does that mean?" James asked.

"Trust me," Duane said.

Outside the main part of town, the roads were in even poorer condition. Junk lined the gutters. Homeless people camped out on several blocks, and dogs and cats roamed about. He wondered how the dogs and cats had survived. Had they not carried the virus? Sheilah, like he, had believed they did, although he never personally had seen one dead in the street. Perhaps they were killed as a precaution. His empty stomach growled. Everything felt sterile.

As they passed a rickety shuttle, James noticed the faded directions to the 101.

Duane led them to two different apartments as well as a small house that Cleo supposedly had lived in at one time. Two of the residents had not heard of Cleo, but the friendly woman who occupied the house said Cleo had lived there six months earlier.

"What the fuck, Duane." James had given up everything to do this, and Duane didn't even know where she lived. Duane left him with no choice but to distrust him.

"We'll find her," Duane said.

Next, they pulled up to a sprawling house with a manicured lawn. The large, diverse houses in the neighborhood appeared to be in excellent condition.

James jumped off the bike and knocked hard on the door, but no one answered. "Cleo. Cleo." He peeked through the window and noticed a blond cat inside. "She loved cats," James said as D'Arcy appeared next to him.

On the side of the house was a locked door to the garage, and Duane inserted a straight, stiff tool into the bottom lock and played with it until the door unlocked. The deadbolt had not been secured.

The garage was empty, so Duane picked the house door lock.

"I don't think we should be doing this. There might be cameras," D'Arcy said.

Duane turned to D'Arcy and smiled. "There are no security cameras anymore."

"I don't see any," James said.

"That doesn't mean they're not there," D'Arcy said.

Duane nodded. "We'll do a quick search and get out."

James was on Duane's side, though he believed D'Arcy was right; it wasn't a good idea to break in, but committing a minor crime to find out if Cleo lived there overrode everything else.

Inside they found ornate furniture and a print of a lion on a grassy plain hanging above the fireplace. Nothing in the home suggested Cleo lived there. It wasn't until James was in the bedroom that he found on a dresser a framed snapshot of himself, Cleo, and their mother.

He took it to the front room, where D'Arcy and Duane were. "This is my mother and sister."

D'Arcy studied it and touched his shoulder. He looked into her translucent eyes and at the colorless eyebrows he had not noticed before. She maintained a punk attitude, but he trusted her. She seemed honest, unlike Duane—you never knew what he was hiding.

Duane moved past them and peered out the window at the backyard.

James hurried back to the bedroom and sifted through the closet. He didn't recognize anything as Cleo's, but they were her size.

D'Arcy found fruit and vegetables in the refrigerator. There was nothing that said anything about who lived here.

"They're hiding something," Duane said after searching a desk.

James didn't care. He knew Cleo was alive. He had never given up hope, and his heart raced at the thought of seeing her soon.

"Let's get out of here," D'Arcy said.

After a couple of hours, Duane and D'Arcy took a break, and James waited alone on the patch of grass alongside the home. Eventually he strolled the neighborhood, hoping to find a neighbor who might have seen or spoken to Cleo.

An angry man with a scruffy graying beard marched out of a house across the street straight up to him. "Why are you hanging out here?"

The man seemed like he meant business. James eyed him without fear, eager to find out if he knew Cleo. "I believe my sister Cleo lives here. I'm waiting for her to come home."

The neighbor turned to the house, as if he was thinking.

"Do you know her?" James asked.

"I've seen her, and I see the resemblance."

He shrugged. "She's my sister."

The man glanced back at Cleo's house. "All right. I just wanted to know what was going on." He stalked back across the street to his home.

James didn't see anyone else in the quiet neighborhood.

In the early evening D'Arcy returned in a beat-up SUV. Duane followed, riding his bike, and James joined them at the curb where D'Arcy had parked.

"Why don't you come out and eat?" Duane asked. "We'll have you back in a couple hours."

"I'll wait," James said. Goose bumps popped up over his body, and he buttoned his leather jacket. Fog crept in.

"I have some food," D'Arcy said when Duane rode off.

In the SUV he sat on the passenger side next to D'Arcy and ate an apple and a bag of nuts. He learned that D'Arcy had graduated from UCLA and was well read. She passionately hated the previous government and had been an early protester and resister. She had had to flee the Westside when the pandemic and fighting hit their peaks, just before you had to isolate or die.

He sensed a closeness building between them, but part of his energy was absorbed by Sheilah's constant presence—that amorphous lump in his belly. The way she had responded when he broke up with her convinced him that she hadn't been acting and that she truly did love him.

"Do you like living here?" he asked.

"It sucks less than anyplace else."

A Toyota Prius pulled into the driveway.

"She's here."

It almost felt like an out-of-body experience as he watched Cleo step out of the Prius and turn toward him. She looked amazing. A tall, dark man appeared outside the driver's side, and Cleo started to smile, then stopped.

In a scream three SUVs and a van slammed up to the sidewalk. James's immediate thought was for Cleo, and he said her name, and then someone cracked him into the cement sidewalk. He heard gunshots and felt warm blood at the back of his head and on his hair.

He could see D'Arcy on the ground, muffled in a choke hold. The men gripped his limbs, powerful and tight. A mask was pulled over his head, and he was handcuffed. He fought passing out. Faraway voices mumbled as he was slid into the van. The claustrophobia of the mask panicked him. He hyperventilated until darkness twirled him deeper and deeper, and it all went black.

When he regained consciousness, the mask was off, and his nose and cheek brushed up against the coarse black carpet. He realized he was still in the van and traveling at a high rate of speed. A woman's voice was speaking. It was D'Arcy, but he couldn't make out what she was saying. He opened one eye and could see a huge black army boot, ideal for stomping him in the face. He thought it was only minutes later, but he wasn't sure.

For what seemed like a long time, he lay half awake, his upper back and his head throbbing. Did he have a concussion? He tried to think about Cleo, but everything was fuzzy and dreamlike.

When he was able to sit up, he examined the curly light-brown hair streaming down in a rich tapestry over his sister's face next to him. He gazed through the hair at her closed-mouth smile. He smiled too, though he winced when his back spasmed.

Her eyes were glassy. He could see that she had been crying. She seemed listless, and everything hung on her as if gravity was yanking her down.

"Hey."

"Hey."

"What happened?" he asked.

"They finally got him."

He didn't have to ask. The man she was with was dead. He obviously had meant something to her. She shook her head in a defiant way, as if to say that she wasn't going to break and that she didn't care what happened to her. She glared at the four beefy guards sitting in a ready position. Each had a bully stick and a revolver and pepper spray on a thick black belt. Two carried assault rifles. An additional two were in the front seats of the bulky vehicle, which must have been tricked out; whatever was under the hood purred powerfully.

D'Arcy's red face told James how she felt, but she cocked her head at him and his sister, then fixated on the carpet.

The van swerved and knocked them about.

D'Arcy scrunched up her face and screamed. "Duane must have sold us out. I never saw that coming." She thrust her cuffed hands forward. "This can't be happening."

Two guards faced D'Arcy, and the other two focused on James and Cleo.

"You two should talk here. They'll separate you when we arrive," D'Arcy said.

James pushed himself with his feet back toward the partition separating them from the front. Cleo followed, and they leaned into each other. He reassured her that he was all right.

"Who was he?"

"My husband."

He had a million questions.

"He saved me," she added.

"Why wasn't I invited to the wedding?"

She smiled and touched his face with her cuffed hands. "I tried to call you that night, but my phone had stopped working."

"It was complete chaos. I looked everywhere for you."

"I was trying to get to your place and found myself in the middle of the fighting, and Alex, that's his name, protected me. We had to run for our lives, and then the pandemic ripped the world apart."

She told him she'd never stopped trying to find him, but it had been impossible to learn anything. "I received anonymous messages and images last month telling me you were alive, but I couldn't cross over," she said, starting to cry, but recovering. "I guess it was a setup to kill Alex."

James had been used to locate him. "I'm sorry."

She grasped his hands. "It's not your fault."

"What's going to happen to us? I don't understand what is happening," he said.

Cleo shook her hair as if to say she didn't know.

"What secrets do we have to give? I'm just a brother looking for his sister."

Cleo seemed like she wanted to say something, but she stopped as the van slowed and continued at a snail's pace.

He pressed his nose into Cleo's shoulder, then sighed and fell back, passing out again.

James woke groggy in a small cell: latrine, sink, and cot. His head had been bandaged. He felt weak. "Cleo? Cleo. It's James." His voice was raspy and didn't carry far.

A male voice in the cell next to him called out, "James?"

"Who are you?"

"Daniel."

"Daniel?"

"Holy shit," Daniel blurted.

"Daniel, have you seen a woman with the same color hair as mine?"

"There're no women on this block."

James sat up despite his pounding head that almost felt too heavy to hold upright. "How long have you been in here?"

"Since the day I spoke to you."

James considered that. "Where are we?"

"A military prison. There's a yard we can walk around in. That's all I know."

"What did they charge you with?"

"There's no due process here."

James remembered what D'Arcy had said. "I think Duane sold us out," he said.

He could almost hear Daniel thinking.

"Hell, no. I've known Duane since grade school."

James didn't respond, and after a long silence, he asked, "What happens in this place?"

"You either stay locked up, or you disappear from the building. That's all I know."

"How's the food?" James joked.

"It's free like Google or Facebook's cafeterias, but it sucks."

After a couple weeks, his head injury had healed enough for him to exercise two or three times a day. When he wasn't working out, he lay on the cot, too fatigued to do anything. His blue prison jumpsuit was too long and loose.

He didn't even crave reading a book.

Occupants rotated endlessly in and out of the prison. When new prisoners arrived, they were often angry about the injustice of their arrest. In this block it was all men, of all ages. The prison population seemed to be skewed toward the educated, he thought. Some had been out to expose or bring down the government, but most were used to voicing their opinion in a democracy, though some were troublemakers, and some may have been criminals.

After two months, Daniel called out to him, "You know, I think they put us next to each other on purpose. It's no accident."

James did a pushup, then pulled back into a down dog pose. "Why do you say that?"

"I'm in prison, man," Daniel said. "It's the kind of truth that comes to you when you're locked up."

James fell into a resting pose. He thought this was true at the office as well, and Jens must have been in on it. He didn't know why or how, but he knew that now. Daniel was right. Insights came to you in prison. The way Jens had looked at him, so smart and ingratiating. He had been hiding right in front of James. They'd wanted information on his sister from the moment he came up.

Daniel believed they had forgotten about him rotting in there. Then one day, Daniel never returned to his cell, and someone else moved in. The guards shrugged when James appealed to them for information. They appeared to have strict orders about conversing with prisoners, since they rarely spoke except to order the inmates around. He would see them now and then joking among themselves.

He felt hard, both inside and out. He imagined himself unbreakable, but he knew that wasn't true.

Then it was his turn. In the middle of the night, three guards forced him to the ground with his hands and legs crossed and slipped cuffs on his wrists.

"Where are you taking me?"

The guards didn't answer. Grim-faced, they escorted him out. This was a death march—anything else would have been done during working hours.

James yanked away from them. "Don't touch me," he said. He did this several times, but one guard kept roughly returning his hand to James's elbow.

After a short van ride, they escorted him down a hall. He spotted D'Arcy in one room and Cleo in the room next to it. They both approached their windows as he passed them and entered a third room.

He must have been in the white-walled room for two hours when Jens entered. The bags under Jens's eyes were significant.

"I'm sorry, James, that it has to end like this," Jens said. For the first time Jens had difficulty looking him in the eye. "I did everything I could," Jens went on, "but too many people have died because of these terrorists. It seems people want more than being left alone."

James glared. "No one is left alone here."

"I don't want to argue. The decision has been made. I'm sorry, you have one hour."

"How does it happen?"

"Lethal injection."

"Why, why do this? You have no reason to do this." James's voice rose in a burst of anger.

"Your sister was married to a terrorist."

Knowing his sister was alive should have been enough for James. He could have found another route to see her. At least he'd kept Sheilah out of it. He wanted to ask about Sheilah, but he didn't know what to say.

"We also believe you had no idea who your sister married," Jens said, filling the silence.

"I was just searching for my sister," James said again, more indignantly.

"Yes, and you found her, and we were waiting along with you."

"You know she's a good person. She wouldn't hurt anyone."

"Unfortunately, she is connected to people who accelerated the violence and may have helped start the worldwide pandemic." Jens tapped his chin.

"But you had a vaccine the entire time? How did that happen if someone else was at fault?"

He was guessing, but by Jens's small smile, he knew he was right.

Nothing fazed Jens though. He had nothing to lose. It was James who had everything to lose. He wondered if Jens didn't care, or if he had a little Pontius Pilate in him and would always take the politically expedient way out of everything.

"I want to help you, I do," Jens said, "but it's out of my hands."

"If Cleo's husband is a terrorist, why have I never seen an attack?"

"Because we have stopped them. You were underground when we were fighting for your freedom. Who do you think

195

kept the power grid going and water flowing and stopped the killing fields?"

James took a deep breath. "I'm not guilty of much."

"The guilt by association is difficult to get around. That suggests to us you're capable of anything."

"Aren't we all before we've done something?"

Jens smiled. "I've always liked you, James. I'm sorry it's come to this."

"You sent Sheilah to spy on me?"

"When did you figure it out?"

"I didn't. I thought she cared about me."

"I think she did."

Annoyance erupted in him. "I know she did."

Jens glanced at him, then checked his phone. Cell towers must still be functional, because James had seen prison personnel using mobile phones too.

"Can I have my sister by my side so we can be together?"

"Yes, that's been arranged. D'Arcy will be there as well."

"Will you give Sheilah a letter from me?"

"No."

"Why the fuck not, Jens? Come on."

"The world isn't fair, James."

"Go to hell," James said.

"Maybe," Jens said, giving his little smile as he walked out.

The dimly lit room was stuffy; any sound, no matter how small, seemed to hang in the air, looking for a way to escape. Three medical gurneys with large straps were lined up.

James felt no drama, like he couldn't possibly die, but many people, particularly the young, believed they were invincible until it happened to them.

Jens was there and armed, a holster visible when he moved. Three new guards had arrived, and Jens quietly asked the original three to leave.

The doctor, a tall, slim woman, instructed them on the procedure. "It is no different than drawing blood. You'll barely feel anything." She turned to D'Arcy. "Do you have any last words?"

"Yeah, fuck off," D'Arcy said, "and fuck you."

James wanted to smile at her and cheer her on, but the doctor didn't wait and injected her. D'Arcy did not acknowledge him. She seemed to fade away, her eyes remaining wide open. Then it was his sister's turn, and he told her he loved her several times.

"I love you, brother," Cleo said.

He watched her shut her eyes and display no emotion. His chest expanded, and he furiously tried to hurl and rock himself up and break out of the straps, but he couldn't. One of the guards came up close; he looked like Duane. It was Duane, who pinned his chest and put his hand over James's mouth.

Jens held out his hand as if to give James a chance to collect himself. "Put him under," Jens said.

They tied the rubber tube around his arm and pricked a vein. Then there was nothing, he felt nothing at all, except the oozing, oozing of going away.

IX

WAS HE DEAD? That was James's first thought as he hazily realized he was conscious. The disorienting darkness gave him a sense of bobbing up and down as if he were on a raft in the ocean, and he heard water dripping. Then he wiggled his fingers. His dull head lay heavy on a pillow. Crisp sheets covered his body.

When he opened his eyes hours later, the second idea that sparked in his mind was the fantastical notion that he would walk outside into a new city or some higher world where his sister, Sheilah, and his parents were waiting for him. This humored him, but when he swung his feet off the bed, he touched cold hardwood. This was a physical space. He peeked through the drapes at an old wooden fence. It seemed to be early morning.

There was a lamp that he switched on. An open suitcase with folded clothes lay neatly on the floor. His clothes, from his home.

He slept for two more hours before he was able to get dressed and creak open the door. It was a big house, older, but kept up beautifully. He smelled coffee and tiptoed down the hall to a large open kitchen, where a sliver of light sifted in through the shutters. He was parched. He poured himself a glass of water and gulped it down.

"You must be thirsty?"

James shifted his focus to the voice in the front room. A light flicked on, and there was Jens, sitting with a steaming mug of coffee next to him. "Pour yourself a cup." Jens raised his mug.

James poured coffee to give himself a moment to think. He felt like he was still dreaming, but it was Jens, sitting there like nothing had happened. The thought of escaping entered his mind, but Cleo and D'Arcy had to be nearby. "Where are we?" he asked.

"In Hollywood."

"Where in Hollywood?"

"West Hollywood."

"And my sister?"

"Sleeping."

"Here?"

"Yes."

"D'Arcy?"

"Same, in another room."

"Are they searching for us?"

"You're dead." Jens smiled. "We put you in body bags, and you've been cremated."

"No one checked our pulse or breath?"

"Why would they? The doctor certified your death."

Jens remained seated. He was blinking and wetting his lips, suggesting to James that he was tense and perhaps unsure of himself.

James ran his fingers across the stubble on his face. "How long have I been under?"

"Two days."

"Why? Why do this?"

"We planned and built a sustainable society. I'm proud of that, but we're at a tipping point toward totalitarianism and perhaps mutual annihilation. I didn't sign up for either, and I'm not a murderer."

"Who is in charge now?"

"Hardliners with backing from many in the military."

James heard footsteps. It was Cleo, her wild hair in tangled curls, a curious smile on her face. "Am I dreaming?"

Behind her entered D'Arcy. "What is happening? What is he fucking doing here?" D'Arcy gestured to Jens.

"What are we doing here?" James asked.

D'Arcy paced back and forth, glaring at Jens.

James rushed toward Cleo and embraced her. He opened up an arm and D'Arcy joined them too. While they were hugging and crying, Duane strolled in and sat on the edge of the sofa.

"Everyone needs to come clean right now," D'Arcy said in a hoarse voice.

No one answered, so James filled the void. "Were you and Jens in on this from the beginning?" he said angrily to Duane.

Duane raised his arms in the air. "I'd never met Jens before we were brought back."

"How did you get back here?"

"The same way you did, tied up in a goddamn van." Duane's incredulous expression seemed sincere.

Cleo looked dubiously at James, then said, "Someone betrayed us."

"The government betrayed you, which means I betrayed you," Jens said.

"Yeah, we knew that," D'Arcy said.

"Duane had no way of knowing he was dealing with traitors, trained and paid for by the government," Jens said.

"That's why I was in the dark about Cleo's whereabouts," Duane said, spreading his arms, "and why the helicopters didn't stop us."

The government had tracked them the entire trip, Jens told them. The plan was to use James to lure Cleo out at one of the addresses; they weren't sure which one it was, but it was always Cleo's partner, not Cleo, that they were after.

"You killed him," Cleo screamed. She hurled herself forward with clenched fists. James thought she might attack Jens, but she stopped and put her hands on her face.

The blood abandoned Jens's face, but he was quick to respond when Cleo recovered. "That was not supposed to happen," he said in a quavering voice. "That's why I'm on your side and worked out a plan with Duane to save and free you."

"Jens got me out of prison the same way you got out," Duane said in Jens's defense.

"You could have stopped it," Cleo told Jens.

"I did stop it. We're here now."

"Let's get real," D'Arcy said, an edge to her voice.

"I could not have stopped it. I'm sorry. It was not something I controlled, but it has pushed me over the edge. I can't go back," Jens said. "I hope we won't let the past get in the way of the future. We need each other."

James thought they were all contemplating this.

D'Arcy shook a finger at Jens. "Fuck, I don't trust Jens, but I don't trust our chances much without him," she said.

Jens stood and took two steps toward them. He pursed his lips and spoke in an even tone. "I'm on the line now too, as much as or more than you are. There's a real unease and desire for transparency. And people are healthier now, and I think they're becoming bored, to be honest. They want their old freedoms back." Jens's voice became impassioned. "This is our opportunity."

James looked around the room.

"We can't let these hardliners win," Jens pleaded. His phone vibrated wildly in his pocket. He frowned, then grabbed the phone with a quizzical expression. "They're coming for me." He tucked in his shirt as if showing he was resigned to facing them.

"Jesus. They know we're here," Duane said.

"I don't think so. They know I'm here. I'll stay and deal with them," Jens said. "D'Arcy and Duane, take the bikes from the garage and go. James and Cleo, go three streets west down the alley. Huge elm in the back. Enter through the back gate. Jim will be expecting you."

James held Cleo's hand and hurried down the hall and out the back door to the alley. Outside they heard vehicles coming but could not see them arrive at Jens's house. Hugging the fence as a helicopter hovered nearby, they edged down the alley.

A man popped his head out of a gate. "James," he said.

They slipped into the man's backyard, with its thick, leafy elm in the middle. The helicopter was overhead now, and James worried they'd been seen.

He recognized the man, but his head was shaved, and stubble covered his face. "Jim on the shuttle?"

"I'm a colleague of Jens's."

Dangling a revolver in his left hand, Jim appeared much more robust and fitter compared to the older man James had spoken to on the shuttle. "You can hide out here."

Inside, the shutters were closed, but Jim peeked out for a moment. "They might go house to house searching for anyone associated with Jens," he said, still looking out at the street. "Jens has been worried about today for some time. They've been purging the moderates or anyone interested in real democracy since we've come up."

"It was common knowledge on the Eastside that it was an authoritarian state, but why Jens?" Cleo asked.

"He's too intelligent, and they know they can't control him.

I'm surprised it took this long to arrest him," Jim said.

"Sometimes being intelligent isolates you," James said. Seeing what had happened to smart people like Jens and Daniel confirmed to him that he was on the right side.

Jim gestured to the sofa for them to sit.

"Do you two know each other?" Cleo wondered.

"Jim and I met once. I'm guessing that wasn't a random occurrence," James said.

Jim poured them two mugs of water in the kitchen, where hanging pots and pans were visible. He brought the mugs to them. "I wanted to get a sense of what kind of person you were," he said.

"And the baseball talk?"

"All true."

"And here?"

"Jens wanted me nearby in case of an emergency."

A police vehicle pulled up in front of Jim's place.

Jim whisked the mugs away and deposited them in the sink. "You need to hide in my basement. Don't stand straight, stoop. They might spot you."

James and Cleo bent over and followed Jim to a back-office room with books lining three walls.

Jim pulled back a heavy Asian rug and lifted a floor door to descending stairs. "I haven't been down there in a while, but it should be fine. Here's my keys. I'm about to be arrested. When you think it's safe, take my car and get the hell out of here. You can stay at the house Duane first met you at. There is food there. Don't go anywhere. Someone will pick you up."

The basement was cool, with a large bed in the corner and a sofa. Piles of books dominated a wall. They heard the knocks on the front door. When no one answered, the knocks became louder, and they heard Jim walking on the hardwood floors that amplified the sound of his steps.

James grasped Cleo's clammy hand as they listened to the muffled conversation above. Something or someone crashed to the ground.

Heavy boots lumbered down the hall, accompanied by shouting voices. For the next twenty minutes, they listened to the thuds and rips and voices above as the police ransacked the place.

The following evening James and Cleo drove down a dark street and parked.

At the hideout it was quiet, with a crazy number of stars in the sky. They took a moment to appreciate the sight. The door was unlocked, and inside a lamp was on. Food was piled up in the kitchen.

"What do we do now?" Cleo asked.

"We wait."

The first couple of days, they talked nonstop, but after a while they suffered through the boredom and silence of isolation. Loneliness tugged at James. He considered visiting Sheilah's place but didn't do it because it could put Cleo in danger.

He imagined they would be in hiding for a long time. His heart sank at the thought. Cleo's too. Their tolerance for solitude weakened, and after a week passed they decided to go to the Superstore. Before they could leave, a woman appeared at the door.

"Daniel sent me," she said.

The woman chauffeured them to a quiet neighborhood and pulled into an underground parking garage. James was excited to see Daniel, but the woman informed him she was told to use the name to gain his trust. There was no one she knew named Daniel.

James's and Cleo's spirits lifted when they discovered Duane, D'Arcy, and a disparate group of people making signs and flyers: "We Demand Transparency," "Who Is in Charge?" and "Where Can I Vote?" The "Disappeared" flyer had photos of people who had disappeared. On it was a picture of Daniel.

This "Transparency and Freedom Celebration" had been conceived in the past year. Twenty-five volunteers would distribute the leaflets and paste them up all over the city before the start. It would be an all-day occasion filled with music, entertainment, and speeches, set up under the pretense of a government happening. Topics included free and fair elections, transparency in the government, and missing citizens.

Strength and violence would not win this battle against an elite military force. This was their only option.

"We're going to take a stand," D'Arcy said.

Cleo began to cry. "Is this for real?"

"Yeah." D'Arcy smiled, then hugged Cleo. "We're either going to be in prison, or this government is going to change. Are you in?" she asked.

"We are," Cleo said. "Anything is better than waiting to be arrested."

James picked up a leaflet. On one side he read the word "Today" and on the other was the address of the stadium where it would take place. "When is it?"

"Top secret, but soon," Duane said.

D'Arcy informed them at least five hundred hardcore protesters would be there. "Maybe thousands attending," she said, clenching both fists.

James could only look around in wonder at their courage and willingness to do something.

"More people have been arrested and detained the past week than any other period since we've been up," Duane said. "Jens was right. We're at a tipping point."

"Has anyone heard from Jens?"

The muted response suggested that Jens was in prison or worse.

While Cleo and D'Arcy roamed about the room, Duane led James to the opposite corner.

"I have a fake ID for you," he said. "I want you to go into town and report back what you see."

"You think it's safe?" James asked.

"Yeah, they have no idea you're alive, and with an ID you're fine."

Downtown, James was struck by the posters glorifying society and the government. He sensed the chill in the air and the military's heavy hand. Armed soldiers and police prowled about, keeping their eyes on anyone coming and going. He knew he had to get out of there.

James headed to the Superstore to show he was downtown for a reason and purchased a potato and avocado, which he put into a bag he had brought with him. On his way back to the shuttle stop, he couldn't avoid the two plainclothes policemen who demanded to see his ID. He handed over the ID to the taller policeman, who inspected it, then tried connecting through a device to verify it.

"What are you doing out here?" the shorter policeman asked.

"I got hungry," James said, smiling and holding up his bag of food.

The tall policeman could not connect to the satellite wireless. "Goddamn it," he said.

"Where do you work?" the short policeman asked.

"Analytics. It's part of the planning department."

He and James eyed each other, and James got the sense the man knew he was lying.

"Is something going on?" James asked.

"No, you're free to go," the short policeman said, nodding for him to take off.

He walked away as casually as he could, feeling the policemen's eyes on his back.

When he reached the shuttle terminal, he dared to glance back, and there they were; they had followed him. The tall policeman still appeared to be trying to connect his device.

James had taken a seat at the sparsely filled station, when he spotted a tall woman approaching. Before he could see her face, he knew it was Sheilah. She hadn't noticed him; he was certain of that.

She had lost weight and her tan. Her hair hung limp and lifeless. She seemed deep in thought, and she never turned toward him.

He watched her as the shuttle pulled up and she boarded. He was going to board too, but the policemen hopped on behind her.

The shuttle was not crowded, but she did not sit down; she grabbed a strap. Then she gazed out directly at him, her expression completely blank, as if she didn't know him. He parted his lips, wanting to say something.

Her eyes remained fixed on him until she was gone.

Back at the townhouse, James gave Duane and D'Arcy his impressions of downtown, although he left out seeing Sheilah.

D'Arcy became angry, and she and Duane went back and forth.

"No one needs to be going out. Nothing has changed," D'Arcy shouted.

"He doesn't compromise us any further."

"What about Jens?"

"Jens is no longer relevant to what we're doing here."

"Since when?"

"Since he disappeared."

"We can't take any risks. If James gets caught, we're all at risk."

"Safer for him to go out than one of us."

"Reckless, Duane," D'Arcy said, storming out.

"Did anything happen out there, James?" Duane asked.

James had been standing off to the side, understanding that D'Arcy was right. "I told you," he said. "It seemed like a police state, so I got out of there."

"You didn't see anyone you knew or recognized?"

"No." He wasn't going to bring Sheilah into this. He had caused her enough grief.

Stiff with guilt about not being transparent about Sheilah, he wandered into a room with multiple computers, where he found an upset D'Arcy alone.

"I'm sorry, I won't go out again," he said.

She gripped his hand and didn't let go. He felt her breath near his face.

"I can't," he said. Seeing Sheilah had confused him, and his regret at losing her made it impossible for him to consider D'Arcy at that moment.

She let go of his hand just before Cleo entered.

"You all right?" Cleo asked.

"Yeah," he said.

Duane rambled in with an open laptop in his left hand.

"You're on a wanted list," he said. "They know you're alive."

"How did that happen?" D'Arcy's tone was angry again.

"You tell me," Duane said to James.

"It probably happened when they took Jens," James said.

Duane looked at his laptop, then slammed it shut. "It happened today."

"How do you know?"

"We hacked in."

D'Arcy stalked off, then came back. "We can't have you anywhere near us right now. You're too hot."

"Do you think they're aware of Cleo?" James asked.

"If they're aware of one of you, they're aware of both," Duane said.

Cleo shrugged. "We're going to the event. If we get arrested, so be it."

"We'll all be on the line after that, so you might as well be there too," Duane said. "But we need to get you out of here before then. A car's waiting."

James glanced at D'Arcy, but she turned away.

Duane's angry face jutted out at him. "Now."

X

THREE WEEKS LATER, as James and Cleo rode the shuttle downtown, he followed a flyer tumbling down from a four-story building. The wind caught it, and it floated sideways to the sidewalk below. A short woman picked it up.

As they got closer, they saw flyers everywhere. Protesters were everywhere too—five hundred of all ages, at one shuttle stop.

Armed security increased as the protesters neared the city center, and so did the number of protesters entering on shuttles, on foot, or on bicycles. Talkative young people rushed by them in high spirits.

Their shuttle stopped at the direction of a jittery policeman. "I'm sorry, people, but you're going to have to turn around," he said.

"The government was taken by surprise," James whispered in Cleo's ear.

"Why can't we go downtown?" a dark-haired man asked the policeman.

An African American woman added, "We're going downtown."

"You're going to have to turn around. We believe there is a credible terrorist threat. It's too dangerous," the policeman said.

211

The African American woman waved a hand at him. "That's bullshit. You don't want us to go to this event."

"We have our orders."

The pushing and shoving began when the police attempted to force everyone to turn around, but the protesters charged past them. Additional police were dispatched and attacked back, swinging their batons, but there were not enough of them, and they couldn't stop that many determined people. Women, particularly women, were outspoken and kept rushing forward. A tall, thin man with a beard wrestled a beefy policeman to the ground, and then the additional police retreated or began running with the crowd so they wouldn't be steamrolled.

James and Cleo jumped off the shuttle and followed the mayhem.

Stadium police in riot gear in a side-by-side formation blocked the entrance to the stadium as an officer on a bullhorn threatened thousands with arrest. "Please turn around and return home. There will be no event today. I repeat, today's event has been cancelled. Anyone downtown is breaking the law, and we will have no choice but to arrest you."

No one retreated from the stadium police, who were now more than four lines deep and were putting on gas masks. When they charged, the protesters shoved back with threats and fists, lashing out from all directions. Some in the front were bludgeoned, but more were fighting right behind them. James and Cleo remained behind the mania of the crowd.

Security vehicles rolled up, but resisters swarmed in from all directions and jumped on the vehicles when they tried to move.

"Yes!" Cleo cheered on the resisters and raised her left fist.

James was ecstatic to see the people standing their ground and fighting back.

Then orange powder burst and banged inside and outside

the stadium. The protesters' retreat began immediately; they panicked to escape the tear gas, tripping over each other and choking. Many were half blinded or were hit by rubber bullets and collapsed to the ground. James and Cleo weren't far enough back, and their eyes were burning, so they scampered away across several streets to a safer distance.

A convoy of military trucks and personal rolled up, and the screaming and coughing crowd was surrounded and unable to escape.

The military personnel, all in gas masks, emerged and attacked. It wasn't about getting people out of the stadium. It was a free-for-all to pummel resisters. It was a horror show, watching so many people being bloodied or incapacitated.

"Let's go," James said, but when he angled to leave, he was shoved to the ground, a boot in the middle of his back.

He heard Cleo yelling, but her voice was coming from above; she hadn't been knocked to the ground.

"Get the fuck off me," James shouted.

The man kept his boot on his back for a long time, even after another had latched on handcuffs. James could only stare at the shoes and legs trying to sidestep out of there and others being trampled to the ground.

James's eyes began to burn again, and he caught a whiff of the acrid odor. The man replaced the boot with his knee on James's back, which was even more painful.

When they lifted him up, he saw that Cleo had her wrists handcuffed too.

"Didn't you see what just happened? This sort of thing is over, it's all over," Cleo roared.

"You're both wanted by the government," a man with a badge said.

Then James saw her strawberry-blond hair standing out

among the crowd. A few yards behind Cleo was Sheilah, a bitter crisscross of revenge warping her lovely profile. The mousy girl from his work stood next to Sheilah, flipping them off.

"This is my sister," he called out to her, motioning to Cleo.

Sheilah displayed no emotion toward him, her blank face cold and rigid.

"I broke up with you only to find my sister. I didn't mean it," he said as the detective yanked him toward the street.

He wasn't sure Sheilah heard or understood him, but she never took her eyes off him until the detective forced him into the back seat of a car.

Back at the prison, James was interrogated, but it was neither dramatic nor intense. The interrogator was going through the motions.

"We know it was an inside job," the interrogator said.

"If it was, I had no idea what happened."

"Was Jens Ensley involved? We know you and he were close."

"Jens hated me. We were not close. I thought I was let go because I'd committed no crime."

"You're an enemy of the state."

"You had ten thousand enemies this week."

The interrogator leaned back in his seat. "You're not the only one who thinks this is bullshit," he said, not looking at James.

Nothing happened for the next two months. The guards seemed on edge, but they quietly spoke with James and others about their desire for change.

James became depressed, but he found a burst of energy whenever he learned there had been more protests. It turned into a daily ritual for protesters to be incarcerated. Everything was in chaos, including the prison. Now there were two or three prisoners per cell. His new cellmate, a former carpenter named Bill, had participated in all the protests and was eventually identified and picked up at his home. Bill thought the military had grown weary of being policemen, and they now remained in the background for the most part. Something had to give, the man said.

One thing hadn't changed. Sheilah still overwhelmed James's thoughts. He relived their first meeting, their passion, and her desperate love for him and his for her.

But most of all he thought about what he should have done differently. He should have trusted her, damn it, but now that they had betrayed each other, it gave him hope she would forgive him. He had already forgiven her.

One midafternoon, four months after his arrest, James was taken to a waiting room, where there were about thirty men. A woman he did not recognize asked his name and flipped through several sheets of paper. "You're being released. Your house is waiting for you. Congratulations," she said.

He didn't believe it until a guard handed him the clothes he was wearing when he was brought in.

At his house, Cleo greeted him. "What took you so long?" she asked.

"Did we win?"

"We're free."

Two days later, they visited the Superstore. The military was no longer present downtown, and though a few uniformed police were speaking to a couple, it appeared benign. Working people were still going to work; the shuttles were running. A street musician plucked on a guitar, and down the street someone was giving a talk to a small audience. The government propaganda posters were torn down.

A free pamphlet in the Superstore expounded on the themes of the rally. They each picked one up.

"I'd like to go back to my old place and get my things. We could stay there together for a while," Cleo said.

"I'll go wherever you want, but I have to see her one more time," he said.

"I know."

"I'm glad she betrayed me. Now we can start over clean."

Cleo only smiled and touched his back.

The next day, James met with Joan in the human resources department at his former office to see if he could find out where Sheilah lived. He had tried her place, but someone else lived there now. His heart had been beating out of his chest when a blond woman answered the door and let him know she had moved in months earlier and had never heard of Sheilah.

"I don't have Sheilah's current personal information," Joan said. "She left her role months ago, and I don't know what happened to her or how to get a hold of her."

"Can you ask anyone else if they know?"

"Yes, I can do that, and if you leave your address, I'll let you know what I find out." Joan gripped his arm. "She's a sweet girl. I hope you can help her," she said, then added, "I was only doing my job. I never supported what was happening." Her face was desperate, almost pleading for understanding.

"I know."

The next week Duane appeared, dripping wet at James's door. An El Niño–type storm was pounding the West Coast. "I found her."

They hopped on a shuttle in the pouring rain and traveled to the far south of town to a street with rows of run-down apartment buildings.

When they arrived, the rain had subsided, and teenagers were playing out front under the dark storm clouds. Windows with no screens were open. Music blasted and thumped through a stereo with a heavy bass. Men sat on the front steps drinking something out of old milk jugs. Red-eyed, they examined James and Duane, though James didn't sense hostility, but they were not welcoming either.

Inside, the elevator had a note taped to it: "Out of Order," so they hustled up the stairs. Swastikas and anti-government graffiti depicting cops as fascists decorated the stairwell walls. The place was a dump. Why was she relegated to living here? He could save her from this squalor.

He made his way over the dirty carpet down the hall toward what Duane had identified as Sheilah's apartment. He knocked and waited while Duane stood back and out of view of anyone answering the door. He knocked again, and when there was no answer, he twisted the doorknob. It was locked. He turned to Duane, who inserted his little tool and played with the lock, jimmying it open.

The apartment was neat. No art or photos on the walls. An old sofa, scuffed coffee table, and green lamp in the front room complemented an unpleasant odor.

"Sheilah?"

Music with the volume on high came from a corner unit.

He led Duane past the kitchen with clean dishes filling a plastic rack where they had dried.

Before the bedroom was the bathroom where James spotted dark stains edging out on to the carpet. They moved past the bathroom and down the hall.

Trepidation made James more cautious, and he paused before he pushed open the door to a bedroom.

Sheilah lay on her back on the bed, her legs twisted elegantly and her waist thin. She was wearing a sexy, slim-fitting dress that he remembered. Dark pools surrounded her head and white pillows. Her eyes and mouth were shut, and her hair was caked and frizzy with gray matter. There was a handgun near her left hand.

"Goddamn," Duane said.

James leaned near Sheilah. He didn't think she was breathing. He was crushed. He smelled alcohol and vomit and leaned down and inspected the blood. He dabbed a finger in it. It wasn't blood.

When Sheilah opened her eyes, he bolted upright and backed into Duane. He wanted to ask if she was all right, but his throat was too choked up.

James and Duane guided her down the stairs. Duane carried a suitcase filled with her clothes, shoes, and what was in her medicine cabinet.

Sheilah appeared to be drunk and flailed her arms and legs. "Leave me alone," she said.

James didn't respond, until Sheilah wiggled herself to the ground.

"I'm taking you to my house. You can't stay here," James said.

"Leave me the fuck alone. I fucking hate you," she said.

He had never heard her swear before. It sounded unnatural coming from her, and it stung like a sharp arrow through his abdomen because she sounded sincere.

They pulled her up and carried her down the stairs. Her arms and hands slapped them a few times as she resisted.

Sheilah planted her wobbly legs on the ground, but she

218

seemed confused and in a haze. She kept turning to James, as if she couldn't believe what she was seeing.

When they reached the shuttle, she crumbled on to the bench with her head bowed, suddenly humiliated and resigned.

"I need a brush," she whispered.

Duane opened the suitcase and pulled out a brush and handed it to her. Her hair was a mess, and she tugged at it over and over.

"Water," she muttered.

"They don't have water here," James said, "We'll get some on the next stop."

It started to rain, and they all sat exposed to a new deluge. Sheilah continued to brush her hair.

When they reached James's place, he lay a passed-out Sheilah on to his bed. Cleo waited in the hall, and as he closed the door, she gave him a frightened look before they wandered to the front room with Duane behind them.

"I'm going to go. Let me know if you need anything. You know how to find me," Duane said.

When James hugged him, Duane stiffened and stepped back.

"Thanks," James said.

Duane nodded and quickly left.

"Do you want to be alone with her?" Cleo asked.

"No. I need you now more than ever."

The next day in James's backyard, he moved a tomato plant and a dwarf lemon tree that Cleo had potted to a sunnier part of his backyard.

"This feels good," he said.

"Gardens sprouted up all over the east," Cleo said.

Marching out of the house with her suitcase was Sheilah. She didn't look at them and rushed across the yard.

James sprinted to her and blocked her from reaching the cracked sidewalk.

"Sheilah, please. Don't go. We need to talk," he said.

"What's there to talk about?"

"You know what we need to talk about."

Sheilah turned away from him.

"You can't go back to that place. Stay here until you figure something out," he urged.

Sheilah noticed Cleo.

"That's your sister?"

"Yes," Cleo said, approaching Sheilah, who kept her eye on her. "I'd like to get to know you."

Sheilah hesitated. "OK."

Cleo made a salad with fresh romaine, tomatoes, avocados, onions. She set the table with a bottle of white wine punctuating the center.

Sunlight shone through the open windows. James stood poised to bring Sheilah in when she entered quietly and sat.

Sheilah stared at her bowl, so Cleo filled it and smiled. Sheilah didn't look up.

"I just want to say that I'm incredibly grateful to be here with my sister and you Sheilah," James said.

When Sheila's expression remained stoic, they began to eat the meal in silence.

The stillness in the house seemed thick and omnipresent. Every clank, crack, or squeak disturbed James's deteriorating peace of mind. That sensitivity to everything around them put them all on edge, he thought. He sensed the tension emanated from

Sheilah, even though she rarely left the bedroom.

That afternoon, James knocked on the door.

"I wanted to check in with you to see if you're OK?"

"I'm OK," she said.

He imagined her laying on the bed facing the wall.

"Can we talk for a bit?" he asked.

"Not now."

On the sixth morning, Sheilah entered the front room and stated that she wanted to go for walk, so he and Cleo tried to keep up with her through a neighborhood of half-built tiny new homes. Sheilah strode surprisingly fast. She'd lost weight and her tan, but something inside was driving her.

Cleo tried to start a conversation several times, but Sheilah remained fixated on speed-walking and never responded, and perhaps never even heard her.

If she had been healthier James and Cleo would not have been able to keep up as Sheilah led them to the "No Lands."

The "No Lands" appeared calmer with less smoke exhaling from the earth. Most of the junk and wreckage had been cleared out, and a new plain valley had been cleared to the sea. Sheilah halted and peered west. She seemed surprised at the changes, before she turned and started back.

When they arrived back at James's house, even Sheilah seemed worn out after the long jaunt, and before they entered, she turned to them and said: "I needed that."

"Me too," James answered.

He eyed her with a certain neediness, which caused her to turn and enter the house and go directly to the bedroom.

Sheilah stayed in the bedroom the rest of the day and night. James had hoped she would come out to the garden or to dinner, but she never did. It was always eerily silent in the bedroom.

When he woke in the middle of the night, he heard hushed voices coming from the bedroom. He tiptoed closer and realized that Cleo and Sheilah were in a conversation. He hesitated, but he knew it wasn't right, so he returned to the sofa.

He had a hard time getting back to sleep and ended up oversleeping, and when he got up, he wandered down the hallway and saw that his bedroom door was wide open, and the bed was made. Sheilah's suitcase was missing.

That afternoon he and Cleo hiked to the "No Lands," where they were pulled toward the ocean and started to walk toward it.

They reached the Venice Canals in two hours, where the waterways were full, smoky blue, and translucent. Trailers and campers were parked throughout the canals. A few wild-haired groups were grilling something outside.

At the beach, James and Cleo took their shoes off and waded through the cold waves. James was in awe being there, and he and Cleo splashed around in the white water that rushed in and out and soaked them up to their knees.

Their feet sunk into the wet sand, as they continued down the beach toward the broken-down pier.

"Tell me what she said again," James said.

He could tell the question caused Cleo's happy mood to descend.

"I'm sorry," he said.

She kicked at the tide and faced him. "She's confused and destroyed. She needs some time."

"So, you think there's a chance?"

James gazed out at the swells.

"She said she thought maybe you really loved her."

"Of course, I did. Did you tell her that?" he stammered.

"I told you that I did."

"How long do you think it will take her?"

"I don't know."

"If you had to guess?"

"A year."

"Do you think I should try and see her in a couple months?"

"I think that would be a mistake."

He couldn't accept this, but he didn't tell her.

"Give her the time she needs," Cleo stated, laying a hand on his shoulder.

Happy teenagers approached them running down the beach, and they smiled at them scampering past.

XI

AT JAMES'S PLACE, D'ARCY ENTERED and gave him a quick, intense embrace, then hung her head as he took her coat.

A large monitor had been set up in front of the sofa for D'Arcy, Duane, and Cleo to watch the live-streamed announcement from Jens Ensley.

James had not seen Jens, but he had met with Jim, who told him that Jens had been imprisoned, but after the protests a swell of support within the former government as well as the military freed him.

When all the hardliners were forced out of positions of leadership, Jens, who had believed in more transparency and a democratic republic from the early days, was identified to lead the effort in putting together a new government.

"Today is a new day of freedom and openness that will include a free market, a transparent government, and an independent media," Jens said. "All government and military officials will be made public. Elections will be held. Except for violent criminals, of which there are few, all political detainees have been released. The people have spoken; we have listened."

Duane and D'Arcy were holding hands. James couldn't help but watch them, and when Duane noticed, James held up his drink in salute.

They all gave James the eye periodically to see how he, the tragic and pathetic person, was holding up.

"We have survived," Jens went on, "and we will strive to build a sustainable and hopeful future that allows every citizen the opportunity to follow their individual dreams. This new day of openness has come about because of you."

Relief and cheers greeted the announcement. "We did it," Duane said. Tears were in his eyes, and he and D'Arcy embraced.

"It's fantastic," James smiled, but he stopped as soon as no one was looking at him.

In his bedroom the next day, James heard Cleo coming and shut the book he was reading about Venice, Italy. Stacks of books were scattered nearby. Cleo entered and sat on the bed. He loved her sympathetic eyes and the concern in her pursed-lips smile. He knew what she was going to ask, even before she gripped his hand.

"Won't you reconsider coming with me to my place," she said, "just for a visit? Maybe a change in scenery would do you good."

"I just want to be in my room with my books, until she's back.," he said.

"I'll only be gone for a month," she said, bowing her head and walking out.

He opened the book and began to read.

In the backyard, he watered his lemon tree and a new orange tree. The tomato plant's vines ran up the house behind him. The cherry tomatoes on it were almost ripe.

He wiped his brow. The sun was beating down, so he turned on the hose and splashed water on his face.

That evening he tried to read a book, but he couldn't focus, so he wandered in the yard staring at the stars.

On his way to work on the shuttle that Monday, he thought there was more activity downtown. Several coffee shops had opened. Others on the shuttle were engaged in conversations. No one seemed to notice him. He had become invisible to others.

At work he tried to focus on a spreadsheet, but he was bored and distracted and peered out the office window at the sunny day.

After work, he picked up some groceries. Again, that night, he couldn't sleep and tossed and turned. Finally, he gave up and turned on the light and opened his laptop.

This was his life now. Just one lonely event after another. He didn't connect with anyone with Cleo gone, and he felt that he radiated an uncomfortable energy that made people he came across shy away from him. He was a solitary figure.

Four months after Cleo's return, she told him she didn't feel well, so he hiked alone to the "No Lands." He decided against venturing all the way to the ocean since that was an all-day journey, so he lay on his back in a small patch of field, where he fell asleep.

It was silent when he woke up. As he scanned the area, he thought he saw movement in the distance. He waited and realized it was a single person approaching.

James sensed something and stood, then started to walk toward the person. Before he could recognize her features, he knew it was Sheilah.

He wanted to walk faster, but he remained at his patient pace. As they each came within view, it was the Sheilah he had first met. She was in tremendous shape and her hair was lustrous.

When they reached each other, they stopped six feet apart. James didn't know what to say. She seemed a little scared.

"Shall we walk?" he asked

They stepped side by side back toward town.

"How are you?" he asked after a few minutes of silence.

"I'm OK."

"You look healthy."

He tried to display a confident smile, but he didn't pull it off. She didn't react.

Back in town they reached the shuttles and a few people out for a stroll.

"Shall we go to our favorite bar?" he asked.

"OK."

Inside, they sat in a booth and drank a martini, then ordered another. Even though she barely said a word; she seemed as if she wanted to say something. He didn't have a sense what she was thinking until she spoke.

"I hated you for a long time," she said.

"I should have trusted you."

She didn't seem to care that he said this and remained self-absorbed. "I was ashamed you were fighting for our freedoms, and I was not. I've had a hard time dealing with the fact I had lost myself so long ago."

Her face hardened with bitterness, before James's words came rushing out. "It wasn't you. It was an extreme and unprecedented situation. We all lie and do the best we can at the same time."

This seemed to take an edge off her, and the stiffness of her shoulders visibly loosened. She sipped her drink several times.

"My lie was breaking up with you."

She peered out the window for a moment. "I'm glad you're alive. I couldn't have lived with having caused your death."

"I can't really live without you."

"I know."

James waited for her to say more. "I can't help it," he said.

"It's a madness that's inside you that you can't escape," she said.

"Love is a good madness."

They both finished their drinks.

"I feel like walking," she said.

As they left the bar, she angled her arm around his.

"Let's go slow," she said.

James lifted her arm up and kissed the back of her hand, and she offered him a mysterious smile.

"We're free now to go slow," he said.

INSIDE '75

I

THE OPPOSING TEAM'S CHEERS drowned out the groans from our side of the bleachers. This wasn't just any game. It was the last inning of the 1975 Middle League thirteen-to-fifteen-year-olds semifinals. And Jimmy, our slightly built second baseman, had fielded a routine grounder and flung it into center field instead of tossing it to the shortstop covering second base.

Coach Riggins's shoulders were hunched, and he stared downward as he walked out to the mound. He was met by our star catcher, the pale-blond Chris, already six feet at fifteen years old. This was the third year in a row we'd played together, and we were now great friends.

I scanned the parents, brothers, sisters, and friends of the players in the stands—cheering, gossiping, playing, eating sunflower seeds, drinking Coke. I hated it when our hot-tempered coach came out to the mound.

"Christ, look at him," the coach growled, frowning at Jimmy. "Nice going, pussy arm!" the coach screamed at him. "Hell of a job!"

Jimmy's cap was pulled down over his eyes. He had moved to the outfield grass, as far away as possible from the coach's

233

wrath. Jimmy appeared catatonic, and I prayed the next ball wouldn't be hit toward him.

Behind my back I flipped the coach the bird for Jimmy's benefit.

The coach took off his cap and scratched his thick black hair. "It's not your fault; you're getting no support."

"The only support Jay's getting is from his jockstrap," Chris said.

A ridiculous grin burst onto my face.

The coach glared toward center field. "All right. It's good to be relaxed," he said. "All we need is one more out, and we're in the championship."

"I'll get him." I stifled my laughter.

Chris put on his catcher's mitt to hide the wise-ass smile he was known for.

"All right, all right. Get this turkey." The coach clapped and returned to the dugout while Chris jogged back behind the plate.

The pimply kid at bat dug in the box. The umpire, a big-nosed high school student, got set. The opposing players and fans cheered.

Chris flashed me a single finger. I nodded, set, and fired— ball. I did this again and again. After the third ball, the coach frisbeed his clipboard against the wall in the dugout.

"Don't choke, pretty boy...I think he's going to cry!" yelled a rough kid they called Chewy.

I stepped off the rubber, sweat forming under my cap.

On the sidelines stood my good friend Early, a lanky African American, whose team had already won their semifinal game. Next to him was Keith, who always seemed to be hanging around the high school parking lot and teenage weekend parties, where he sometimes supplied the booze and pot. He was nineteen and tough as nails. The blond girl Keith had been talking about was quietly standing next to him, wild hair blowing in her face.

I exhaled and kicked at the mound, then threw two quick strikes, the second one swinging. Both pitches were meat, straight as an arrow and begging to be smacked. The batter's shoulders were up around his ears.

Chris flashed one finger for a fastball. I shook my head. He wiggled one finger again. I waved him off. He wiggled it once more and squinted at me through his mask as if he didn't believe me.

"Time!" He held up his hand and walked over to the mound. "What the hell?"

"I'm throwing a curve."

"One more ball, and they'll tie the game."

"One more strike, and we're in the championship."

"You're crazy." Chris jogged back and flashed me one finger, the middle one. I waved him off again. Finally, he gave up and flashed the two-finger curve signal.

My roundhouse curve rotated beautifully, heading directly at the batter, who flinched. The pitch purled right across the outside corner.

"Strike three!"

I don't know why I wasn't nervous. Maybe because Jimmy was humiliated, and I figured nothing worse could happen to me. Or maybe I wanted the game to be over.

Coach Riggins tossed his cap in the air, tripping into Jimmy as he chugged out to the mound. Chris got there first and picked me up before everyone mobbed us.

When the bats, balls, and equipment lay packed in duffel bags in the locker room, Chris and I walked out past the batting cage and bullpen to the street that ran through the railroad station, behind right field.

"Your dad was at the game," Chris said.

"He see us win?"

He shrugged.

"He must have stopped by before work." I picked up a rock and flung it toward the train station, enjoying the pleasant emptiness inside me. My father stocked groceries at night. It sounded like a terrible job, but he didn't seem to mind it— though he was often in a foul mood.

"My mom said there's a depression," Chris said.

"Recession. It's not a depression." I'd learned this in government class.

"What's the difference? No one has any money."

"We're working."

"Yeah." He laughed.

Past the railroad tracks, a 1969 Nova full of Southsiders approached on the other side of the street. I froze, but Chris didn't react. It occurred to me that he was steeling himself for the confrontation. That his complete focus was on what would happen next.

This was the Garza brothers' gang, all of whom hated Chris.

I turned around, thinking the option of running was not a bad one, but Chris stood there waiting for them.

I had only heard about this feud. I went to the private Catholic school, while Chris went to the public school, which was partitioned between the poor kids—mainly Mexican—and the middle-class white kids, though there were plenty of middle-class Mexican kids on the white kids' side and vice versa.

Why Chris was hated was a mystery to me. I never saw him do or say anything wrong. I knew there had been altercations between him and the Garzas, but he had never mentioned it, and I'd never asked.

I heard the two younger members behind us on foot, closing in. The skinny brothers were as hard as the railroad tracks and the same iron-brown color. A freckled kid with a blue scarf tied around his red hair and a small but speedy pale kid with a shaved head and white eyebrows made up the rest of the gang.

"Let's go through the fence," I said, anxious to get the hell home.

"Let's get out of here," Chris said.

We were outnumbered, which is why I think he made the decision to run.

We snuck through a fence and raced past the railroad station, but before we reached the ballpark, the Garzas' Nova pulled up on the opposite side of the tracks. The younger Garza gang members had stayed up with us from behind.

"What are we going to do?"

"Fight," Chris said.

We were trapped. We watched the Garza leader, a burly guy with a shaved head, jump out of the Nova and cross the tracks toward us. He had on a tight tank top that showed off his weightlifting arms and chest. Even though he was only about twenty, the five-year difference between us made him a lifetime older. He dangled a thick iron chain.

The closer he got, the more fearless he seemed.

"There's five of them," I said.

Chris ignored me.

The sky shrank, as though only the immediate earthly surroundings existed. I lost my breath.

Then Keith's baby-blue 1965 Malibu with chrome Cragars screeched to a stop, sending dust and pebbles flying. Early and

Keith jumped out and marched past the Garza leader. The girl with blond hair covering her face remained in the car.

The Garza leader rattled the chain in his hand. "We don't have anything against you, Early. It's the *whettos* we want."

Early frowned. "There's nothing I can do now, I'm here."

"Why don't you fight me alone?" Chris asked. "Your little brother had the guts."

The youngest kid's left eye was purple and puffy, like he'd been beaten up recently, obviously by Chris.

"You're pretty brave when someone's smaller than you," the leader said, approaching Chris, who didn't budge.

No one seemed to notice me, except maybe the blond girl. Her eyes were gigantic. She got out of the car as if she wanted to help.

Keith stepped forward, like he'd seen enough. He lifted weights, worked on motorcycles, hung out in bars with a fake ID, and played a lot of pool. He had cool dusty-brown hair that he combed straight back and had a reputation for being someone you didn't mess with.

"Christ," Keith said. "Your little brother sucker-punched him. This kid's only fifteen."

The Garza leader flicked the chain toward Chris. "He fucked with my family!"

"He didn't start the fight."

"Are you saying I should blame my bro?"

"I'm saying fight him alone, without the chains. That's fair," Keith said.

"Fair. He attacked my little brother. What's so fair about that?" The Garza leader wrapped the chain around his forearm.

"He didn't start it." Keith shuffled but didn't move forward.

"Bullshit." Garza swung the chain, slicing Chris's head and forearm with it.

My heart rioted. Everything was a blur. I wasn't sure what was happening, but Chris had already charged, swinging ferocious punches, relentless despite the Garza leader's powerful kicks and the chain being whipped at his head.

Keith faced off with another Garza brother and the redhead. The youngest Garza and the small guy jumped me, throwing vicious, hard-edged punches. I heard Keith yell to Early, "Help Jay!"

I dodged back and sideways as Early flew in and knocked them off me. Somehow I'd risen to their level of energy now and swung punch after punch. The smallest gang member's eyes darted around—he was looking for help that never came.

Keith was a better fighter than Chris, but even he couldn't take down two of the gangsters. They hid and bobbed and weaved and jabbed, followed by a flurry of punches.

Everything changed when Chris yanked the chain from the Garza leader and knocked him to the ground. The gangsters Early and I were battling scrambled away to help him.

"Chris!" I yelled.

He pivoted and smashed the younger Garza's face, laying him out motionless on the ground.

Sirens approached in the distance, and the Garzas scrambled back to the Nova.

"You're on my list! You're a dead man!" the Garza leader yelled at us all.

"You're on *my* list, man! You're on *my* list!" Keith screamed back.

"You *putos* fucked with the wrong family!"

Keith answered by throwing a rock at the Nova.

We jumped into the Malibu, and Keith spun out. Far behind us, the black-and-white police car stopped in front of the dust cloud Keith had created.

I had never been in a real fight before and had been petrified as this one started. But at some point in the battle, I had stopped caring. I was proud I'd survived and fought as well as I could. I did wonder what I was doing there. I never felt like I belonged in this town.

On the outskirts of town, Keith slowed. "How is everybody? Anyone need to go to the hospital? Chris?"

"I'm all right," Chris said.

The mystery girl patted the cut on Chris's forehead with her sweatshirt sleeve.

Sitting in the back, I couldn't get a clean look at her. I glanced at Early, wondering who she was.

"Jesus Christ!" Keith shouted.

The Garzas' Nova was back, bumping Keith's Malibu from behind. The Nova had little patches of primer all over its beat-up exterior; they didn't seem to care about denting or scraping it more. Keith was the kind of guy who parked his flawless car a mile away from other cars, in fear of a door ding.

Keith's hot rod was faster, but there were too many turns and too much traffic on the country road for him to race away. The Garza leader was a deft driver. He managed to bump Keith's car again, jerking me forward. I caught a glimpse of the girl. A veneer of isolation seemed to shelter her from what was happening around us. She looked innocent, but if she was with Keith, I figured she wasn't. Her teeth were white and straight, and if she ever smiled, she must have looked like a happy, all-American girl.

"They don't care about that piece of shit," Early said.

"No shit, Sherlock." Keith swerved toward the Nova, catching the leader off guard. They almost spun out into a lettuce field, but the Garza leader fishtailed back onto the road.

Keith jerked us into the right lane, maneuvering so he

couldn't be rammed from behind again. "Everyone hold on," he said.

As Keith pulled parallel to the leader, I looked directly at Garza's eyes, which were more mischievous than angry.

"Watch out, Keith," I said.

"Shut up."

They tried to sideswipe us, but Keith slammed on the brakes. The Nova missed us, and the momentum sent it sliding on its side to the edge of an irrigation ditch.

"Holy Christ!" Keith hooted and laughed.

"You can't leave them like that," the girl said.

"Just wait!"

One of the gangsters struggled out of the window and flipped us the bird.

"I'd say they'll be all right," Keith said, laughing.

II

SAFE AT HOME, I mostly stayed in my room, ignoring my older sister and our dog chasing each other around the house. My father's recliner was empty; a can of Coors and an ashtray lay next to it. My mother was in the kitchen, cooking tacos and warming corn tortillas. She didn't seem to mind my sister's screaming, the dog, and the TV making so much noise.

When I heard Keith's car horn beep outside, I grabbed my jacket and ran out. "Bye, Mom."

The fair was one of the few events for teenagers in town, and I was feeling free, thrilled to be going anywhere.

Keith's Malibu reeked of Old Spice cologne. He had one shirt sleeve rolled up, perhaps to show off the homemade tattoo of his name etched on his left shoulder.

I gazed out at the traffic as older hot rods, 1956 Chevys, 1950s Ford trucks, Gran Torinos, GTOs, and Camaros cruised up and down Main Street.

"Thanks for driving, Keith."

"No problem. I saw you throw a couple punches today," Keith said, laughing and punching my arm. "And I figure I better go in case you peewee leaguers get in trouble. Besides, I'm meeting Lily at the fair." Keith swigged from a bottle of apricot brandy and handed it to me. "Go ahead—it's smooth," he said.

I took a drink and passed the bottle back to Early and Chris. I had started drinking and smoking pot with the three of them in eighth grade. There was nothing else to do.

Chris guzzled from the bottle. Early took a sip, then burped.

"Peewee leaguers. Jesus," Keith said. He turned up the music and sang along to Bowie's *Diamond Dogs*. I joined him.

Keith loved Bowie, and so did I. He had taken me to the Forum in Los Angeles the year before to see Bowie. It was my first concert and probably the greatest day of my life so far.

"Keith, you know what this album's about?" I asked him. I'd just learned myself from an article in *Rolling Stone* and wanted to show off.

"'Rebel Rebel'?" Keith said.

"That too, but it's about the book *Nineteen Eighty-Four* by George Orwell."

Keith looked out the driver's side window for a beat. "Oh yeah," he said without enthusiasm. "Who gives a shit, it rocks."

We rambled off into the crowd of cowboys, Mexican families, and young people that energized the Saturday night fair. The flashing lights, games, freak shows, strangers—this was life, and I had not seen much of it.

Chris, Early, and I went straight to the Kiwanis Lodge hot dog stand, where we had signed up to sell hot dogs for three hours to earn $9.75 each. We were trained in five minutes by our skinny new boss, who wore too-tight polyester pants and a dizzying paisley shirt. Chris hauled and stacked the cases of buns while Early boiled dogs in a wire basket.

"Come on, come on. Get them out of the water. You're soaking them," the boss said. "And what are you looking at, Pretty Boy Floyd?" he asked me. "You got customers."

Chris spilled a box of wieners on the ground.

"Pick them up and wash them off, bozo. You kids ain't sixteen. You're not even my shoe size. If I could get decent help, you'd be fired." The boss flailed his arms, like he wanted to say something else, but then he walked out.

We started to laugh and couldn't stop, even when I turned to the customer, the blond girl, Lily, who had been in Keith's car. Her frightened blue eyes seemed to encompass everything and nothing at the same time.

"Hi," I said. "I'm Jay."

"I know."

Two fifteen-year-old girls I'd seen at baseball games, Melinda and Monica, appeared behind her.

"Can I get a—" Melinda began.

"Wiener?" Monica finished the sentence.

"Oh my god. Shut up!" Melinda said.

I smiled at the blond girl.

"I know you. You go to St. Luke's," Melinda said.

"Yeah, I do, but they don't." I gestured to Early and Chris, who abandoned their jobs to join me. I ignored a woman who was considering ordering a hot dog.

"You were in Keith's car," I said to the blond girl. She nodded.

"Her name's Lily. She's shy," Melinda told me.

"Have you guys ridden the Zipper?" Monica asked.

"Monica! They're working!" Melinda said, shoving her.

"Not all night. There's three of them and three of us," Monica said.

"I can't believe you. Besides, Lily has a boyfriend." Melinda put her finger down her throat and mocked gagging.

I watched Lily while the others gossiped. The revelation that Keith was her boyfriend made her face flush, and she wouldn't look at me anymore.

"Sure, we'll meet you," Chris said.

"By the Zipper," Monica said. "And bring wieners."

"Oh my god!" Melinda screeched.

The boss's mustache and wild shirt appeared over my left shoulder. "What's going on here? You have customers waiting!"

Monica and Melinda giggled and then grabbed Lily, pulling her along toward the rides.

After our work shift ended, the boss paid us ten dollars each. Because he was so pleased with the job we did, he gave each of us a hot dog.

Flush with cash, Chris stopped at a booth, grabbed some softballs without paying, and knocked down the pins.

Keith, Lily, and Monica appeared behind us. Keith had his brandy bottle tucked in his waist, and his arm was around Lily.

"I know someone who likes Early," Monica said, squirming and twisting as if she had something we wanted.

"Give me a break," Early said.

I knew he was pretending to be upset. "Who is it?" I asked.

"I'm not supposed to tell."

Keith winked at me. "She's not supposed to tell."

"It doesn't matter," Early said.

Keith laughed. "It doesn't matter."

I leaned into Monica, who bit her lip. "Come on, you have to tell us. It's Melinda, isn't it?"

"I don't need to know," Early said in a defensive tone.

Melinda wandered toward us, eating cotton candy.

"Don't tell her I told you," Monica said. "You have to promise."

"I promise," I said.

Early pushed me.

Monica smiled at Early. "It's Melinda. She thinks you're cute."

I could see that Early was uncomfortable; he grimaced and glanced around like he was looking for some reason to change the subject.

"What?" Melinda appeared, wide-eyed and suspecting something.

Silence.

"What did you say? Tell me," Melinda said.

Monica shrugged. "We're waiting for you."

"What did you say? You better not have been talking about me."

"We're going on some rides." Monica pulled Melinda and Early toward the Zipper. "Come on, you guys. There's no line."

"I'm not going on these stupid rides. I don't trust the carny freaks who run them. You go with Jay," Keith said to Lily.

Lily edged toward me.

Keith lit a Camel cigarette.

A stringy-haired guy with a lopsided face strapped us into the Zipper, leering at Lily's breasts with a yellow-toothed smile.

As the Zipper rotated higher than any building in town, I saw Keith below, gazing up. When he noticed me looking down at him, he flicked his cigarette at the guy. The guy said something to Keith, who stepped toward him as if he was itching for a fight. The guy flipped Keith off and then ran, weaving away through the crowd. Keith walked in the other direction.

"Keith's your boyfriend?" I asked.

"I guess." Lily's voice was a whisper.

"How long?"

"Not very long," she said, as if she were far away from herself.

City lights dotted the landscape. Goose bumps rose on my arms from the ocean breeze. We were stuck up here now because the guy working on the ride had run off.

"You get kicked out of school?" I asked.

"Yeah. Smoking pot."

We both looked down at the sea of people and the bright lights flashing everywhere.

"I've been taken," she said.

I wanted to ask what she meant, but the guy returned, and the Zipper started revolving, haphazardly sliding from the sky to the ground and around again. Lily and I bobbed and dropped, rolling in the iron cage until I threw my arm around her. We embraced each other, a little unit. Our noses could have touched. And when the Zipper stopped, I didn't want to let go—and didn't until they opened our cage. We wobbled out, giddy. She bumped up against me, maybe because she was off balance.

A cigarette dangled from Keith's lips as he waited with a teddy bear he had gotten somewhere. He handed it to Lily.

Monica and Melinda, both clearly dizzy, clutched at me for balance. "Jay, let's ride on the bumper cars."

Keith spun Lily around and wandered off.

After two hours of rides, games, junk food, and the curiosities of Sealo and Penguin Boy, we wandered toward the parking lot, through the stables with the 4-H animals. Most of the animals had settled down, but an occasional grunt came from the barns.

"My brother thinks you guys are cool," Melinda said to Early.

"I know your brother. He comes to all the games," Early said.

I kept turning around to monitor Keith kissing and rubbing up against Lily. They had finished the bottle of apricot brandy, and both were drunk. Lily's head was tilted up, her mouth open and kissing Keith back. She was offering no resistance or seemed to have no willpower to object.

"She's so dumb," Monica said.

Melinda kicked the dirt and leaned against a fence, no longer watching. "He's an asshole…and she's drunk."

"She's a weak little whore!" Monica shouted.

Keith steered Lily into one of the stalls lined with hay. On the way, Lily dropped her teddy bear. I almost ran back and picked it up, but I chickened out and stepped in a cow pie instead. "Crap."

Early and Chris laughed at me as I tried to scrape the mess off my Chuck Taylors.

"She better come. We gotta go home," Melinda said.

"Lily, we're leaving!" Monica called out.

I nodded. "Yeah, we got to get home too."

"You don't have to be home," Early said.

I ignored Early and walked toward the stables. "What are they doing?"

"What do you think?" Monica said snidely.

I shuffled back, a burning sensation in my chest. I'd known it was a stupid question. "We've got to go, don't you think, Chris?" I asked.

"Keith is our ride home," Chris said.

"Lily, we're going!" Melinda shouted.

"Maybe you should go get her," I said.

"I'm not going in there."

"Forget Lily," Monica said. "Tell the drunken whore she can have Keith take her home. I can't let my parents see her like that. They'll ground me for a month."

Monica skipped off, and before Melinda joined her, she spun in front of Early. "I'm in the book."

"What book?" Early asked.

Melinda smiled. "The phone book."

"Yeah, we are too."

I knocked on Early's head. "Do you have rocks in there?"

"Shut up."

When the girls were out of sight, I backtracked behind the stables, Chris and Early following between the wooden planks. Keith was on top of her now. He had pulled her pants down.

"They're doing it," Early said.

Lily wasn't struggling, and her thighs were thrusting up. Sorrow streaked through me. My gut churned.

"You ever see anyone do it before?" Chris asked.

"Have you?" Early said.

"I asked you first."

Early shook his head and turned away.

"Listen to her," Chris said.

I bolted and heard Early behind me saying, "I'm outta here." My mind was racing so fast that I couldn't breathe. Panic overwhelmed me.

"She was wasted," Chris said when he'd caught up to us.

I plunged both hands into the pockets of my Levis. "So what? Keith's uncool to take advantage of her like that."

I should have walked home, but I couldn't leave. I was leaning against Keith's car when he appeared, walking fast. Lily trailed behind him, her shoulders slumped, her gaze focused on her feet. I had been fantasizing about kicking Keith's ass when he showed up, but I didn't say a word.

"Hey, get off the car," Keith said.

I stepped away. Keith checked the dented Malibu for new scratches. He didn't find any.

"We gotta go home," I said.

"The peewee leaguers got to go home," Keith said, unlocking the car. He didn't look at anyone.

Early and Chris silently slipped into the back seat.

Lily's blue eyes were moist, vulnerable. She got in front,

keeping her head down. Keith clicked in the *Diamond Dogs* 8-track. He mumbled along to the tracks, perhaps trying to avoid thinking about Lily, who never took her chin off her chest. Maybe it was his way of dealing with it. I did not sing along.

When Keith dropped her off at a large two-story house in one of the nicest neighborhoods in town, he said, "I'll call you."

She looked at him but didn't speak, and as soon as she got around the car, Keith sped off.

For years I had admired Keith. He'd given us rides and advice and booze and pot, always generous with the wad of cash he had in his leather wallet. He also looked so cool in a James Dean sort of way, and he seemed unafraid of anything. I thought I hated him now, and even though I feared him, I knew I might try to hurt him, despite my confusion about him.

III

EARLY, CHRIS, AND I PEDALED our bikes up a dirt road on the outskirts of town. The sun seemed extremely close today. Tall, sharp white grass layered most of the valley. To the south were a forest and several barely visible ranches.

"I don't believe it," I said.

"Believe it," Early said.

Chris pointed to an isolated oak tree in the distance. "There it is, the hanging tree."

The oak was huge, its branches twisting every direction. A dark moss that I didn't see on any other tree hung off it.

"Who told you about this place?"

"Man, everyone has heard about it."

"I never heard about it." I had barely been out of the house for a week, except for baseball practice. I didn't want to see anyone. Eventually boredom and the news about Lily had brought me out that afternoon. Early had told me a witch spoke through a Ouija board and possessed her. "It opens the door to evil," he'd said.

I stared at the tree. "What?" I acted as if I thought it was crazy, but I felt something in the bottom of my stomach that scared me and made me feel empty of even who I was.

"I heard a candle flamed up for no reason and caught the room on fire," Chris said.

"Who said that?" I asked.

"Monica told me."

"Monica is an idiot."

Early and Chris ignored me.

The closer I came to the tree, the spookier the moss and the huge size of the tree seemed. That and the eerie silence made me believe what they were saying.

"She better see a psychologist," Early said.

"Or a witch doctor," Chris said.

"The weird thing is…" Early started to say.

"The weird thing?" Chris asked.

"Yeah." Early faced me with a defiant tone and intense, wide-open eyes. "There was a woman named Sylvia a hundred years ago that was hung on a tree out here."

"No way," I said.

"Yeah way," Early said.

"I don't believe it."

"It's in the library, check it out."

At the tree, I dropped my bike and inspected the noose strung up on a branch. It looked about a hundred years old, thick and coarse, hanging amid the dark moss that blanketed the tree.

It was almost always windy in this area. We'd gotten used to it and learned to deal with it, but today there was no wind. Nothing. A strange tremor rushed through me. "Someone put that there!" I said, unable to take my eyes off the noose. "I'm gonna hurt Keith if he did this."

"Keith didn't think it was funny," Chris said. "He's pissed."

I stood directly under the noose, sensing my own mortality crawling through me. My youth seemed to be slipping away. I wanted to run from this place.

"My mom says things like that happen to vulnerable kids.

They go crazy, join cults or gangs or something," Early said.

"I'm going to take it down." I climbed the wide trunk toward the branch where the noose hung.

"Someone's coming," Early announced, his voice cracking.

I plopped to the ground, and with some trouble, we hid our bikes behind heavy bushes maybe twenty yards away. Chris and Early fought to stay out of sight and get the best view of the still-distant car.

"Move over," Early said, elbowing me.

I slid forward. "It's probably passing by."

"To where?" Chris asked.

The paved road wound around the mountain, seemingly to nowhere. Dust rose from the ground when the car crawled onto the dirt trail and up to the tree. The three of us stopped moving and our apprehension kept us silent, but I knew who was in that car.

A large, important-looking man in a suit and no tie stepped out of the car and gaped at the tree. A tired blonde with a pained expression joined him. Her motions were jerky, as if she were in a constant state of desperation. She folded her arms and would not get any closer to the noose. Lily, wearing blue jeans and a black T-shirt, hopped out. She slammed the door shut and leaned against the hood.

"Lily's parents," Chris whispered.

I could not imagine what Lily's father was thinking. He glanced at his wife, then back at the tree.

I wanted to let Lily and her family know I was on their side, that we hadn't put it up. I looked at Early, who put his index finger to his lips.

Lily's father punched the air below the noose. "This is a hoax."

"It's real. I've felt it!" Lily shouted. She stomped off a few feet from the tree toward the road.

Lily's father paced about, running a hand through his hair. Lily's mother twisted her fingers. Wind appeared from nowhere, stirring up dust and the bushes around us.

"That rope could've been found anywhere," he said to his wife.

"I don't care!" Lily said.

Her mother approached Lily as if to comfort her, but Lily pulled away.

Her father seemed to sense someone watching him. He looked over the surrounding area and even kicked at the ground that we'd just ridden over near the tree. My bike reflected the sun. Had he noticed it? What would Lily think of us being there? That was what worried me the most.

"Bill, come on. We've seen enough. Let's go," his wife said.

Lily's father stepped toward where we were crouched down, and stared straight at us. We were about to be caught. Then Lily screamed, "I don't care if you believe me or if that stupid psychologist believes me! She talks to me!"

"We know you believe it, honey," her mother said.

"You don't understand. It comes through me."

Her father jerked his head toward Lily, then ordered them all into the car. Finally the doors slammed, and the engine started.

When they were out of sight, I surveyed the dry grass and ugly trees, the dirt road, and the oil rig silently hammering up and down in the distance. I went down on one knee. "Let's get out of here."

"It's coming," Early said as Chris placed a nickel on the track. The train chugged toward us, making the nickel fall. Chris picked it up like he had all the time in the world.

"Don't mess around," Early said.

Chris set the nickel on the track again.

"Hurry up!" I waved for Chris to get back, but he leaped to the other side. The train chugged by, spinning the nickel intro the air.

When it had passed, Chris was standing across the tracks, smiling and holding up the flattened nickel.

The nickel was stretched out, creating a caricature of Jefferson.

"Someone told me you can derail a train that way," Early said.

"I told you that," Chris said, laughing.

Early had his hands on his hips. "It could've slid off and killed you."

"Who cares?" I said.

"I care. I want to make it to sixteen."

Chris tossed the nickel in his left hand. "I care because I want a cool car."

I wheeled my bike past the hangar where train cars were once loaded and unloaded. It was abandoned now, with rows and rows of small windows at the top, many of them broken. Hundreds of pigeons rested on the beams. I dumped my bike, picked up a rock, and threw it through a window. The ruffled pigeons fluttered and cooed.

"You're going to get us in trouble," Early said.

"Who cares?"

"Yeah, who cares," Chris said, joining me.

Small rocks and pebbles lay scattered around the train station and tracks. We smashed four or five more windows, watching the old glass rain to the ground. The pigeons rioted now, their wings flapping in protest.

"The fuzz!"

A police car edged up at the end of the street, to the left of the railroad station.

I tried to take off on my bike down the tracks, but riding over the pebbles slowed me.

"Dump them," Chris said.

The police car bumped along on the opposite side of the tracks, where the Garzas had headed us off a week earlier.

Fortunately, a slow train provided cover. Early skidded to a stop, forcing Chris and me to stop too.

"Which way?" Early asked.

"We'd better backtrack."

"Let's go downtown. They'll never find us there."

"They'll catch at least one of us before we get there," I said, not wanting to split up.

"The park."

It seemed like a brilliant idea. We raced to a fence plank that slid out so the initiated could squeeze themselves into the ballpark for free. Inside, we scrambled up the stairs to the unlocked announcer's box above home plate.

"My dad's gonna kick my butt if I'm caught," Early said.

"We're safe here."

I peeked over the box to see the neighborhood's Spanish-style rooftops and tree-lined streets, and the distant mountains.

"How long do you think they'll be looking for us?" Early asked.

"All day," Chris said.

"What's the big deal? We get a whipping and laugh about it in a month. How about Lily? She might never be all right." My voice cracked as I sank into the corner.

"What do you want us to do about it?" Early asked in a practical tone.

"Help her. I don't know…be her friend. Nothing, I guess."

"She'll be all right," Chris said.

"I hope so."

We hung out there for an hour, then ventured onto side streets until we reached downtown. There we sat in front of Fosters Freeze, munching on hamburgers and fries at the table outside while traffic cruised by on the busy street. A line of cars waited to fill up at a cheap gas station across the way. Exhaust permeated the air.

Early had his mouth full when Keith appeared, grabbing him in a headlock.

"Let me go, you asshole," Early choked out, kicking and flailing his arms, but Keith was strong, too strong for Early.

"What the hell are you peewee leaguers doing on Broadway?" Keith let go of Early. "You have a death wish?"

I glanced at Chris and Early. "The cops know who we are?"

"What are you talking about? You triplets better hide out at my house," Keith said.

"Why?"

"Because I said so." Keith gestured with his thumb toward his car.

I wasn't about to follow him. "Who died and made you king?"

"I'm having a party, and Melinda and Monica are going to be there." Keith winked at me. "Lily's going to be there too—or whoever she is."

I grabbed his arm. "That's pretty uncool, Keith."

Keith spun around and bumped me hard. "Don't tell me what's uncool, you little pipsqueak. You haven't seen nothing. I've been through thick and thick."

His fury paralyzed me for a moment, but I held my ground. "You humiliated her, and now she's all screwed up."

"She humiliated herself. I ain't got nothing to do with that. I don't mess around with her anymore," Keith said, getting in my face before backing off. "You punks don't appreciate nothing I've done for you. Who's gonna save your little asses when the Southsiders find you? The Garzas' father died, you little fucks, and the family is blaming you, especially Chris." Keith shook his head, disgusted. "I've been driving all over town looking for you to help you out. Thanks a lot, Keith. Thanks for thinking of us and giving us all those rides and wrecking your car for us." Keith tossed his cigarette on the ground, then waved at us as if to say, *Get lost*. He strutted to his car.

Chris chased him down and stopped in front of him. "What are you talking about?"

"You want to be on your own, then you're on your own," Keith said.

"Come on, Keith," Early said, standing alongside Chris. "You were acting like an idiot with that girl."

I was proud of Early, but Keith flipped around and glared at him. I put my hand on Early's shoulder.

The veins on Keith's forehead and neck were huge and bulging. "You don't know where I've been. I don't owe anyone anything."

"What are you talking about?" I asked.

Keith turned slowly to me, and I swallowed my fear, believing Keith might beat the crap out of me this time. "I'm getting really tired of you. The way you look at me as if I'm dirt." He poked me in the chest.

I jumped back, then jerked toward him as if I were attacking him, screaming, "She never did anything to you or to anybody!"

Keith kicked the ground. He suddenly didn't seem angry. "I fucked up. I know I fucked up. So shut the fuck up. I'll deal with it my way."

Chris angled himself between Keith and me. "All right, it's cool. It's over."

Chris, Early, and I glanced at each other.

"Okay," Early said.

"The Garzas' father died. What's that got to do with us?" Chris asked. "It's not our fault."

"Tell the Garza brothers that. I'm sure they'll understand." Keith lit another cigarette and stepped back from Chris.

"How'd he die?" Chris asked, moving Keith away from me.

"Day after the wreck, the old man's heart overheats. They said if he dies, you three aren't going to be around much longer either. He croaked this morning. They're blaming you lucky lizards—especially you," Keith said, nodding at Chris.

"Let's get out of here," Chris said.

Keith lived in the oldest part of town. He had painted his two-story Victorian house white with blue trim. The lawn was mown and manicured. The backyard was huge—four times the size of the house.

Keith's party was a mixture of rough-looking characters: surfers, punks, farmers, and a few construction and city workers. I was the youngest one there and stuck out. Early, Chris, and I sat against the backyard fence, watching a scuffle between two drunken losers who stumbled every time they missed each other with a punch.

"Keith sure knows how to throw a party," Early said.

I stood and brushed the grass off my pants.

"You going to break it up?" Early asked.

"It's been a long day. I think I deserve a beer, like my old man says."

"Get me one too," Chris said.

Early smacked me on the shoulder. "Me three."

I wandered over to the keg, which stood behind a brawny guy with a mustache.

"What's your name?" he asked.

261

"Jay."

"Did your old man used to own a grocery store?"

I nodded. My father did have a market that went out of business when the big chains opened two stores nearby.

"Damn, that was a nice market. I know your father," the guy said. "He used to give me free wieners when I was a kid." He slapped my back. "He's a good man. If anyone gives you trouble, let me know."

"Cool," I said.

"Let me get you a beer."

"I need three."

"Whoa!" The guy held his hands out for me to stop.

"They're not all for me."

I spotted Melinda and Monica running into the house. The guy poured me three big cups filled to the brim with beer.

"Thanks a lot."

"Be cool."

I carried the beers to Chris and Early. "Melinda and Monica are here," I said.

"You gonna bogart those?" Early asked.

I handed them over. "Let's go inside and see what they're doing." I sipped mine. I didn't like it, except that it was cold.

"I don't want any part of them," Early said.

"Me either," Chris said.

I looked back and forth between them several times, then stopped, knowing how desperate I must appear.

"You're thinking about her, aren't you?" Early asked.

"Oh, forget you both," I said, and hurried to the house.

Inside, I searched for Lily but found Keith smoking a cigarette at the bottom of the stairs.

"If it ain't the Boy Wonder." Keith started to sing the Batman theme: "Doo-doo-doo-doo-doo-doo-doo doo doo." Next to him stood a girl who kept twisting her curly hair around her finger. She laughed for no reason, then kissed my cheek and put her hand on my neck.

I tried to ignore her.

"Where's Melinda and them?" I asked.

"Don't you mean 'Where's Lily?'" Keith laughed along with the girl, who took her arm off me.

"All right, where is she?"

"I'll only tell you if you have a drink with me." Keith waved his beer in my face.

"I'll drink with you, Keith."

"You will? That's all I wanted to hear."

Keith raised his plastic cup and tapped mine. I drank, but then he shoved my cup back, forcing beer down my throat. It spilled when I pulled my head away.

"You asshole." I threw a punch at him but hit only air.

Keith grinned. "I owed you one."

I kept my fists raised.

"Relax, come on. You want to see? I'll show you," Keith said. "Come on, Boy Wonder." He hummed the Batman theme again and headed up the narrow stairs to what looked more like an attic than a second story.

Keith gestured to me. "Go on in. I don't want anything to do with this."

I was suddenly concerned about entering. I swallowed hard, worried I would see something I didn't want to see.

"Go on, Boy Wonder."

I cracked open the door.

Candles everywhere lit the room, casting throbbing shadows on posters of Led Zeppelin, Black Sabbath, and Blue Öyster Cult. Lily, Melinda, and Monica sat around a board with a thin, long-haired guy I had never seen before.

I didn't think they noticed me come in. Lily glanced up, but it was as if she didn't recognize me. Her hands were on something that seemed to swing them to certain letters on the board—a Ouija board.

"S-Y-L-V-I-A." Melinda spelled out the letters.

Monica's hair was long and parted in the middle. Her gaze darted between Melinda and Lily. "Ask her a question. Ask her what she wants," she said.

"What do you want?" Lily asked in a slow, deep monotone.

It was her voice, but I sensed an oppressive presence in her mind and in the air. As Lily's hands shot across the board, the candles brightened as one. At that moment I felt a force aligned against me—staring right at me.

"S-A-C-R-I-F-I-C-E. Sacrifice," Melinda interpreted.

"Who? Sacrifice who?" Monica asked, her eager eyes reflecting the candle flames.

Lily's bizarre behavior was a game to them, but it wasn't her causing this. It was outside her. "This ain't right," I said.

"Shh," Monica said.

Something inside me ticked and burned, a fuse in my mind. "This is bad."

"Shut up or get out, Jay."

"You get out!" I shouted. "All of you, get out!" I lunged for the Ouija board, but Lily grabbed it first and held it down like she was fighting for her life. I don't know how I did it because it didn't feel like me, but in one swift motion I flung the board into the air.

"You idiot, Jay," Melinda snarled. "Get out of here."

"What an asshole," Monica said.

I switched on the light. The guy moved toward me, but I hit him twice, and he rushed by me to get out the door.

Keith appeared behind me. It was only then I realized Lily was screaming.

"Jesus," Keith said.

I reached down and touched the whimpering Lily, who had curled up on the floor.

"Get out and stay out, Jay. This is all your fault," Monica yelled.

Keith seemed contrite, though, and bent down near Lily, then laid a blanket over her. "You better go. I'll take care of this," he said softly to me, nodding toward the door.

I ran down the stairs, past Chris and Early, and through the curious crowd. My two friends followed me out onto the street.

"What happened?"

I didn't stop.

"Jay, wait up!" Early shouted.

I kept on running.

IV

I DIDN'T SHOW UP to the championship game against Early's team. I took the phone off the hook because it rang constantly starting an hour before game time. No one was home, so I lay on my bed listening to Bowie's "Rock 'n' Roll Suicide" and the entire *Ziggy Stardust* album on my little cassette player.

Chris and Early showed up at my place after the game. Early dangled his huge trophy from his hand. Chris and I each received a trophy about half the size. He had brought mine with him.

I put my trophy in my room, and we decided to walk downtown to Taco Bell.

"Why didn't you show up?" Early asked.

"I forgot," I said.

"Bullshit," Chris said.

"I hate sports and everything right now."

Chris laughed. "The coach is pissed," he said.

Early threw his trophy against the cement sidewalk, cracking off the gold batter on top.

"What the hell, Early," I said, throwing out my arms.

"Come on, Early, you still deserve it," Chris said.

"I don't want it." Early looked at me indignantly and kicked the trophy to the curb.

"It's just a game," I said.

"It was just a game. Now it's something different." Early waited for my explanation. When he didn't get it, he marched off.

"Early, come back."

I knew he wouldn't.

I returned home while Chris continued to Taco Bell and went straight to my room to lie on my bed. At some point, I looked out through the thick blinds, as I often did.

Across the street, trimmed olive-green trees lined the neighbors' backyard fence. Lily crouched between the trees, her wild locks covering her face.

She wouldn't see me if I exited out the back, so I went through the rear gate and walked straight across the street. I hesitated before I reached the trees.

"Hi." She was already standing waiting for me.

"Hi," I managed. "What are you doing here?"

"I don't know."

"No one's home. You want to come in and listen to Bowie?"

"No." She shook her golden hair.

"You like Bowie?"

She nodded.

"He's my favorite."

"Mine too," she said, and smiled.

"You want to walk to the park?"

She nodded again.

Behind my house, an ivy-lined path the width of a driveway led to a large grassy area. We strolled in silence toward the children's playground, then sat beneath a pungent eucalyptus tree.

"How did you know where I live?" I asked.

"I looked it up in the phone book." She floated her palm above the grass.

"I'm sorry about the other night."

When she didn't reply, I wondered if I should have kept my mouth shut.

Then she stared at me. "All those spirits ran from you," she said.

"Where did they go?"

"Back in the board, I guess."

The wind stopped; the air was calm, almost serene.

"They came for me again, you know," she said. "The spirits."

I let her know I believed her because I had felt it too.

She flipped her hair. "They were fighting for control of my mind, and I thought, 'They can have me.' Then I thought about what you did. You wrestled with them, and you jumped up and turned on the light. So that's what I did too. I knew they were angry, but I kept thinking of you, and they couldn't do anything to me."

Part of me vibrated with life. "Do you think they'll come back?"

"No. Keith told me he burned the Ouija board."

I tightened at the mention of Keith's name, but I let it go. "That's good. I hate that thing."

"I want to go away where no one knows me. I'm going to be a freak here forever."

"You're only fifteen."

She flashed a smile. "I don't know where, not here."

"I think you're cool."

I walked Lily home to her parents' large white Colonial-style house.

At the open garage, Lily's father and a cute little girl, who must have been her sister, appeared. Her father glared but said nothing. Lily walked past him without a word.

V

AS I NEARED HOME, I saw Early, wearing all black and a baseball cap, pacing near the entrance to the park. His bike and mine—he must have retrieved them from the train station—leaned against the fence. A woman wearing a robe appeared to be monitoring him from across the street.

"Hey, man, I'm sorry about today," I said, glad to get it off my chest.

Early paced, skittish and nervous, and I started to think it was a big mistake to not show up to the game because of how it had affected him.

"We'll worry about that later," Early said, talking fast. "Did Chris's parents call yours?"

"They're working. Why?"

"He's in the hospital. Beaten up pretty bad," Early said.

The woman across the street slammed her door.

"Garzas?"

Early started pacing again. "We're not supposed to be out right now. The police are looking for us, trying to make us stay in."

"Let's go."

In the hospital we hurried through the corridors, halting when we saw Chris's father and a doctor exit a room on the second floor. When they moved out of view, Early and I slipped inside.

In the first bed was an older man with a tube up one nostril. He got a bit wide-eyed when Early and I passed him.

A curtain was drawn between the two beds; Chris was on the window side.

"Early, Jay," Chris said, smiling.

His ribs were taped, his left arm was in a big cast, and his face was bruised and cut. A heavy weight pushed against my chest, and I didn't feel like I could move.

"It took all of them to get me down. Took them a while, too," Chris said.

"That's cool," Early said.

"It's not so bad," Chris continued. "I'm not going to die or anything. Didn't even get a concussion. Guess my head was too hard."

"I guess there's nothing in there," I said.

It looked like it hurt Chris to laugh.

"Garzas," Early said to no one.

"It doesn't matter. It's over," Chris said.

"They don't care. They hate you...us," I said.

"It's over," Chris said.

Early took off his hat. "There's no way Keith will take this lying down."

Chris turned to the window.

"He's right," I said. "We'll try to be cool."

Early nodded. "Maybe the police will take care of it."

Chris glanced back toward us, but this time he looked sad.

Outside, we walked our bikes across the parking lot.

"What are we going to do, Early?"

"We got to do something."

"You heard what he said."

Early threw phantom punches. "We can't act like something didn't happen."

"Uh-oh. Early!"

A rusty old gas guzzler with a hood the length of a boat was cruising right at us and making a deep, popping rumble.

We pivoted and walked in the opposite direction.

"How many are in there?" Early asked, walking faster.

The car followed. "I can't tell."

The closer we got to the hospital, the faster we walked. The car kept the same pace. "You ready?" I asked.

"I'm ready," Early said, dropping his bike.

I dropped mine, and we sprinted across the grass and back inside the hospital. I heard the engine rev.

We hurried through the hospital to the exit in the back.

The car was waiting for us.

Smiling and revving the engine of the dented, souped-up wreck was Keith. "Come on, peewee leaguers. We got business to take care of."

Keith cruised through what he called the Southside badlands, which, except for a couple homes, looked like any other neighborhood to me.

"We'll pick them off one at a time," Keith said, pulling the car to the side.

Early and I exchanged a glance. "We don't think that's right," I said, speaking for both of us.

"You got a better idea?" Keith asked.

Two young men with shaved heads strolled by, scowling at us.

"I don't know about coming to their neighborhood to fight them," Early said.

"What, do you think I have rocks in my head? We're not going to fight them here," Keith said in a belligerent tone. He lit a cigarette and took a long drag. "We're looking for them," he added calmly, as if he wasn't worried about anything. "Then we'll see what happens."

Several guys raced across the street into a house that had three beat-up cars parked on what was left of the lawn.

"All I'm saying is, I have a bad feeling about this," Early said.

Keith hit the steering wheel with his palm. "How do you think Chris feels?"

"He wants us to forget about it," Early said.

Keith pulled out a revolver. "That's exactly what I'm trying to do—forget about it for good."

"Oh, man. No. No way." I wanted no part of it. Chris was right, I thought. Nothing good would come from this.

Keith played with the chamber and rolled it around in front of my face. "Is Chris your friend?"

"He's our best friend," Early said, his tone suggesting Keith was not part of that friendship.

"Take me home, Keith," I said.

"Me too."

"Of course you have a bad feeling," Keith snarled. "You're in their stinking neighborhood."

I cracked open the door. "This ain't right. I'm getting out of here one way or another."

"We're not that far from Main Street," Early said.

Keith played with the bullets and the gun. I waited to see if he would drive us home.

Early kicked open the back door. "I'm walking."

"When it happens to you two, don't come crying to me, you hear?" Keith shouted.

"We'll see you, Keith," I said, opening the door.

Keith pointed the gun at me and pulled the trigger. *Click.* My heart stopped. Then I got out and slammed the door.

I brushed my hair into my face. Early lowered his baseball cap to hide himself. We ran for several blocks, finally slowing when we neared a busy intersection.

"You think he'll be all right?" I asked.

"He'll be all right. Who knows about anyone else."

The sound of two gunshots echoed around me.

Early and I looked at each other. We knew we had to get out of there fast.

When we reached the corner, I saw Keith driving wildly, turning left and away from us. He must not have seen us. Four or five of the Garza gang were in the Garza leader's Nova, which screeched to a stop. Perhaps they'd thought better of chasing a guy who was carrying a gun.

A woman across the street pointed at Early and me. "Northsiders!"

Early and I ran for our lives, across lawns and streets. I turned around, and they were jumping out of the Nova, which had stopped behind us. I heard the footsteps and curses. I wasn't far behind Early. The Garza gang—four of them, anyway—tackled me. I threw a couple of punches and kicks, but they swarmed me, and I couldn't see much, the blows coming from every direction.

I curled up and protected my head, giving them only my back to pummel.

"Get out, Jay! Run!"

That was Early's voice. I squirmed and rolled and saw him throwing wild punches. They were all over him too, but Early wouldn't go down. Someone kicked me in the gut when I tried to get up. Then I saw it: a shiny three-inch blade swinging toward Early.

"No!"

Early was cut. The blood must have scared them because they all stopped fighting.

"Let's get out of here. This is too hot," one of them said.

They jumped in the Nova and raced away.

Early was on his back. I heard sirens as I crawled to him. Blood soaked his shirt.

"You shouldn't have come back for me," I said.

"I guess not." Early tried to stand.

I hovered over him. "Stay down."

He stopped trying to move.

"Does it hurt?" I asked.

"Only when I do this." Early flapped his right arm like a chicken.

"Then don't do that," I said, laughing and breaking into sobs.

He laughed, then started to cry too.

At the hospital, the medics rushed Early into the emergency room. I didn't think I had any broken bones, just lots of lumps and bruises, but sharp pain throbbed in my left hip and shoulder. The police officer who had driven me over was speaking to a nurse. No one paid attention to me as I limped toward the corridor.

"Where you going, Jay?" the police officer called out to me before I got around the corner.

"To make a phone call," I said.

"We're already trying to get ahold of your parents."

"I'm gonna call my girlfriend."

The officer nodded. I turned the corner, then walked to the back door as fast as I could. I made it to the parking lot, found my bike, and rode through the field behind the hospital.

I was really hurting by the time I reached Lily's street. I laid the bike on someone else's lawn and sat on the curb under a streetlamp for half an hour.

"Jay?" Lily called down from a second-story window.

I waved, and she came right out and sat next to me. I couldn't speak. I shook my head, dizzy, and she wrapped her arm around me and helped me up and inside.

Her mother found us fifteen minutes later. My head had started to ache. They rushed me back to the hospital, where my crying mother met me.

I found out that night that Early was going to be okay and there would be no permanent damage.

The next week, the kids in town made us out to be heroes, especially Early. I guess that's what happens when you're stabbed. But Early's local fame didn't last long. His family moved three months later.

Chris and I drifted apart too, although we remained friends, and Lily became my first girlfriend. Something changed in me after that summer, though. Except for Lily, I retreated from the world into books and music; a certain otherness surrounded me. I didn't understand what that meant until later.

SEEDS FROM '79

1

SNAP. SNAP. SNAP. Jay danced, watched, waited. He jabbed. *Snap.* The burlap punching bag careened back and forth, swinging from the huge wooden beam. *Snap, snap, snap.* A left-right-left combination. Keeping his guard up, he grunted and side-kicked the bag. On the dryer, a boom box blared Bowie's "Look Back in Anger."

Jay stalked the bag, his wet hair matted against his cheeks. Perspiration rolled down his back.

The music clicked off.

"He's asleep. I don't want to wake him," Jay's mother said, standing on the steps next to the dryer.

Jay lost focus and energy without the music. He snapped the bag one more time and glared at his mother. She was slim, with a beautiful smile and gorgeous hair. A lot of men were attracted to her.

He strutted to the front of the open garage, his spine burning as if his feelings were a raw nerve. Damn, he hated her eyes, that hurt gaze. It made him feel at fault for her pain. Hands on his hips, he scowled through the open garage door, past the '65 Chevy Malibu he'd purchased when he turned sixteen and his mother's 1978 BMW. A grumpy neighbor was raking his lawn across the street.

"Are you done yet?" Jay asked, glancing at her.

"Give me a minute," she said, pulling towels out of the dryer.

"Jesus." He turned back around.

After a long shower, he was out the front door without a word to his mother, who sat at the kitchen table. She glanced at him but didn't say anything. He shoved his hands in his tattered jeans, searching for his lighter, then lit a cigarette.

The guy raking next door frowned at him as if he disapproved of the smoking. Jay took a long drag and flicked the cigarette toward the neighbor.

Fifteen minutes later, in his friend Brian's back room, he blew smoke rings up at the wall-to-wall posters of the Clash, Blondie, and Bowie. Across from him was an elaborate stereo system and hundreds of records organized in alphabetical order. Brian, a slim Mexican American who had gone to Catholic school with Jay since the first grade, shared one of the three thrift store sofas in the room. Kevin—a surfer with extremely long hair—and Billy sat on the other two.

Brian threw back his silky black hair and nodded at Jay.

Kevin fingered through the records, picking out a Donovan album.

"None of that sixties shit, Kevin," Billy said, patting his pompadour.

Jay had his drawing pad and pencil out. He began to sketch.

"I hate that sixties crap. Put on the Clash," Billy said.

"I want to hear myself think." Kevin's voice cracked as if he were upset.

"Hear yourself think?" Brian said. "How does that work, Jay?"

Jay ignored him.

"It doesn't. Put on the Clash," Billy said.

"'Put on the Clash. Put on the Clash.' That's all you ever want to listen to. Why don't you try and expand your horizons for once?"

"Donovan will expand my horizons?"

Jay set down the pencil and laughed. Billy emptied a Thai stick on an album jacket to clean out its seeds. Kevin, well over six feet tall, held the Donovan record over his head, then dropped it at Billy's feet. Brian scrunched up his face at Jay and the familiar scene.

"'Put on the Clash. Put on the Clash,'" Kevin said.

As Brian slipped the Donovan record back in its sleeve, Jay chose Bowie's new album, *Lodger*, and put it on the turntable.

Kevin crossed his arms and glared at Jay and Billy.

"Seeds. This is loaded with seeds," Billy complained.

"Asshole," Kevin said.

Billy smiled. He seemed pleased.

Jay took his sketch of a spiky-haired David Bowie and pinned it to the wall. "The Thin White Duke" was written on Bowie's shirt. It looked cool, he thought, but no one commented on it.

Billy kept loading the bong and passing it around. Jay must have taken four hits. Everything was funny: Brian lighting the wrong end of a cigarette, Kevin's coughing attack, Billy's wisecracks.

Their fun ended when Brian warned that his stepmother would be off work soon, and they should leave for the party. Jay didn't want to go, but what else was he going to do? Go home?

Outdoors, the stars seemed within reach to Jay. The fresh air made him feel higher. He imagined himself still in control but separate from the world. He heard voices far behind him, but when he turned, Kevin and Billy were only a couple of feet away, leaning against the hood of his Malibu.

Jay and Brian climbed in the front seat while Kevin and Billy jumped into the back. Jay turned to Billy. They had not spoken much all night. "What about this party?" he said. There might be people who didn't like the Rio Madre kids, especially Billy. He was disliked by a lot of people for good reasons, particularly for being manipulative, lying, and never paying for anything. "We'll be outnumbered, and we're pretty stoned."

"We'll be okay," Billy said without looking at him.

Jay smelled something—Kevin puffing on a joint.

"Pass that up here," Jay said.

"You got it."

Jay grabbed it and heaved it out the window.

"What the hell are you doing, man? I've been saving that," Kevin yelled.

Jay pulled the car to the side. The moon was full, stars thick in the luminous country sky. Moonlight reflected off the water that separated rows of lettuce running into the distant frame of the mountains.

"I've been pulled over twice this month," Jay said. "I'm not going to jail for anyone or anything."

"You didn't have to toss it out the window. That was the last of my allowance."

Jay took a five out of a wallet full of bills and dropped it on Kevin's lap. "This should cover it."

Outside the party, he parked behind an old muscle car. At the back gate a big, bearded character collected money in a Folger's coffee can.

"Two bucks for you guys," the bearded guy said.

"Here's four. I got this dude," Jay said, nodding at Brian.

The backyard population consisted of dropouts, bikers, construction workers, surfers, heads, losers, and jocks. It was mostly guys standing around drinking beer and smoking something.

The house itself was dilapidated, with parts of the roof missing and no screens on the windows. The pulse of the party beat around the three kegs set up next to the sliding glass door.

Kevin immediately gravitated toward a surfer chick with stringy blond hair who he was always hooking up with. Brian met his longtime girlfriend, Karla, who was Lily's best friend. Billy had entered the house as soon as they got into the backyard.

"I'll get us some beer," Jay said.

Lily skipped up to him—now Jay's ex-girlfriend. She had grown a few inches the past year, and she had let her straight blond hair grow to the middle of her back. "I called you the other day," she said, sounding as if she might cry.

"I know."

At the keg, he pumped the tap and filled her cup.

"I can't help it," she said.

"I can't either."

"I still don't understand," she said, her eyes enveloping him with her pain.

Jay didn't understand either. They *were* perfect. He'd broken up with her because she didn't graduate high school and wasn't considering college. He wondered if that was shallow. They had been together more than three years. Did he love her? He did, but he wasn't ready to settle down. He wanted to experience life first. This town oppressed him. He was only here because the local junior college was the best he could afford, even though he'd gotten into UCLA.

"I want to talk about what happened to us," she said, stroking his arm. They moved to a corner of the backyard for privacy.

"We've talked a hundred times," he said.

Anger narrowed Lily's eyes. "You want to be with that chick you work with."

He had no idea she knew Ellen existed. "She's a friend. We understand each other." As soon as he said it, he knew it was a mistake. In fact, Ellen didn't understand him, and he didn't understand her. He didn't know why he'd said it.

"And we don't?" Lily huffed and strode into the house.

"I didn't mean that," Jay said feebly.

Jay chain-smoked, waiting for Lily to come back out so he could apologize, but then he saw Ellen. She wore high-top Chuck Taylors, which he liked, and her auburn hair was hanging loose. Ellen attended UCLA and was majoring in English. Her slinky, beach-tanned friend, Ann, followed her into the yard. Jay waved them over to the grassy slope. The girls were out of place at this party.

"So, this is a three-kegger?" Ellen asked.

"Four." Jay nodded to a skinny guy who was carrying another keg in.

Ellen frowned. Jay nodded at Ann, who had the pinched expression of someone repulsed by everything, including the air around her.

"I'm glad you could make it," he said to Ellen.

"If I hadn't seen your car outside, I wouldn't have come in," Ellen said. "Besides, I want to know if all those stories you tell me are true."

"Are Charles and David coming in or not?" Ann asked, looking over her shoulder toward the entrance.

No one in Jay's circle came near them. Karla hated girls like Ellen and Ann. Lily didn't hate anyone, Jay knew, but when she came back outside, she saw him talking to Ellen, then ran back into the house. Out of the corner of his eye he saw Kevin sneaking out of the party with the surfer girl. God knows what Billy was doing.

Ellen's and Ann's boyfriends, Charles and David, appeared—preppy, wealthy, and tall. Jay detested them.

"I paid five dollars to come in this…backyard. It's obviously worth it," Charles said. He ignored Jay.

"We are going to die," David said.

Ellen smirked. "Stop it, Jay's here."

"We are going to die," Charles said, looking at David, then stuffing his hands in his chinos. "If we leave now, we can get to the game before the second quarter."

"Come on, Ellen. Let's get out of here," Ann said.

Charles and company were right. It was a party for losers.

"Fight!" The word echoed everywhere. Most of the party scrambled toward the excitement, somewhere out front.

Jay looked for Billy and didn't see him. Damn, it had to be Billy. He considered Ellen. "I gotta go."

"Where are you going?"

Jay pushed his way through the crowd to the ring of spectators in the front yard. Billy was beating up a smaller guy, smashing the kid's face with his fist, pummeling him long after there was anything left in the guy. Jay pulled him off. Only Billy's hands were bruised.

"Jesus, Billy."

Billy backed up and strutted away. Jay didn't want to follow him, but his car was parked in the same direction. He watched several girls trying to help the poor guy stand.

A skinny girl pointed at Jay. "He was with him."

"Where's your friend?" a guy with a marine crew cut asked Jay.

"I ain't a part of this, man," Jay said.

"I'm going to ask you one more time. Where's your friend?" The marine bent his thick neck and stuck his tight, regimented face in Jay's.

Police sirens wailed, closing in on the neighborhood.

"Tell your friend if I find him, I'll kill him," the marine said. He spat in the gutter and marched away.

Jay crossed the street right in front of a police car. Two blocks away, he found Billy and shoved him. "Fuck you, Billy. I told you there'd be trouble."

Billy pushed him back. "It wasn't my fault."

"Don't give me that shit!"

"The little prick insulted Lily."

Jay turned, and there was Lily with dark, tear-stained eyes. "Well, fuck 'em, then." He trudged to his car to find Kevin in the back seat on top of the surfer girl. "Jesus!"

Jay wandered away onto someone's front lawn. Brian and Karla joined the group, and when Brian started to laugh at Kevin, Karla slapped her boyfriend on the back of the head.

"Ouch!" Brian said, then walked over and knocked on the car window. "Come on, Kevin. We have to go."

Jay approached Lily and lit a cigarette for her. "Are you all right?"

"Yeah, I'm all right."

II

JAY FLICKED OFF THE ALARM and lobbed it into a pile of dirty clothes. He was lying on top of his bed in the same clothes he'd worn the previous night. David Bowie and Bruce Lee posters dominated his room. Books he'd read recently—*Nineteen Eighty-Four*, *The Hustler*, *The Man Who Fell to Earth*, and *Christiane F.*—were stacked above his cheap record player and his albums.

He had loved Bowie's performance in the film *The Man Who Fell to Earth*, so he read the book, which moved him more than the movie, which he'd had a hard time understanding. He'd read *The Hustler* in one day. He had read *Christiane F.* twice and related deeply to her alienation and dive into the Berlin junkie underground. When you started falling, you kept plunging lower. He felt the same in himself sometimes. Bowie's *Diamond Dogs* album referred to Orwell's *Nineteen Eighty-Four* many times, so he had read it on his own as well as for school. Jay sensed it had changed him, but he wasn't sure how, exactly. He was certain that he loved to read, and he was always searching for a new book.

Jay got up and opened the door, but he waited when he heard his mother's whispered telephone conversation in the kitchen.

"I know. I can't. What can I do? Of course, I want to see you again."

On the way to the bathroom, Jay peeked in at his father, who lay on his back in a gurney-type bed. He closed his father's door.

"There's cereal in the cupboard," his mother said, hanging up the phone as Jay strode through the kitchen.

"I'm going to work." He grabbed an apple and rushed past, making sure not to touch her. His sister had married earlier in the year and moved out of the house. He had to get out soon. He was too damn angry living at home.

When Jay arrived at the B. Dalton Bookstore, Ellen was standing behind the counter, working on the schedule. She had been named assistant manager, even though she was only in town for the summer.

"I once kissed a guy who smoked," she said. "It was revolting. I never let him come near me again."

She must have smelled it on him.

Jay squished up the pack in his pocket and tossed it into the wastebasket. "I quit."

"Right," she said.

"I'm serious."

Ellen laughed.

"I discovered an amazing writer," Jay said, eager to talk books with her because she loved reading too, and he had no one else to talk to about literature.

"Oh yeah?" she asked, her voice rising. "Who?" She stopped working and eyed him.

"Walter Tevis. He wrote *The Man Who Fell to Earth* and *The Hustler*."

Ellen pondered the titles. "I saw the movies," she said. "They're both so different. Who does that?" She gestured with both arms.

"That's what I was thinking. The guy is a genius."

She gazed at him curiously until a customer approached the counter.

When Jay finished helping the customer, Ellen sidled up to him. "That's cool that you read both those books."

He smiled. "Thanks."

"I'm going to read them too." She swayed as if off balance, maybe wanting to say more. "I'm sorry, I have to go. I only came in to put the schedule together and go to the bank."

The deflation must have been clear on his face.

"I'll see you later," she said sweetly, then stood close to him and held his hand for a moment.

III

IN THE AFTERNOON A FEW DAYS LATER, Jay sat on
his bed and poured buds onto Bowie's *Heroes* album cover. He
had read in *Rolling Stone* that Bowie had been living and recording in Berlin. Jay knew nothing about Berlin, except what
he read in *Christiane F.*, but there was something about Bowie's
last three albums, which the magazine called Bowie's Berlin
Trilogy, that obsessed him. He considered these his personal
coming-of-age albums. They were so outside the mainstream,
so strange and different and powerful.

Maybe he would find people like himself or Bowie in Berlin,
so he would lose this god-awful gloom that pervaded him.
Despair appeared on the albums, but so did hope.

He cleaned up the bud and separated the seeds, then rolled
a joint with Zig-Zag papers.

In the front room, his father slouched in the recliner, clicking the remote control. He looked so frail, Jay thought.

"Hey, Dad. What's on?"

"Same old shit."

Jay couldn't think of anything else to say. Spirits sagging, he
went out the sliding glass door into the backyard. "*Same old
shit.*" That was his father's favorite phrase.

Jay hurried across the backyard and around the corner, where a row of marijuana plants and weeds led to his ancient play-house. In his facile, little-boy writing, the faded front door read "No Mothers Allowed."

Crouching in front of the playhouse, he torched the joint and inhaled deeply, ignoring the awful blue sky. A seed lay on the ground. Jay flicked it toward some wildflowers.

Like reading, getting high took him outside himself. He doodled in the dirt for a while, and when he looked up, his father was outside, leaning into his walker. Jay was too dumbfounded and stoned to respond. His father seemed puzzled; he stared at Jay as if he hadn't seen him in a long time. Jay thought his father might say something, but he averted his gaze and pushed the walker back to the house. Jay himself wanted to say something, but there was nothing to say.

He left through the back gate, where he found his mother taking golf clubs out of the trunk of her car. She waved, probably curious, but he ignored her and jumped into his Malibu. He wondered who her boyfriend was and if he was married too. He shoved in the Bowie cassette and burned rubber out of there.

Jay drove east along the rich farmland, down a lonely road bordered by fields of cabbage, strawberries, and lettuce. The speedometer hit ninety before the hairpin turn next to a large dairy. He felt no fear, only concentration, as the g-forces pulled him to one side.

A couple of hours later, he drove through a neighborhood full of tract homes and turned up a long driveway. Past the elaborate garden, he pulled up next to Kevin's broken-down Volkswagen with a surf rack on top.

Kevin's tall mother answered the door, wiping her hands on her apron. She was always so friendly to him.

"Jay, what a surprise. It seems like forever since I've seen you." She stepped back to let him in. "You've been working hard on your studies?"

"I have been, Mrs. Johnson." He stepped in. "Is Kevin in his room?"

Kevin's mother seemed interested in speaking with him. The house's decor was clean and comfortable. In the adjoining room, Kevin's balding father slept in a recliner, a newspaper draped over his potbelly.

Jay started toward Kevin's room.

"Do you still go to Mass, Jay?"

"Sometimes."

"Does Kevin go every Sunday?"

"Yes," Jay lied.

She headed toward the kitchen. "He's not here. He left early this morning, probably to go surfing."

Five blocks from Kevin's, Jay parked beside a silver-blue Mercedes, which was next to a long, sleek speedboat. A Datsun 240Z that Billy no longer had a license to drive was angled haphazardly in front of the endless house.

When Jay reached the front door, it was ajar. From the back, disco music sifted through the air. Jay passed the pool table, wet bar, and library and walked out across the patio. Four or five teenagers were horsing around by the swimming pool, and nearby was Jennifer, Billy's leggy twenty-three-year-old sister, lounging in a bikini.

When she saw him, she took her black shades off.

"Hey, stranger," she said. Her eyes seemed to embrace him.

Even with her sagging chin and upturned nose, she stirred Jay's sexual desire. He surveyed the pool. "Is Billy around?"

"Who knows where that bastard is?" She scoffed. "Grab one of his suits and join me. You could use some sun."

"I can't."

Jennifer rose. "Come on, I'll make you a drink."

He followed her swaying gait.

"Do you really like my brother?"

He didn't answer.

"Margarita?"

At the portable bar under the umbrella, she poured him a drink.

He sipped around the crushed ice. "I used to."

"Used to what?"

"I used to like him, but he's changed a lot."

Her jaw dropped. "No one likes him, but everyone hangs around him. Why is that?"

The drink cooled his burning desires, and he relaxed. "He has energy. Lots of it. And I've known him all my life."

"You haven't known him all your life. That's my excuse."

Jay shrugged. "I have nothing else."

She grinned for no reason he could understand, and then she reached out and massaged his hand. "Remember when we went skinny dipping? You said you loved me."

"I was fifteen." He thought about Lily, whom he'd met after his fling with Jennifer.

She leaned into him. "I think about that summer all the time. No one has ever loved me like you did. And believe me, I've looked." Her eyes bugged out at him.

He finished the drink. Jennifer was his first sexual experience.

"You don't know what I've been through," she said, laying her hand against his chest. "Love me like you used to? Even if it's just for one day."

He squirmed, probably as desperate as she, but he couldn't let go. "I can't love like that again."

"We could try." She took his hand, and he let her lead him into the house.

Inside, raised voices came from the kitchen. Jennifer pulled him toward the commotion.

Alcohol, steaks, cashews, and cartons of Salem cigarettes covered the drainboard next to two half-empty grocery bags. Billy's mother, whose blouse was unbuttoned and hanging below her flat left breast, leaned forward with a glass of what looked like hard liquor. She was plastered enough to make Jay wonder how she'd gotten home.

A bag filled with Catholic communion wafers lay nearby. Jay knew the Candales donated them to the church. Matt, a smaller, younger version of Billy, spit a communion wafer into the sink.

"Those aren't cookies, you idiot. We buy them for the church," Mrs. Candale's scratchy voice proclaimed. She slapped Matt across the nape of the neck.

Matt gagged into the sink.

Jennifer let go of Jay and pushed her little brother. "You're throwing up. God, you idiot. Matt's throwing up Jesus."

"Shut your trap," Mrs. Candale said before she noticed Jay. "What do you want?"

Stone-faced, he watched Matt wash his mouth out with a Coke.

Jennifer stood with her hands on her hips. "You better go to confession, Matt. Spitting out God. You're more pathetic than Billy," she sneered.

"You're the one who needs to go, you whore," Matt said.

Mrs. Candale threw her glass into the sink. "What a goddamn mistake you two were."

"I better go," Jay said, sidestepping toward the door.

"Why?" Jennifer stroked his waist. "We don't have to see them anymore. It'll be just like it was." She pulled him into her.

He grabbed her wrist and held it down hard. "I'm sorry."

"Fuck," she said.

They stared at each other. She almost seemed to be pleading with him, but then she stamped her foot and returned to the kitchen.

He opened the door while Mrs. Candale screamed at Matt, "You little shit! Stay the hell out of my cigarettes!"

Jay drove through a neighborhood of modest tract homes, past the kids playing basketball in their driveways and riding bikes. He cut the engine in front of Brian's parents' house.

Brian's father, a large, wavy-haired man with a moon-shaped face and kind eyes, opened the door. Brian had left three or four hours earlier, he said, but his soft, pleasant manner caused Jay to linger. "Brian tells me you're going to school."

"Yeah," Jay said cheerfully.

Brian's father leaned forward and nodded as if he was truly interested. "What are you majoring in?"

Jay shrugged. "Journalism, art maybe. I'm not sure yet. I'm doing my general ed right now."

"You don't want to be a working stiff like me, do you?" Brian's father gave him another wise nod. He had started to say something else, when Brian's nervous, suspicious stepmother squirmed in.

"What do you want? Drugs?" She sniffed and looked him up and down disapprovingly.

"Margaret?"

"Don't 'Margaret' me," she said. "That boy comes home every night reeking of marijuana. Why do you think he has money all the time?" She gestured at Jay.

Jay held up his hands and smiled, which seemed to infuriate Brian's stepmother.

"They're good kids," Brian's father said.

"For Christ's sake, him and those other two fools are the biggest dopers in town. Open your eyes."

Jay did not sell dope. He earned his money working at the bookstore; he was the only one of his friends with a job. But Brian sold weed sometimes.

Jay rocked over the speed bumps in the park. Sunlight filtered through the bird-and squirrel-infested hundred-year-old pines. Families and young couples were cleaning up after a day of picnicking. To them, Jay was one of the long-haired, loud music–playing troublemakers who sometimes ruined the park for families, but today he was withdrawn. He passed the tired ponies walking in a circle with children riding them and the parents holding the reins or taking pictures.

The park housed a small zoo, where a bird sanctuary reached up seventy yards high. Getting out of the car, he admired the magnificent hawks and other birds cawing, whistling, singing, and soaring, stuck below the nets strung across the sky.

Alongside were dreary cages for a toothless lion, sheep, deer, and some bored monkeys. Next to them a lone scraggly buffalo inhabited a fenced dirt area with nowhere to hide.

Jay watched the monkeys, who peeked back at him. Then one bent over and mooned him.

Suddenly he was shoved face-first against the fence by an unseen foe. The monkeys went ape, howling with delight. Jay remained limp without fighting back until the grip relaxed;

then, spinning, he knocked off one attacker with an elbow and charged the other. Then he heard the laughter.

"Jay, it's us."

Jay controlled himself enough to realize it was Brian's voice. Jay must have hit him because Brian was sitting on his ass, rubbing his chin.

Kevin smiled. "We scared the piss out of you."

"That hurt," Brian said.

Jay helped Brian up and dusted himself off. "Assholes."

Kicking back, the four of them rested on a small mound of grass that overlooked the haggard buffalo. Kevin offered Jay a cigarette, but Jay waved it away.

"I'm serious. What are we going to do with our lives? Come on, Brian, what do you want to do?" Jay asked.

"Sex, drugs, and rock 'n' roll," Brian said.

"What else is there?" Kevin added, lighting a cigarette.

Billy sat up. "What the hell do you want us to do? Go to school? 'Hi, what's your major?'"

"Um, my major is accounting with a minor in boring," Kevin answered in a squeaky voice.

Brian got up and leaned against the buffalo's fence. "If I get this job in two weeks, I'll be making eight hundred bucks a month building houses, plus selling weed, while they're taking bullshit accounting classes."

"You have to be really boring to want to work with numbers," Kevin said.

"You're the creative type," Brian told Kevin.

"Did you know creative people dream every night?" Kevin asked.

"I dream all the freaking time."

"Fucking A!" Billy rose and swaggered over to the buffalo.

"What's his problem?" Brian said.

Jay couldn't believe how stupid these guys were.

Kevin looked at Jay, then Brian. "What time is it?"

"Five," Jay said.

"My mother has spies making sure I go to Mass. If they don't see me, she won't let me live at home."

"I'll go with you, man," Jay said, knowing Ellen went to Mass with her family.

"You going to the drive-in later?" Kevin asked.

"Yeah," Jay grumbled. The only place he didn't want to be more was home.

Billy began throwing rocks at an already-jittery buffalo, which flinched every time it was hit. It stared at Billy with a mixture of what looked like hate and fear.

Jay jumped up. "Knock it off, Billy."

When Billy flung another rock, hitting the buffalo in the ribs, Jay marched over to him.

"Oh shit, here we go," Brian said.

"If you throw one more rock, we're going at it."

"Like you've never hit it."

Jay pushed Billy and grabbed him by the shirt.

Brian squeezed between them. "Relax, man. He's only fooling around," he said to Jay.

"What's your fucking problem?" Billy shouted.

"You are motherfucker."

Billy pushed off him. "You have to be a prima donna everywhere you go?"

"Come on, we're going to be late for Mass," Brian said half-jokingly.

Jay tried to stare Billy down. He knew he couldn't beat up Billy.

"You guys don't need to fight, you just need to get laid," Kevin said.

"Fighting won't prove anything," Brian said. "Come on, it ain't worth it, man. You've known each other since second grade."

Brian pulled Billy away and drove Billy home because he didn't want to go with them to church.

Inside the church were stained glass saints, hardwood floors, white marble statues of angels, candles flickering in corners, and a rainbow of flowers surrounding the statue of the Virgin Mary. Jay dipped his fingers in the holy water and crossed himself. Kevin and Brian giggled behind him as they entered.

When Jay sat in the pews, he spotted Ellen next to her father and mother. Her mother seemed nice, but her large father sat stiffly, unhappy, like he was contemptuous of the world.

Ellen's eyes were huge, enveloping Jay. The spell was broken when her father nudged her and nodded toward the priest at the altar.

He would have waited outside if Ellen hadn't been there. He caught only fragments of the readings and daydreamed through the sermon. He did focus when the priest read: "The Kingdom of Heaven is like this: A man takes a mustard seed and sows it in his field. It is the smallest of all seeds, but when it grows up, it is the biggest of all plants. It becomes a tree, so that birds come and make their nests in its branches…"

Jay had always liked that sermon, maybe because he often felt small and insignificant himself.

When Mass ended, Jay tried to catch up with Ellen outside, but she was in the back seat of her father's car by the time he made it through the crowd. She turned and waved to him as they drove away.

IV

AT THE DRIVE-IN, Jay, Karla, and Brian sat in the front seat and Billy, Lily, and Kevin took the back. Lily was curled up in the corner. Every time Jay turned around from watching *Alien*, she stared at him with love-starved eyes.

"This movie is freaking me out!" Karla said.

Brian fidgeted and put his arm around Karla. "It got amazing reviews."

Jay heard stamping in the back seat; Kevin was trying to put out the cherry he'd dropped from his pipe or cigarette.

"Freaking Kevin," Brian said.

Jay attempted to focus on the movie. Karla glanced at him, then at Kevin and Billy. "You guys go to church, and an hour later, you're getting stoned. That's so hypocritical."

"I haven't touched it," Jay said.

Kevin laughed. "All you did in church was stare at Ellen Weber."

Karla gave Kevin a dirty look.

"She's a stuck-up bitch," Billy snapped.

"I work with her, so what?" Jay shouted for Lily's sake.

"Is that why you chased after her in the parking lot?" Kevin asked.

"I don't chase after anybody."

Karla folded her arms. "Are we going to watch this movie or talk?"

"I want to watch it," Brian said.

"Let me out please," Lily whispered.

Billy offered to go with her, but Lily said no and slid out of the car and walked toward the concession stand.

Jay stared at the screen.

"Go talk to her, Jay," Karla said, elbowing him.

"I don't see why you don't like Lily," Brian said.

"What am I supposed to do, marry her?"

"All you care about is yourself," Brian told him.

"I care about her."

"The fuck you do," Billy said.

Jay turned violently toward Billy, but they were all peeved at him.

"The least you can do is go talk to her," Karla said.

Kevin tried to hand Jay the pipe.

"Get that out of my face."

"Excuse me for breathing," Kevin said.

"You're a son of a bitch," Karla said, facing Jay.

Brian didn't look at Jay. "You can really hurt people, man."

Jay's stomach fell; he hated hurting Lily. "All right, all right. I'll talk to her."

He trudged across the pebbles that paved the drive-in. Lily wasn't inside, and when he walked around the building, she wasn't outside either. He did see Ellen at the snack bar counter. "Jesus."

When Ellen came out, he walked alongside her.

"Are you following me?" she asked, displaying no surprise.

"Yes."

She bent over slightly, as if to control her laugher. His spirits were lifted. He thought he would walk her back to her car, but then Lily showed up.

Lily exited the women's restroom right in front of them and froze. Jay stiffened too. He couldn't think of anything to say.

"Hello," Ellen said.

Lily ran with her hand over her mouth toward Jay's car.

"Never, ever say that to her."

"That's not funny, Jay. She's hurt."

"What am I supposed to do? We broke up."

"I feel sick for her," Ellen said, leaning against the cement building.

"Me too."

"You have to say something."

"I know," he said, watching Lily walking head down in front of rows of headlights. Life would have been easier if he'd stayed with Lily.

"I know exactly how you feel." Ellen pointed to the cars. Something had loosened in her, or maybe seeing Lily had chipped away at her remarkable control. "I'm right over there with Charles," she said.

"That's a nice boat."

"I hate it. I feel like I'm my mother in my father's car." The words rushed out of her, and she hugged herself before smiling again. "Only a couple more months before school starts," she said.

"I can't wait to move away and go to school," Jay said.

After she left, Jay sat on a car mound alone, peering in the direction of the movie.

Thirty minutes later, he opened the door of his Malibu and found the seating arrangements had shifted. Kevin appeared comatose in front, Brian and Karla cuddling next to him. In the back, Billy had his arm around Lily. All of them stared at

Jay as if he were a leper. Jay pulled out his keys and tossed them to Brian.

"Leave them in the ashtray. I'll get it tomorrow."

No one said a word.

On his way home, Jay crossed the street toward the redbrick church. The light was still on in the steeple. Shadows and flower gardens mysteriously flowed together. Jay sat next to the pearly statue of the Madonna and lit a cigarette, blowing smoke away from the statue. He flicked the cigarette into the gutter.

The heavy church doors swung open, and someone wrapped in a long, dark coat hurried out. It was his mother, half hidden, her high heels clicking. She glanced at the burning cigarette in the gutter but never noticed him sitting next to the Madonna.

Entering his house later, he ventured down the dark and narrow hallway to find his mother doing her duty, making his father more comfortable in his gurney bed. Jay stood in the doorway. She glanced at him, her eyes full of anger, as if to show she was not going to take any disrespect from him tonight. The phone rang and his mother picked up.

"I can't talk right now. I'm tired. I'll call you tomorrow," she said.

In bed Jay tossed and turned on his hot pillow. He considered getting up and watching *The Tonight Show*, but that might wake his parents. He switched on the light and picked up *Christiane F.*, which he had just read. It was at least three o'clock before he fell asleep.

The next day at work, Jay was stocking and rearranging books when roses were delivered to Ellen.

She opened the card. "It's signed J. Gatsby," she said, and wrote the *J* in the air. "This isn't like Charles," Ellen told him.

"He's probably trying to make up with me. I've been awful to him lately." She slouched as if in pain.

Jay stuck his nose near the flowers. "Maybe it's a secret admirer," he said.

"There you are!" Charles entered through the back door and hugged Ellen. "I've been trying to get hold of you all morning. Is your phone off the hook or what?"

"I've been around." She shrugged.

Jay returned to shelving books but stayed close enough to listen.

"Why don't you want to go down and find a place this week? You have to get one now, or you'll never find a decent place," Charles said.

Ellen folded her arms. "Give me a break. You're just like my father."

"Okay, I'm sorry. Let's talk about something fun. Have you picked up your dress for tonight?" Charles asked, his hands on her shoulders.

"Tonight?"

"My parents' party for us. You forgot?"

Jay pretended to read a book.

"It slipped my mind," Ellen said.

"That's all I've been talking about this month. What's wrong with you lately? Your father and I have both noticed it."

Charles's back was to Jay now.

Ellen stared at her Chuck Taylors until Charles lifted her chin. "Thanks for the flowers, J," she said.

"What?"

"Whoops," she said, twisting her lips.

"Who's Jay?"

"Jay Gatsby."

307

"Who's that?"

Jay laughed.

Charles kissed her. "Look—whatever you're thinking, I'll support you. Just don't shut me out, all right?"

"All right. But I better get back to work." She picked up a book and glanced at Jay.

"We'll have fun tonight, I promise," Charles said.

After Charles left, an awkward silence separated them.

"Have a good time tonight," Jay said.

"Is that what you were thinking before he walked in?" Sarcasm dripped from her words.

"Yeah, I'm telepathic," he said, looking at the roses.

"Tell me what I'm thinking right now."

Jay looked out into the mall. "I don't know what you see in that guy."

"He's got a full ride to USC."

"Yeah, and I've got a ride with a full tank of gas that will take me anywhere I want to go. That's all I need."

Jay didn't want this to happen. He didn't think she wanted this to happen, but the pressure inside him made him want to explode, so he hurried away and out of the mall, Ellen calling out behind him.

At home, Jay nursed a quart of apricot brandy. What should he say in his letter to his parents? Draft after draft. Drink after drink. He wrote and revised: "*I don't belong here. I've decided to move. I will write to you as soon as I am ready. It has to be this way for now. Please don't worry about me. I can take care of myself. Love always, Jay.*"

He left the note on the kitchen table.

Jay couldn't remember how he'd ended up on Brian's back room floor, surrounded by Brian, Karla, Kevin, Billy, and Lily. A different brandy bottle lay next to his ribs. He tried to get up, pushing off the sofa where Billy and Lily sat arm in arm. He slurred something but had no idea what he was saying.

Jay fell into Kevin, who was changing the record.

"What are you doing, man?" Kevin screeched, pushing him down.

"Jay's wasted," Brian said. "I've never seen him this drunk, unless you count the time he drank all that Boone's Farm in eighth grade. Remember that?"

Kevin tore down Jay's David Bowie drawing and tossed it at him. "Yeah, his mother called mine. The police found him wandering down the freeway."

Jay managed to climb onto the couch.

"You were the class president back then, weren't you, Jay?" Brian asked.

"And Billy was the flag football stud," Kevin said.

Billy nodded. "Remember Early? That guy was cool."

"Kevin was vice president," Brian said. "He gave the morning report."

Kevin broke into a smile. "Those were the good old days."

"Remember those ten-dollar bags when we were freshmen?" Brian asked.

"Best buzzes I ever had," Billy said.

Jay stared bleary-eyed at Lily kissing Billy. "Billy's a loser. They're all losers. Losers." He wobbled to his feet and tried to push Billy's arm away from Lily.

Billy hit him, then flung him against the opposite wall. Jay fell into a sofa and hung off the edge of it, unable to focus on anything or anyone.

Brian stepped in. "Fight fair, Billy."

"He started it," Billy said.

"That's enough, man," Kevin said to Billy.

"He's the one who's unfair." Billy jabbed a finger in Jay's face. "If he can't handle his own life, don't tell us what to do with ours. We're young and having a good time. What's wrong with that?"

"That's right," Lily said.

Jay wiped the blood off his mouth. "Right, that's right."

Jay's next memory was in his bedroom at his parents' house. The TV and radio were blaring. He staggered to his feet and found dirty dishes piled up in the kitchen. The phone rang, but he was too wiped out to answer. His note was no longer on the kitchen table. He held on to the walls all the way back into his room, then curled up on his bed and fell asleep.

Jay woke, startled, when someone touched his cheek. He sat up, squinting through the topaz darkness. The light came on. Shading his eyes, he saw his mother wearing an old robe.

"Mom." When his eyes adjusted to the light, he noticed her pursed lips. "What's going on?"

"We got your note. Your father's worried sick."

Jay leaned on his elbow, his head spinning.

She ran her hand through his hair. "I know you don't like me too much," she said, looking as if she was holding back tears.

"That's not true," he said in a rush.

"I'm doing the best I can." She was crying now.

Jay wiped away her tears. "I know. Me too. I'm sorry."

"It wasn't like this when you were a baby. He was strong and handsome like you," she said.

"I remember."

She glanced around the posters in his room, perhaps trying to formulate her thoughts. "He loves you. He cares so much, but he feels he's failed. We both do."

His father appeared in the doorway, leaning against the wall. Jay could tell he was trying to stand tall and proud.

"Hey, Dad."

His father's hand shook for a moment, and he braced it against his chest. "We want to help you get through college."

Jay choked up. "Thanks, Dad."

"We'll get the money," his father said.

"I can get student loans." He rose and embraced his parents until they all stopped sobbing.

Jay's tears were hot. He used his palm to wipe his cheeks, streaking the tears away. He smiled at his father, who held his hand for a moment before shuffling back down the hall to the bedroom.

"Oh, I almost forgot," Jay's mother said. "Some girl, Ellen, has been calling all night and day. She wants you to call her back."

Jay grabbed his coat.

"Where are you going?"

"I'm going to see her."

"Jay?"

"Yeah, Mom?"

"Take a shower first."

Jay pulled up to Ellen's two-story redbrick home with a courtyard and fountain out front. He had never been there before. Her father answered the door after a couple minutes of knocking. He stared at Jay as if he didn't know what to make of him being at the door.

"Hi, is Ellen home?"

"She's asleep, but here's Eleanor," her father said, retreating into the house.

Ellen's mother appeared, smiling sympathetically. "Ellen's in bed, but I know she would like to talk to you."

Jay took a deep breath. "Thank you. Tell her I came by."

As Jay walked back to his car, he turned to stone when he saw Charles, half dressed, race to his BMW parked down the street and drive off.

"Jay?" Ellen jogged out the door, wearing sweatpants and a polo shirt. "I'm sure I look great."

"Did you call me?"

"Did you come over for a reason?"

"I don't know."

"I'm sorry about yesterday," she said.

"I am too."

She took a breath and looked off into the distance. "I wanted to let you know I'm quitting B. Dalton," she said.

He shrugged. "I can quit if you want instead."

"No, that's not why. I think you're cool. It was fun working with you. But I got the chance to travel Europe for a month," she said, twisting her lips.

"That sounds amazing," he said.

"Yeah," she said without excitement.

"I'm sure you and Charles will have a great time."

"It was a surprise gift I got last night."

"That's great. Send me a postcard from Berlin."

She grabbed his arm and leaned into him. "I really like you, I do, but it's just the way it is right now."

With her revelation, he wanted to leave.

"Don't hate me," she said.

He thought of Lily and her eyes that had yearned so painfully for him. "No, I understand. Enjoy your trip."

He walked away smiling.

"Jay, wait."

He stopped smiling and didn't look back.

ENDNOTES

1 John Hall, "David Bowie Dead: German Government Thanks Late Singer for Helping to Bring Down the Berlin Wall," *Independent*, January 11, 2016, https://www.independent.co.uk/news/people/david-bowie-death-german-government-thanks-late-singer-helping-bring-down-berlinwall-a6805931.html.

2 Jones, *David Bowie: The Oral History*, (Penguin Random House, 2018), 554-559.

3 Jones, *David Bowie: The Oral History*, 54-55.

4 Andrew Trendell, "David Bowie's Earliest Years—As Told by the People Who Knew Him Best," *NME*, February 6, 2019, https://www.nme.com/features/david-bowie-a-portrait-of-the-artist-as-a-young-man-as-told-by-those-who-knew-him-best-2443649.

5 Jones, *David Bowie: The Oral History*, 34.

6 George Simpson, "Tom Jones SHOCK: How Music Legend Is the Real Reason for David Bowie's Stage Name," *Express*, April 11, 2020, https://www.express.co.uk/entertainment/music/1267996/Tom-Jones-David-Bowie-stage-name-David-Jones-Davy-Jones-Monkees.

7 Kurt Loder, "Straight Time," *Rolling Stone*, May 12, 1983, https://www.rollingstone.com/music/music-news/david-bowie-straight-time-69334.

8 David Hepworth, "How Performing Starman on Top of the Pops Sent Bowie into the Stratosphere," *The Guardian*, January 15, 2016, https://www.theguardian.com/music/musicblog/2016/jan/15/david-bowie-starman-top-of-the-pops.

Endnotes

9 Katie Rogers, "Was He Gay, Bisexual or Bowie? Yes," *The New York Times*, January 13, 2016, https://www.nytimes.com/2016/01/14/style/was-he-gay-bisexual-or-bowie-yes.html.

10 In Music, "David Bowie Sings 'Fame' & 'Golden Years' on Soul Train (1975)," *Open Culture*, November 8, 2016, https://www.openculture.com/2016/11/david-bowie-sings-fame-golden-years-on-soul-train-1975.html.

11 Sue Carter, "Curator Geoffrey Marsh on David Bowie's reading habits," *Quill and Quire*, September 26, 2013, https://quillandquire.com/events/2013/09/26/curator-geoffrey-marsh-on-david-bowies-reading-habits.

12 Randall Colburn, "David Bowie Book Club launched by his son, Duncan Jones," *Yahoo! Entertainment*, December 30, 2017, https://www.yahoo.com/entertainment/david-bowie-book-club-launched-191552879.html.

13 Andy Greene, "Flashback: David Bowie Rips into MTV for Not Spotlighting Black Artists," *Rolling Stone*, June 14, 2020, https://www.rollingstone.com/music/music-news/david-bowie-rips-into-mtv-for-not-spotlighting-black-artists-62335.

14 Cameron Crowe, "The Playboy Interview with David Bowie," *Playboy.com*, January 11, 2016, https://www.playboy.com/read/playboy-interview-david-bowie.

15 NME Blog, "Aliens, Nazis and Cocaine: Six 70s Myths about David Bowie," *NME*, January 10, 2018, https://www.nme.com/blogs/nme-blogs/six-70s-myths-about-david-bowie-761066.

16 Rob Smith, "David Bowie's Tragic Real-Life Story," *Grunge*, August 2, 2018, https://www.grunge.com/130199/david-bowies-tragic-real-life-story.

17 Alan Light, "How David Bowie Brought Thin White Duke to Life on 'Station to Station," *Rolling Stone*, January 23, 2017, https://www.rollingstone.com/music/music-features/how-david-bowie-brought-thin-white-duke-to-life-on-station-to-station-125797.

18 Bill Keller, "Major Soviet Paper Says 20 Million Died as Victims of Stalin," *The New York Times*, February 4, 1989, https://www.nytimes.com/1989/02/04/world/major-soviet-paper-says-20-million-died-as-victims-of-stalin.html.

19 History.com Editors, "Berlin Wall," *History*, December 15, 2009, https://www.history.com/topics/cold-war/berlin-wall.

Endnotes

20 History.com Editors, "Berlin Airlift," *History*, March 9, 2011, https://www.history.com/topics/cold-war/berlin-airlift.

21 History.com Editors, "NATO," *History*, April 14, 2010, https://www.history.com/topics/cold-war/formation-of-nato-and-warsaw-pact.

22 History.com Editors, "Berlin Wall."

23 James M. Markham, "A Lot Better Than a War," *The New York Times*, February 8, 1987, https://www.nytimes.com/1987/02/08/books/a-lot-better-than-a-war.html.

24 Thomas Putnam, "The Real Meaning of Ich Bin ein Berliner," *The Atlantic*, https://www.theatlantic.com/magazine/archive/2013/08/the-real-meaning-of-ich-bin-ein-berliner/309500.

25 John F. Kennedy, "Remarks of President John F. Kennedy at the Rudolph Wilde Platz, Berlin, June 26, 1963," *John F. Kennedy Presidential Library and Museum*, June 26, 1963, https://www.jfklibrary.org/archives/other-resources/john-f-kennedy-speeches/berlin-w-germany-rudolph-wilde-platz-19630626.

26 History.com Editors, "Berlin Wall."

27 History.com Editors, "Berlin Wall Built," *History*, March 4, 2010, https://www.history.com/this-day-in-history/berlin-wall-built.

28 History.com Editors, "Berlin Wall Built."

29 Joel D. Cameron, "Stasi, East German Government," *Britannica*, July 20, 1998, https://www.britannica.com/topic/Stasi.

30 Des Shaw, "Bowie's Berlin: the City That Shaped a 1970s Masterpiece," *HistoryExtra*, January 10, 2018, https://www.historyextra.com/period/20th-century/bowies-berlin-the-city-that-shaped-a-1970s-masterpiece.

31 Shaw, "Bowie's Berlin: the City That Shaped a 1970s Masterpiece."

32 Rob Hughes, "David Bowie Remembers Berlin: "I Can't Express the Feeling of Freedom I Felt There," *UNCUT*, January 6, 2017, https://www.uncut.co.uk/features/david-bowie-remembers-berlin-cant-express-feeling-freedom-felt-98780.

33 Hughes, "David Bowie Remembers Berlin: "I Can't Express the Feeling of Freedom I Felt There."

34 Hughes, "David Bowie Remembers Berlin: "I Can't Express the Feeling of Freedom I Felt There.""

35 David Buckley, *Strange Fascination*, (London: Virgin Books, 2005), 277-278.

36 Hughes, "David Bowie Remembers Berlin: "I Can't Express the Feeling of Freedom I Felt There,"

37 Mesfin Fekadu, "Legendary Musician David Bowie Dies of Cancer At 69,"*AP*, January 11, 2016, https://apnews.com/article/22cb6b3e3b64476daf-8d4ece21bd2496.

38 Eli Hetko, "We Could Be Antiheroes," *Slate*, January 15, 2016, https://slate.com/news-and-politics/2016/01/mitki-the-soviet-era-youth-movement-that-loathed-david-bowie.html.

39 Nikola Budanovic, "Bowie Behind the Iron Curtain – His Bizarre Trip Through the Soviet Union," *The Vintage News*, Dec 11, 2018, https://www.thevintagenews.com/2018/12/11/david-bowies-soviet-union.

40 Ilya Krol, "5 facts about David Bowie's Russian life," *Russian Beyond*, January 11, 2016, https://www.rbth.com/arts/2016/01/11/david-bowie_558255.

41 Alan Paul, "Photos of David Bowie in Russian, 1976" *alanpaul.net*, January 11, 2016, http://alanpaul.net/2016/01/photos-of-david-bowie-in-russia-1976.

42 Lorraine Boissoneault, "The True Story of the Reichstag Fire and the Nazi Rise to Power," *Smithsonian Magazine*, February 21, 2017, https://www.smithsonianmag.com/history/true-story-reichstag-fire-and-nazis-rise-power-180962240.

43 Andy Greene, "Flashback: David Bowie Sings 'Heroes' at the Berlin Wall," *Rolling Stone*, June 9, 2016, https://www.rollingstone.com/music/music-news/flashback-david-bowie-sings-heroes-at-the-berlin-wall-90149.

44 Andy Greene, "Flashback: David Bowie Sings 'Heroes' at the Berlin Wall."

45 John P. Rafferty, "Mr. Gorbachev, Tear Down This Wall!": Reagan's Berlin Speech," *Britannica*, https://www.britannica.com/story/mr-gorbachev-tear-down-this-wall-reagans-berlin-speech.

Endnotes

46 William Tuohy, "Radicals, Police Clash as Thousands of West Berliners March to Protest Today's Visit by Reagan," *Los Angeles Times*, June 12, 1987, https://www.latimes.com/archives/la-xpm-1987-06-12-mn-3968-story.html.

47 Inyoung Kang, "A Look Back at Reagan's Berlin Wall Speech, 30 Years Later," *New York Times*, September 12, 2012, https://www.nytimes.com/2017/06/12/briefing/ronald-reagan-berlin-wall-speech.html.

48 Lucy Madison, "Remembering Reagan's 'Tear Down This Wall' speech 25 years later," *CBS News*, June 12, 2012, https://www.cbsnews.com/news/remembering-reagans-tear-down-this-wall-speech-25-years-later.

49 Jeffrey Fleishmann and David Holley, "Loss Evokes Memories Bitter, *Los Angeles Times*, June 7, 2004, https://www.latimes.com/archives/la-xpm-2004-jun-07-na-worldreax7-story.html.

50 Sarah Pruitt, "How Reagan's 'Tear Down This Wall' Speech Marked a Cold War Turning Point," *History*, June 9, 2021, https://www.history.com/news/ronald-reagan-tear-down-this-wall-speech-berlin-gorbachev.

51 Lesley Kennedy, "How Gorbachev and Reagan's Friendship Helped Thaw the Cold War," *History*, October 24, 2019, https://www.history.com/news/gorbachev-reagan-cold-war.

52 Ryan Chilcote, "Gorbachev: Pope Was 'Example to All of Us'," *CNN International*, April 4, 2005, https://edition.cnn.com/2005/WORLD/europe/04/03/pope.gorbachev/index.htm.

53 Strobe Talbott, "Reagan and Gorbachev: Shutting the Cold War Down," *Brookings*, August 1, 2004, https://www.brookings.edu/articles/reagan-and-gorbachev-shutting-the-cold-war-down.

54 History, Music, Politics, "Bruce Springsteen Plays East Berlin in 1988: I'm Not Here For Any Government. I've Come to Play Rock," *Open Culture*, October 8, 2014, https://www.openculture.com/2014/10/bruce-springsteen-plays-east-berlin-in-1988.html.

55 Austin Davis, Marcel Fürstenau, "The Demonstration That Took Down East Germany," *DW*, April 11, 2019, https://www.dw.com/en/november-4-alexanderplatz-largest-demonstration-east-germany-1989/a-51086517.

56 Michael Meyer, "Günter Schabowski, the Man Who Opened the Wall,"

Endnotes

New York Times, Nov 6, 2015, https://www.nytimes.com/2015/11/07/opinion/gnter-schabowski-the-man-who-opened-the-wall.html.

57 Albinko Hasic, 'The Gates in the Wall Stand Open Wide. What Happened the Day the Berlin Wall Fell," *Time*, November 7, 2019, https://time.com/5720386/berlin-wall-fall.

58 Bill DeMain, "The Story Behind the Song: Heroes by David Bowie," *Classic Rock*, February 4, 2019, https://www.loudersound.com/features/the-story-behind-the-song-heroes-by-david-bowie.

Made in the USA
Las Vegas, NV
23 February 2024